## Praise for *Second T*

"The uplifting latest from Carlson follows a fortysomething empty nester who moves from her stylish Victorian to a fixer-upper. This is perfect for fans of clean romance."

*Publishers Weekly*

"This read is the perfect book to cuddle up with during a stormy weekend."

*Interviews and Reviews*

## Praise for *Looking for Leroy*

"Carlson's latest inspirational novel is a sweet toast to second chances. Missed opportunities and misunderstandings abound in this heartwarming tale that's sure to appeal to Carlson's many fans."

*Booklist*

"No one writes clean, contemporary romance quite like Carlson, who delivers another winner with this novel."

*Library Journal*

"Melody Carlson paints a vivid yet beautiful tale of finding old love and of forgiveness."

*Urban Book Reviews*

## Praise for *The Happy Camper*

"Memorable characters and a satisfying inspirational core make this one a winner."

*Publishers Weekly*

"*The Happy Camper* is a cute, fun story filled with family drama and romance. Carlson's writing pulls readers in and keeps them invested in the drama."

*Life Is Story*

# BOOKS BY MELODY CARLSON

*Courting Mr. Emerson*
*The Happy Camper*
*Looking for Leroy*
*Second Time Around*
*Just for the Summer*

## FOLLOW YOUR HEART SERIES

*Once Upon a Summertime*
*All Summer Long*
*Under a Summer Sky*

## HOLIDAY NOVELLAS

*Christmas at Harrington's*
*The Christmas Shoppe*
*The Joy of Christmas*
*The Treasure of Christmas*
*The Christmas Pony*
*A Simple Christmas Wish*
*The Christmas Cat*
*The Christmas Joy Ride*
*The Christmas Angel Project*
*The Christmas Blessing*
*A Christmas by the Sea*
*Christmas in Winter Hill*
*The Christmas Swap*
*Christmas in the Alps*
*The Christmas Quilt*
*A Royal Christmas*

# Just
## for the
# Summer

A NOVEL

# MELODY CARLSON

**R**
**Revell**
*a division of Baker Publishing Group*
Grand Rapids, Michigan

© 2024 by Carlson Management Company

Published by Revell
a division of Baker Publishing Group
Grand Rapids, Michigan
RevellBooks.com

Printed in the United States of America

Library of Congress Cataloging-in-Publication Data
Names: Carlson, Melody, author.
Title: Just for the summer : a novel / Melody Carlson.
Description: Grand Rapids, Michigan : Revell, a division of Baker Publishing
    Group, 2024.
Identifiers: LCCN 2023022698 | ISBN 9780800744717 (paperback) | ISBN
    9780800745615 (casebound) | ISBN 9781493444755 (ebook)
Subjects: LCGFT: Christian fiction. | Novels.
Classification: LCC PS3553.A73257 J87 2024 | DDC 813/.54—dc23/eng/20230518
LC record available at https://lccn.loc.gov/2023022698

This book is a work of fiction. Names, characters, places, and incidents are the product of the author's imagination or are used fictitiously. Any resemblance to actual events, locales, or persons, living or dead, is coincidental.

Scripture used in this book, whether quoted or paraphrased by the characters, is from The Holy Bible, English Standard Version® (ESV®). Copyright © 2001 by Crossway, a publishing ministry of Good News Publishers. Used by permission. All rights reserved. ESV Text Edition: 2016

Baker Publishing Group publications use paper produced from sustainable forestry practices and post-consumer waste whenever possible.

24  25  26  27  28  29  30      7  6  5  4  3  2  1

# one

## HOTEL JACKSON, SEATTLE

Ginny Masters rarely blew her temper. Today could prove the exception. She silently counted to ten while studying her boss's frosty expression. Diana Jackson, owner of Hotel Jackson Seattle, had to be one of the most difficult people on the planet. And working in the high end of the hospitality industry, where most guests at this boutique hotel acted overly entitled, Ginny had met more than her fair share of thorny people.

"I *know* I already informed you of that reception, *Genevieve*." Diana's nostrils actually flared. "I'm absolutely certain of it."

"If you *had* told me, I would've scheduled it accordingly." Ginny fingered the edges of her tablet, standing her ground, but knowing full well that Diana would win. Never mind that Diana had totally blanked on her best friend's daughter's last-minute wedding reception. It made no difference now. Ginny would receive the brunt of the blame for Diana's blunder—and be forced to pick up the pieces.

"Oh, I'll admit it was short notice when I told you." Diana's voice softened ever so slightly as she placed a placating hand on

Ginny's shoulder. A familiar gesture when Diana was about to manipulate the opposition to her advantage. "Poor Vivian was so distraught that her dear Rebecca planned to elope, I promised her the Skylight Room as a way to coax Rebecca back to sanity. After all, they are a very influential family in Seattle." Diana paused to stare up at the chandelier, rubbing her chin as if deep in thought or perhaps inspecting for dust.

Ginny decided to try empathy. "I can understand you wanting to help your friend out, but I—"

"I am certain Vivian booked this in early April. Maybe even March. And I told you about it the same day." Diana's softness turned brittle as she locked eyes with Ginny. "Rebecca's reception will be held right here. On Saturday night." Her hand slipped from Ginny's shoulder. "I will try to overlook your negligence to schedule it as you were instructed. It's not the first time you've let me down. *Now fix this!*"

"But the Bremmers' fiftieth wedding anniversary is booked here on Saturday night. It's been locked in since early February." Ginny tapped her tablet, pointing at the date.

"Then *unlock* it." Diana stepped back with a stony expression. "I don't care how you do it, just straighten out your mess!"

Ginny watched as Diana briskly crossed the ballroom, her clicking heels echoing up to the high ornate ceiling. To argue was pointless, but Ginny's heart went out to the Bremmers. The sweet couple attended her church. She'd known them for years. The most undemanding folks, always helping others. And although the Bremmer children had planned this wingding, she knew how much the elder Bremmers were looking forward to it. She also knew they'd be completely gracious about this double-booking. But their children . . . not so much.

As she hurried back to her office, she formulated a plan to "fix this" as Diana had commanded. And since Diana had said she didn't care how it was done, Ginny did what she often did. She took the matter completely into her own hands. By the end of the day, she had convinced the oldest son, Thomas Bremmer, to accept the Skylight Room, gratis, for a rescheduled early afternoon celebration. To sweeten the deal, she promised if their festivities wrapped up by five o'clock, hotel drinks and hors d'oeuvres would be on the house as well. Knowing this was mostly a church crowd, she wasn't too worried about the bar bill, which is where most tabs ballooned.

"And the wedding reception flowers will be delivered Saturday morning," she told Thomas before hanging up. "So your party can have the enjoyment of those as well. I can assure you they will be gorgeous." And expensive, she thought, as she looked at the name of the florist in charge.

"Well, that's an offer that's hard to refuse," Thomas admitted. "I'll let my younger sister handle the task of notifying the guests."

"I'm truly sorry for this inconvenience. Thank you for understanding."

"Mom and Dad and their older friends will probably appreciate the earlier time anyway. No night owls in that crowd." He chuckled. "I hope you'll be able to join us, Ginny. I know my parents would love to see you there."

"I'll do my best," she said. "But that'll be a busy day for me." She closed her tablet. Thomas Bremmer was a nice enough guy and a successful CPA with his own firm. She'd even dated him a couple of times a few years ago. But he just wasn't her type. As she thanked him again and hung up, she vaguely wondered . . . What exactly was her type? Even if she found her type, would she ever have time for a real romance? Not as long as she was managing Hotel Jackson for its cantankerous owner. Diana Jackson assumed that Ginny was gratefully married to this job. Always treating her like it was such a privilege to be the head manager here. Maybe it was at first. But that was more than ten years ago.

"Ginny?" Adrian Jackson poked his head through her cracked open door. "Busy?"

"No more than usual," she told him.

He grimaced. "So Mom told you about Rebecca's wedding reception?"

She nodded grimly.

He entered her small, cluttered office and, leaning against the edge of her console table, folded his arms in front of him in a totally Adrian pose. "So you're okay, then? I mean, I tried to warn Mom you already had something booked. I even had it on my schedule." He shrugged with a furrowed brow. "But she seemed pretty determined. Sorry."

"It's all worked out now, Adrian. Don't worry about it."

"Oh, good. I figured you'd handle it, Ginny. You usually do." He brightened. "I don't know how you do it though, and I'm sure I could use some customer service lessons from you." He chuckled. "But I'm just the bean counter here. I don't have to be nice. Especially when it's time to shake someone down."

She couldn't help but smile. Adrian wasn't the type to shake anyone down. Sure, he was a reliable CFO for the hotel, but not highly motivated. Growing up rich probably hadn't helped him in that department. Although she suspected even if he'd grown up like she had, his lackadaisical nature would still be laid-back. In a way, it was probably one of his best qualities. He was always calm. Sometimes irritatingly so.

"Any dinner plans tonight?" He stood up straight. "I know you're supposed to get off at seven. I could probably get us into Le—"

"No thank you, Adrian." She checked her watch. "I, uh, I already have a date tonight."

"You do?" He looked just as crestfallen as he usually did when she turned him down. Wouldn't he have gotten used to it by now? "Who with?"

"My bathtub." She shoved her notepad into her bag.

"Aw, come on, Ginny. When was the last time you did something *just for fun*?"

8

She considered this. Of course, he was right, but she didn't plan to let him know that. "I'm exhausted, Adrian. It's been a long day, and I have to come in early tomorrow."

"How about a rain check, then?" He grinned. "It even goes with the weather."

"Oh, I don't think—"

"But my buddy Jean Pierre is managing Le Jardin now. I can make reservations for—"

"No, please, *don't.*"

"Okay, how about this? I'll give you a ride home," he offered. "Then I'll call Ono's for takeout."

As tempting as that sounded, she knew she had to decline. For Adrian's sake. "No thanks."

"I don't get you, Ginny. Honestly, you're the worst workaholic I've ever known. Don't you remember what happens when you're all work and no play?"

"Yeah. Ginny's a dull girl." She forced a smile. "So you've told me before. Thanks."

He brightened. "So I can make us a reservation for, say, next week? I know you're going to love what Jean's done to the menu."

"As lovely as that sounds, please, let me think about it." She wouldn't have to think too long but didn't want to let him down too hard all at once . . . again.

"Okay, fine. If you don't want to go out tonight, why can't I bring sushi by your place?"

"No thanks, Adrian." She gave him her sternest look.

"Is this because of Mom?" His lower lip protruded slightly. "Has she said something to you recently?"

"No . . . I'm just really tired."

"Then just let me get you sushi." He reached for his phone. "I'll call it in now. I can still drive you home, and then I'll bring it back to you. I won't even stay to eat with—"

"No thanks." She grimaced and grimly shook her head.

"I know this is because of Mom."

"I'm just really tired," she tried again. "Sorry to be such a party pooper."

"Oh, Ginny." He leaned forward, peering into her eyes. "Why do you let Mom keep you under her thumb like this?"

How many times had she told Adrian she liked him but wanted only his friendship? Yet he continued to blame Ginny's coolness on his mother. To be fair, he wasn't entirely wrong. Diana vehemently opposed Ginny dating her only son. Not that Ginny had ever wanted to seriously date Adrian. She simply tried to be politely friendly with him. "Look, Adrian," she kept her tone gentle. "You know as well as I do that your mother doesn't approve of—"

"What Mom doesn't know won't hurt her."

"But it might hurt us." Ginny felt relief when her phone rang. Waving Adrian away, she answered it. "This is Genevieve Masters," she said in her usual courteous but efficient tone. Naturally, it was housekeeping again. Still complaining that the laundry was extra slow today. "I know they're shorthanded, Rosaria. There's a flu bug going around down there," she told her head housekeeper. "I'll speak to Lindsey again, but *please* try to make do in the meantime."

"In the meantime, we're nearly out of towels and pillowcases."

"Right . . ." Ginny paused to think. "Hey, can you spare a couple of housekeepers? Ones who'd be willing to go down there and lend a hand for a day or two? I'll even offer a little bonus."

"That might tempt the Johnson twins. They're always scrabbling for money."

"Great. I'll call down to the laundry to arrange it and get back to you ASAP."

Several phone calls and a little job juggling later, the linen problem was being resolved and everyone was moderately happy. But this was only Tuesday. As Ginny removed her heeled pumps and pulled on her walking Keds, she realized the hotel would get busier by the end of the week, and even more so with graduations and weddings around the corner. It was just life in a popular boutique hotel in the heart of Seattle. But sometimes it felt exhausting and never-ending.

Not that Ginny was complaining. Managing Hotel Jackson more than ten years was pretty impressive for someone without a hospitality management degree. Something Diana regularly reminded Ginny of—usually right before job review time. Ginny's educational status always provided Diana with her standard excuse for denying more than a minimal cost of living raise. Ginny knew that managers of similar hotels made more. Much more.

But it wasn't just about the money. After all, Ginny had learned frugality as a child. Before becoming manager, she'd gotten lots of pinching-pennies practice working her way through the ranks in the hotel. But those experiences in the laundry, housekeeping, and restaurant all proved valuable to her later on. She understood the ins and outs of hotel management personally. And attaining the top management position here was no small deal for a girl with only two years of college.

At least it had felt that way when she was still in her twenties. Sometimes, especially of late, she wasn't so sure. Diana was notorious for pulling a fast one like she'd done today. Almost as if she derived pleasure from watching Ginny squirm and then scramble to pull a rabbit from her hat. Sure, the challenges could be fun . . . sometimes. Especially when she succeeded.

But the stress was starting to catch up with her. And the demands of an unpredictable work schedule had taken their toll on her personal life. She laughed out loud as she pulled on her trench coat. *What personal life?* Adrian was right . . . Ginny didn't know how to have fun. Had she ever?

Slipping out the rear employee exit, she frowned to see the deluge increasing the already oversized puddles on the sidewalk. Why hadn't she worn her rain boots this morning? Wet weather wasn't unusual for Seattle in spring, but the low clouds loitering atop the Sound looked gray and dreary . . . and gloomy and cold.

She was almost to her apartment complex when her cell phone

chimed. Seeing it was her baby sister, she eagerly answered. Gillian was Ginny's only flesh-and-blood relative in this world. And although Gillie was ten years younger, they had always been close. Even more so after their single mother died when Gillie was only eleven. That's why Ginny quit college and went to work full-time. It was the only way to take guardianship of her kid sister. But it had all been worth it. Especially now that Gillian was just finishing her last year of med school. The light at the end of their long, dark tunnel.

"What's up, sis?"

"Best news ever," Gillian gushed. "You're not going to believe it, Ginny!"

"Tell me!" Had Gillie already gotten a job?

"I've been invited to work at the Howard Institute."

"The Howard Institute?" Ginny stepped under an awning to avoid the rain and hear better. "A real job? Already?"

"Yes! The Howard Institute is this amazing cancer research clinic."

"That's awesome, Gillie! Congratulations!" Ginny was suddenly imagining the two of them moving into nicer housing outside of the noisy city.

"But one thing, Ginny. The institute is in Boston."

"Boston . . . really?" Ginny tried to keep the disappointment out of her voice.

"I know it's a long way off, Ginny, but this is a huge opportunity for me. The Howard Institute is renowned for its cutting-edge research."

"I know you've always wanted to specialize in oncology."

"And Dr. Billings is one of the most respected oncologists in the country."

Ginny took in a deep breath, willing enthusiasm as she stepped out from the protection of the awning. Feeling the cold runoff water going straight down the back of her neck, she hurried toward her apartment building just a couple doors down. "Then even more congratulations are in order, Gillian. I'm so happy for you. You go, girl!"

"*Go girl*—across the country? So you're really okay with this, Ginny? I mean, we always talked about getting a house together after I finished—"

"Oh, those were kid dreams. The new dream is for you to go to Boston. Become a world-famous oncologist. And save lots of lives. We can always get a house together when we're old women with nothing better to do." Ginny forced a tinny laugh as she hopped past a mud puddle. Stopping by her apartment building, she ducked under its frayed canvas awning.

"I'm so glad you're okay with it, Gin. I promised to give them my answer by the end of the week. They want me to start right after graduation. This summer I'll be a research doctor!" She let out a happy squeal. "I'm so excited."

"I'm really, really proud of you."

"You know I never could've done it without you. As soon as I'm in a place where I can, I plan to pay you back for all—"

"Don't be silly. The way you pay me back is by succeeding. And I get bragging rights. I can tell everyone my baby sister is a famous oncologist."

Gillian laughed. "I'm so relieved you're okay with this. I have to go now. I'm on night shift at eight."

Ginny told her goodbye and went into her building. The cold lobby, damp with rain, smelled mustier than usual. One of the light fixtures appeared to be burned out, and the other flickered as if it were about to join it. As she removed and shook out her soaked trench coat, she tried not to think of how eagerly she'd been waiting to escape this dreary place. They'd moved here after Mom died. Mostly because of the proximity of Ginny's job. Plus, it was cheap.

Ginny would never tell Gillian, but she'd been perusing real estate websites lately. Printing a few photos out, filing them in a folder . . . and dreaming of the starter house they would buy together as soon as Gillian started to practice medicine. Ginny had even managed to accrue a meager savings account to contribute to a down payment. She knew they'd have to start small. But she'd hoped for a little house with a big view, a cook's kitchen, and a real wood-burning fireplace. Well, that dream, like the rest of her life, would have to remain on hold for now.

# two

Jacqueline Potter was fed up. Seriously! What was Grandpa Jack thinking? That she was his indentured servant or personal slave . . . or just an overworked, underpaid employee? She dumped his dirty clothes from the basket onto the laundry room floor and growled. She checked the fitness tracker on her smartwatch. Already, she'd put in more than six thousand steps and it was after five o'clock. Quitting time! Except Grandpa wouldn't be satisfied until his favorite Carhartt shirt was washed and ready for tomorrow.

If it wasn't bad enough to be stuck managing Grandpa's decrepit fishing lodge for the past six years, he now expected her to do his stinking laundry too? She held her breath as she shoved his old fishing shirt, which smelled like rotten sardines, into the washer, followed by a few other ripe items. She tossed in a soap pod, then slammed the door, pressing the electronic button so hard that the stupid machine refused to cooperate.

"Okay, fine," she told the stubborn washer—the same modern model she'd insisted the lodge needed last year. "See if I care." She kicked the empty laundry basket across the room, then, feeling a smidgen of guilt, tried the On button again. A little more gently, and this time it worked.

Oh, sure, she knew she had a bad attitude. And she should feel sorry for Grandpa. Laid up with a swollen ankle and bruised elbow. But that's what you get when you go traipsing around in the river at his age. Good grief, the man was in his seventies! Why on earth hadn't he retired by now? Maybe this was the perfect time—while he was limping around—to urge him to sell this run-down old lodge and move into some sensible senior living place where he could enjoy the rest of his golden years in pampered leisure. Maybe meet a nice old lady.

"Anyone in there?" Margie the cook called from the nearby hallway.

"Just me," Jacqueline grumbled back. "The new laundress."

Margie came into the laundry room with arched brows. "I didn't realize you knew how to do laundry, Jackie."

Jacqueline tossed her a look as she pushed a loose lock of hair behind her ear. "Who do you think washes *my* clothes?"

"Your French maid?" Margie smirked. "Well, that's real nice you want to help out with the laundry. But I need—"

"I don't *want* to help out. I'm only doing Grandpa's clothes because Cassie seems to have disappeared from the planet, and his *favorite* flannel was dirty. He has dozens, of course, but do you think he can live one whole day without his favorite shirt? Apparently not."

"Well, if you're done in here, I could use a hand in the kitchen. The Brower party is coming in earlier than I expected and now I—"

"*What?*" Jacqueline demanded. "They weren't supposed to arrive until tomorrow afternoon."

"Not according to Kent Brower. He and his buddies are outside right now, checking out the dock and the boats, and they're hungry for supper."

"You're kidding." Jacqueline planted her fists on her hips. "I'll send them packing!"

"Mr. Brower said you booked him to arrive *today*."

"No way. I booked them for tomorrow through Sunday."

"Yeah, you might wanna double-check that." Margie picked some soiled towels from the floor, tossing them into the empty basket. "When I couldn't find you, I took a little peek at your reservation book. Turns out Mr. Brower was right."

"Well, that book isn't always up-to-date. I keep reservations on my iPad too."

"Maybe so, but the Brower party is here now. I'm just glad they didn't get here before lunchtime. That would've been slim pickin's. Anyway, those fellas are hungry, and I need help getting supper ready." Margie pointed at Jacqueline. "That means you."

"Oh, Margie." Jacqueline let loose with a loud moan. "I'm done for the day."

"No you aren't." Margie gave her a gentle but firm shove toward the door. "Come on, Princess. You know this is men's week at the lodge. Seems like they eat twice as much with no women around. Anyway, I got a pile of potatoes that need peeling. And then there's—"

"Can't you get someone else—"

"Ain't nobody here but you and me, girlfriend. You can just thank your lucky stars the Riverside Cabin was vacated and that Cassie got it all cleaned and ready, or you'd really be scrambling."

"Why can't Cassie help you with supper?"

"She already went home. Some kind of birthday party or something."

"I wish I'd already gone home," Jacqueline mumbled as she shuffled toward the kitchen.

"You *are* home, honey." Margie laughed. "Welcome."

"I mean home in my own cabin." Jacqueline had planned to start streaming a new series about British royals tonight. Anything to escape the reality of her own pathetic life.

"I know where you live, darlin'." Margie handed her an apron.

"This is so not fair. Being forced into menial labor. That is not in my job description."

"Send your complaints to the management."

"I *am* the management!" Jacqueline sputtered as she tied the apron.

Margie pointed to a large bag of potatoes next to the sink. "I want that whole bag peeled—pronto!"

"Potatoes? Seriously? Why do I have to do—"

"Less talk, more work, *Cinderella*."

"Yeah, where are those helpful little mice when you need them?" Jacqueline picked up a big potato, glaring into the spud's eyes. "This is going to ruin my manicure."

Margie's laugh was not sympathetic. As Jacqueline peeled the potato, she wondered why she'd ever accepted this job in the first place. Sure, it had sounded fun . . . in the beginning. And sometimes it was kind of fun. Most of the visitors here were fishermen, and she'd enjoyed all the attention she'd get from them. But, like most of the guests, it had grown old. And the fun had steadily deteriorated over the years. Even with a new season ahead, she didn't feel the least bit hopeful that life would improve for her. Let alone offer any sort of fun. She couldn't even remember the last time she'd had any real fun. Would she ever have fun again?

GINNY'S ROOMMATE USUALLY worked evenings during the week, but judging by the wet umbrella dripping outside the front door, it looked like someone was here. Hopefully it was Rhonda. They'd been roommates for almost two years, but thanks to different work schedules, they were barely acquainted. That worked for Ginny, because after having had a variety of roommates who eventually moved on, she'd learned not to get too attached. Plus, Rhonda was pretty young—even younger than Gillian. And much more immature.

"Hello?" Ginny called out as she went inside the shared apartment. Observing the trail of various items of clothing and a pair of soggy shoes, she surmised that the sound of water running in the bathroom was Rhonda taking a shower. So much for having the place to herself tonight. Hopefully Rhonda wouldn't use up all the hot water.

Ginny kicked off her soaking-wet Keds and hung her trench coat on a hook by the door, then went over to look out the window. Not for the view, but to peer up at the sky to see if this storm appeared to be breaking up anytime soon. According to her weather app, it was supposed to be sunny tomorrow. Of course, that could change by then. Seattle weather was dependable in one way—it was always changing.

Ginny sat down at the tiny dining table and opened her laptop, absently perusing her personal email, which, as usual, was mostly filled with junk that needed to be trashed. But just before she dumped the last one, its headline caught her attention: *Find Your Dream Job*.

She rolled her eyes as she clicked it open. Dream job? Really? What would that be anyway? The email briefly explained the concept of job swapping, describing the exciting opportunity to try out a different job for a limited time. "Like a working vacation." According to the satisfied reviews, if they were genuine, it was becoming a popular trend in some professions. Including, she read, in the hospitality industry.

Out of curiosity, she decided to check out their website. After reading more happy reviews, she decided JobSwap.com sounded like a legit business. Ginny felt her interest piquing as she went into the hospitality industry section. Photos of exotic locations looked tempting. What would it be like to manage a hotel in Barbados? Before she knew it, she was filling out a questionnaire, and with a simple click, she had registered herself as a JobSwap applicant for hotel management.

# three

By the time the rowdy Brower group was fully fed, Jacqueline was fully fed up. If the men hadn't all been middle-aged and better, it might've been somewhat fun. But the only thing on their male minds—besides eating everything on the table—was fishing, fishing, fishing. Well, that and escaping their wives for a few days. Now all she wanted was to escape them. And she didn't even feel guilty leaving Margie with all the cleanup. After all, Cassie would be back first thing in the morning. She could help with the aftermath. And the breakfast.

As Jacqueline walked down the dark path to her cabin, she glanced at the cabin next to hers. Ben Tanninger lived there, but his windows were dark. No surprise there. Ben, the lodge's fishing guide, usually went to bed with the chickens. Of course, he also got up before the crack of dawn. Apparently the fish did too.

She sighed as she unlocked her door. Giving Ben's cabin one last glance, she imagined a happier scenario. Ben would be sitting on his porch, quietly watching her walk by. He'd call her over to visit with him, perhaps even apologize for his earlier rude behavior . . . and then, who knew? But even with only the moonlight to see by, she could tell his porch was vacant.

She went into her cabin and turned on the light. Of course, the first thing she saw was the enlarged photo of Ben in his fishing gear, holding up a trophy-size trout and grinning like he'd just won the lottery. She'd swiped that photo from Grandpa Jack's collection several years ago. Holding the framed photo, she sank into a chair and just stared into his smiling eyes. With his dark and wavy hair, short beard, and strong build, she thought he looked just like Chris Hemsworth.

She remembered the first summer Ben had come to work here. She'd been managing the lodge for almost two long years and was ready to call it quits. Even with her unimpressive résumé, she'd figured her degree in hospitality would help her land something. A roadside motel would be better than this place. Not that she'd gotten any offers.

But when the drop-dead gorgeous Ben Tanninger showed up, Jacqueline's plans changed. Her half-hearted job search was over. Sure, he was about twelve years her senior, but that only added to the mystique and attraction. It didn't hurt that the other part of his year was spent in his own law practice in Boise, or that he was working on a novel.

At first Ben had seemed to really like her. And why not? She set down the photo and went into the small bathroom, peering at herself in the mirror. Sure, she didn't look her best with her hair pulled back in a messy pony and smudgy mascara that hadn't been touched up since noon. But with her thick blond mane and big blue eyes, she knew that even at her worst she was eye-catching. And when she cleaned up and dressed right, some thought she was downright glamorous. More than once she'd been told she resembled Margot Robbie. Even tonight, the men had complimented her looks as she served them. Not that she'd particularly cared what those old geezers thought.

As she turned on the bathtub faucet, she realized that she still cared about what Ben thought of her. Probably cared too much! But she knew she'd caught his eye back when he first came here.

It hadn't hurt that she was Jack's only granddaughter. Well, until he discovered she had zero interest in fishing and a serious fast-water phobia. But she'd even made a couple brave, albeit failed, attempts to get over that these past few summers.

So last winter, well aware of how the river was near and dear to Ben's heart, she became determined to conquer this thing. She'd purchased an attractive turquoise life vest that matched her eyes and a helmet that didn't totally flatten her hair. She'd even been listening to an app to help overcome her river anxieties. It was particularly effective while immersed in a hot bath. She dropped a rose-scented bath bomb into the tub and swished it around, watching the water splash and bubble . . . pretending it was the river rapids and she was completely relaxed . . . and Ben was impressed.

Jacqueline knew most of Ben's story. He'd met Grandpa as a boy when he'd spent fishing weekends up here with his dad. It was no secret that her grandpa had been his hero. After his divorce, Ben began coming back to the lodge. He was so happy here that Jacqueline suggested he should work as a river guide—for free food and lodging. Ben had loved the idea of a seasonal job with a flexible schedule to work on his novel. And since then, Jacqueline had eagerly looked forward to summers and getting better acquainted with their handsome, hunky guide.

She and Ben had enjoyed some fun times together too. Playing cards, sharing stories, drinking beers by the campfire. By his second summer here, she'd even gone on the river with him. The first time, although she tried to hide her white-knuckled terror, he saw right through her. She pointed out that her mom had probably passed this unexplainable fear down to her, but Ben didn't understand. The second time was even worse.

But she'd really hoped that this summer would be different. To that end, she'd pulled out all the stops on her appearance. Her honey-colored hair was trimmed and highlighted, her complexion was glowing from a week's worth of nightly facials, her nails all gleamed from her latest mani-pedi, her teeth were whitened, and thanks to a fabulous new self-tanning lotion, she was golden brown. She'd never looked better! This was supposed to be her big chance to hook the man of her dreams. But so far it wasn't looking too good.

Jacqueline turned off the tap and slid down into the fragrant hot water. She knew it was futile, but she was determined to take this "sentimental journey" and try to understand what had happened . . . What had gone wrong?

When Ben had arrived last week, she'd been all ready for him. She was casually dressed in cute, faded-denim short shorts that showed off her long tan legs and a lacy white crop top that showed off her trim, tanned waist. Knowing he planned to arrive in the late afternoon, she sat out by the dock, just waiting to welcome him. As soon as his SUV pulled in, she eagerly jumped up and waved warmly, even offering to help him back his boat down the launch. But ignoring her, he'd turned to Grandpa to guide him. So she stood by and watched as Grandpa limped around, pointing this way and that until the boat was in the water and secured to the dock. She could tell, for some unexplainable reason, something had changed. Something between her and Ben felt different.

Since that afternoon, beyond a cursory hello, Ben turned the opposite direction whenever he saw her coming. Still, she'd been unwilling to give up. Maybe he just needed some chill time on his beloved river. She waited until Tuesday, the day he usually took off to work on his book. After observing him out on his porch with his laptop, furiously typing away, she decided to play the good fairy. Dressed in a new pale-pink sundress, she carried out a plate of still-warm blackberry scones—made by Margie, of course—and even offered to make him a fresh pot of coffee to go with them.

"Thanks, but I already ate," he told her without looking up from his screen. And then, when she'd lingered there, attempting some light, pleasant conversation, he simply closed his laptop and carried it into the house without another word. Practically slamming the door in her face.

That, she decided, had been the writing on the wall. Some people thought she was a ditzy blond, but she could take a hint! It was time to move on. Get out of this dead-end job. That night, she went online to see about returning the stupidly overpriced rafting vest and helmet—with no luck! Feeling even more discouraged and downhearted, she decided to check out new career opportunities. That's when she spotted the ad for a website called JobSwap.com. She went to the hospitality section and was swept away by beautiful photos of exotic locales.

Suddenly she was imagining herself in a brand-new life. Maybe on the French Riviera, or the Bahamas, or Hawaii, or Tahiti. Some amazing beachy resort that would be crawling with handsome eligible men. Where did wealthy young bachelors go to relax?

Before she knew it, she'd filled out an application to trade jobs in hotel management. Oh, sure, she'd probably painted her résumé in overly bright colors. Calling Grandpa's fishing lodge a "full-service river resort" and saying they "regularly hosted large group events," and a few other slight exaggerations that were a stretch, but if it got her out of here, it would be worth it.

That was several days ago, and so far, she'd received no bites. She checked several times a day. As she leaned her head back against her inflatable bathtub pillow, she decided not to check the website again tonight. She needed to relax and de-stress and start a new binge on the latest royal miniseries. She would watch until the wee hours of the morning if she liked, and tomorrow she would sleep in until noon. And if Grandpa didn't like it, he could just fire her! It would be her pleasure!

# four

Sometimes Ginny thought the main reason Diana kept her so busy was a passive-aggressive move to keep her from quitting. Diana probably knew no other manager would tolerate the nonsense she regularly dished out to Ginny. Or maybe Diana had other motives. She probably assumed if she buried Ginny in work, she wouldn't have time to date Adrian. Mostly Ginny didn't have time to seriously think about any of that. She also hadn't had time to check back with that job swap website.

In the past few days, she'd been forced to arrange several last-minute events—urgent requests from Diana's personal friends. "Important people of influence," Diana had told her, as if that made it okay. Despite futile attempts to dissuade Diana from creating a crazy, packed schedule that could blow up in their faces, Ginny had managed to squeeze in these impromptu affairs, including a huge baby shower on Thursday and a sorority reunion on Friday—both which sent everyone scrambling to keep up.

In the midst of that and her normal responsibilities, Ginny had also managed to convince her friend Zenith, owner of Happy Daze Weddings, to have all the flowers and decorations for Rebecca's reception in place by early Saturday morning. Ginny's plan was to photograph everything, then have her staff carefully remove and stow everything except the floral arrangements, which could do double duty for the anniversary party. After the anniversary guests left, Ginny and her crew, with her photos to guide them, would reassemble everything in time for the evening reception and before anyone in the wedding party was any the wiser. Hopefully.

By Saturday morning, Ginny was a bundle of nerves. Although the shower and reunion were behind her, Diana had been full of nitpicky complaints. Not a word of gratitude for miraculously making Diana's "important friends" happy—well, maybe not exactly happy, but at least they'd claimed to be satisfied. Considering the short notice, they should've been thrilled. But besides the stress of that, more of the hotel staff had gotten sick. They were seriously shorthanded now. Ginny would have only her favorite concierge, Andrew, to help her.

Zenith and her crew were just finishing the setup when Ginny and Andrew went to check on them. "Thanks for doing this early," she told Zenith.

"This early start is actually helping my schedule," Zenith admitted. "I've got two other weddings to set up today." She adjusted one of the flower arrangements. "Aren't these gorgeous?"

Ginny nodded. "I've never seen such a lovely assortment of blooms together."

"This florist is a real artist." Zenith stepped back to admire the room. "And she better be, for what she charges. She's the most expensive floral designer in town." Zenith called out to her crew, announcing it was time to move on.

"Good luck with all your weddings." Ginny followed Zenith to the door, then closed and locked it behind her. She nodded to Andrew. "Let's get to work."

Ginny pulled out her phone and began snapping photos. Because there were only the two of them, it was almost noon by the time she and Andrew had disassembled, carefully sorted, and safely stowed the decorations in a locked storage room. As they replaced the pale-lavender tablecloths with crisp white ones, setting each beautiful floral arrangement back into place, Ginny asked Andrew to be sure to round up a couple of helpers to redecorate for the wedding reception.

"By five o'clock," she said as she set a bouquet in the center of the last table.

"Will do," Andrew assured her.

Ginny paused to look around the pared-down room, then headed for the door. "I actually like it better like this."

"Me too." Andrew waited as she unlocked the door. "Too much glitz and glitter before."

Ginny led the way out. "Well, the bride must've wanted it like that. We just need to be sure we get everything back together in time. See you at five." As she headed for the elevators, she wondered what she would want if she were a bride . . . not that she ever expected that to happen. Besides, she had too much on her plate to think about such frivolities now.

It wasn't long before Ginny returned to the ballroom. It was time to congratulate Mr. and Mrs. Bremmer, see that the gratis drinks and appetizers were in place, greet a few guests, admire the pretty cake, and then return to work. So far, so good. All she had left was to put the wedding reception décor back into place, and then it was home for her.

It was a bit before five when she headed back up to the ballroom. Hopefully most of the anniversary guests would be cleared out by now. As she approached the door, she noticed Thomas Bremmer and a middle-aged couple just leaving.

"Thanks so much for everything," Thomas told her. "It was all terrific. Mom and Dad had a really great time." He nodded to his friends. "We're the last ones to leave."

"Oh, good." Ginny stared down at the floral arrangement in the woman's hands. "I'm so sorry, but those flowers need to stay here." She reached for the vase.

"But they said we could take them home with us." The woman pulled the vase closer to her. "And they're so beautiful."

Ginny looked past the woman and into the ballroom. By now her kitchen crew was at work, clearing tables of dishes and glassware. And to her horror, there wasn't a single bloom in sight. "Where are all the flowers?" She looked at Thomas in horror. "Where did the arrangements go?"

He shrugged. "Mom told the guests to take them home. She thought they'd just go to waste."

Ginny grabbed on to the doorframe to support herself, feeling slightly sick.

"Wasn't it okay?" Thomas asked.

"Those floral arrangements belong to the wedding reception that is scheduled for this evening." She tried not to glare at him. "I told you that on the phone."

"Oh? I guess I forgot." He reached for the flowers still in the woman's hands. "Sorry, Liz, we better give this back."

"Well!" The woman clutched the vase. "Does it even matter now? After the rest are all gone?"

"Yes, it does." Ginny gently but firmly extracted the bouquet from her grasp. "I might be able to use this as a pattern to get new arrangements made. If that's even possible."

"Well, I guess we should've left sooner," Liz said huffily as the three walked away.

Ginny stared down at the surviving arrangement, wondering where on earth she could find flowers to match these, let alone get them all arranged in an hour. She pulled out her phone and started calling florists, explaining the urgency, but eventually realized no one could deliver so much on such short notice. She knew that nearby Pike Place Market had flowers, but probably not like these. Still, what choice did she have?

She quickly gave instructions to her crew regarding setting up the room and even transferred her phone photos to Andrew, placing him in charge. Then, hoping for a miracle, she had the hotel van driver take her down to Pike Place, and together they gathered as many blooms as she could find that fit the color scheme of the pilfered wedding flowers.

As they drove back to the hotel, she knew that Diana would throw an enormous hissy fit over this embarrassing debacle. She might even fire her. At the moment, Ginny wasn't sure she cared. She just wanted to do whatever she could to ensure the wedding reception was as good as possible. After all, she tried to convince herself, they were only flowers . . . here today, gone tomorrow. A marriage should last forever. Well, in fairy tales, anyway.

At the back entrance of the hotel, Ginny texted Andrew, asking him to round up as many clear vases as he could find in the storage closet and to get them to the ballroom and fill them with water. Then she recruited some kitchen staff to help the driver get the flowers upstairs, explaining it was an emergency.

Eventually, with the help of her limited staff, each table was graced with a vase of flowers. Along with the other decor that Andrew had managed to get back into place, they all agreed that the ballroom looked very pretty. And festive. Sure, the makeshift floral arrangements looked very little like the original ones, but they would have to do.

To Ginny's relief—although the band was warmed up, the beautiful, tiered cake prettily situated, and food and drinks ready to be served—the wedding guests, including Diana, were running late. Ginny had time to make a swift getaway down the service elevator before anyone could arrive and react to the switcheroo. Hopefully no one would notice. She'd already given her staff some last-minute instructions and put Andrew in charge, and praying the wedding guests would all have a wonderful evening and that God would bless the happy couple, Ginny headed home. The wind blew hard and cold and bitter as she hurried toward her apartment, but it was probably nothing compared to what the weather in Diana's office would be like tomorrow. If Ginny had a hole to climb into, she would climb into it now.

# five

Between the Brower party's hot demands and Ben's cool indifference, Jacqueline was more than fed up. She was already packing her bags, making plans to "steal" Grandpa's old Ford pickup, and getting prepared to clear out for good. Maybe in the middle of the night.

"Did you get those clean towels to the Browers yet?" Cassie asked as Jacqueline came into the kitchen. "They called again, just a few minutes ago. Sounded pretty impatient too."

"What's new? Yeah, they got their towels. But now they want more plastic cups and ice for their *before-dinner drinks*." Jacqueline pointed at Cassie. "*You* should be taking care of this—not me."

"Take over here and I will." Cassie shook an onion at her. "I prefer housekeeping over KP any day."

"And Margie prefers your help to mine." Jacqueline scooped ice out of the icemaker, loudly dumping it into a galvanized bucket. "When will she be back with the groceries anyway?"

"Before now." Cassie frowned at the kitchen clock. "Think there's a problem?"

"A problem?" Jacqueline set the bucket on the counter and reached for her phone, checking to see if she'd missed a call from Margie. "If there is, then what happens?"

"Then it's you and me fixing dinner for twenty-seven hungry men."

"Hungry, ill-mannered men." Jacqueline retrieved a package of plastic cups from the pantry.

"Hungry, ill-mannered, *drunken* men," Cassie added.

"Don't remind me."

"I think men's week brings out the worst in some guys."

"It might not be so bad if any of them were under forty."

"Hey, there's Margie's van now." Cassie pointed out the window.

"That's one thing to be thankful for." Jacqueline picked up the bucket and headed back out. She hadn't checked her fitness app lately but felt certain she must've gotten ten thousand steps in today. At least with Cassie here, she wouldn't have to serve supper.

As she trudged back to Riverside Cabin, some men gathered around the smoldering firepit called out to her for more firewood.

"There's a big pile on the other side of the lodge," she said, as in *hint, hint*. Not that she expected it would do any good.

"Great. Bring us a load or two," one of them called back.

She wanted to yell, "Bring it yourself, you big lazy oaf," but noticed Ben walking toward her. It looked like he was walking toward her, anyway. At least he wasn't heading the other direction. Maybe he'd offer to fetch the firewood.

"Hey, Ben." She smiled.

"Better get that wood before the fire dies out," he said in a no-nonsense tone.

"Right." She paused in front of him, blocking his path and glaring up at him. "I suppose your arms are broken?"

"No, my arms are fine. I'm just on my way to meet with Jack. He wants to go over next week's itinerary before dinner."

"Oh, I wouldn't want to make you late for that," she said sarcastically. She was done acting polite around him. What difference did it make? "*Excuuuse* me!" She marched up to Riverside Cabin, knocking loudly on the door. It opened wide and she saw the men in various stages of dress, some playing cards, most of them drinking. "Here." She shoved the ice and cups toward the closest man, then turned and stormed off. She was done, finished, through with this place!

As she stomped off to her cabin, she regretted the fact she hadn't been more frugal . . . or started a savings account like Grandpa had advised. But she'd never been good at finances. Blame it on online shopping and exquisite fashionable taste, but her bank account was seriously low and her credit card was nearly maxed out. She didn't have enough to make it for very long on the "outside." That's what she'd begun to consider anything beyond Grandpa's fishing lodge—the outside.

Still, as she went into her cabin, she told herself she didn't even care if she had to find work at the greasy-spoon café down the road, flipping burgers and fending off truck drivers. Grandpa had already lectured her about sleeping in. She hadn't mentioned quitting just yet. But hopefully he wouldn't make her give up her cabin right away. She slammed the door and, blinking back tears of frustration, opened her tablet and checked her email . . . hoping for a miracle.

So far she'd received only one response from that job swap site. A manager from a Seattle boutique hotel had sounded mildly intrigued. But when Jacqueline eagerly responded, expressing genuine interest and overblown descriptions of the lodge, she never heard back a word. Even when she followed up by sending some picturesque photos of the lodge at sunset, and the shimmering river, as well as her own most glamorous selfies, hoping to encourage whoever this G. E. Masters person was to give her the time of day, she got nothing but crickets.

Feeling more desperate than ever when she saw no other hotel manager had bothered to reply, she decided to make one last-ditch effort to communicate with G. E. Masters. Trying not to sound as hopeless and frantic as she felt, she pointed out that the managerial position here included "free independent lodging and great opportunities for unlimited outdoor recreation." As she hit Send, she hoped—and even prayed—that would make the difference. Because, as much as she loved her quirky, old, persnickety grandpa, she was done with this place. Then she closed her tablet, turned off her phone, and ran a nice hot bath.

# six

Ginny knew something was wrong when a text from Diana disturbed her sleep at 10:37 p.m. But she was so exhausted, she silenced her phone and decided to ignore the message until morning. By the time she got up at 7:00, Diana had texted and phoned her sixteen times, but Ginny read only the last text, sent around midnight, telling Ginny to report to Diana's office at 9:00 a.m. Well, fine. If Diana wanted to scream and shout, let her.

Bracing herself for what lay ahead, Ginny went to work early. Her plan was to straighten her office and sort some things out. Just in case Diana gave her packing orders. But first she picked up a latte at the hotel coffee shop. Sequestered in her office, as she sipped her coffee with door closed and blinds down, Ginny decided to pass time by skimming through her own neglected email.

To her surprise, Jacqueline Potter had sent her three more emails about the job swap. The most recent post had several photos attached. Ginny studied the first two, shots of the lodge and river setting. The river was gorgeous and the log lodge with its big covered porch appeared rustically charming. This manager had even sent several selfies. But they looked more like glamour shots than from someone seeking a hotel management position. Well, it was almost nine now, and Diana was waiting.

Saying a silent prayer for self-control and patience, and with her notepad under her arm, Ginny rode the elevator up to the top floor. As owner of the hotel—actually co-owner, although that was top secret, Diana had an office that was part of a custom suite on the top floor. And very swanky. Feeling like she was going down death row, Ginny walked down the long hallway and past their most elegant suites. Finally, taking a deep breath, she rang the bell by Diana's door. As always, she waited for what felt like ten minutes but was probably only three before the door slowly opened.

"Come in, Genevieve," Diana said coolly, her expression even chillier.

"Good morning." Ginny forced a timid smile, following her in.

"Don't *good morning* me," Diana retorted as she sat down in the high-backed chair behind her fancy desk. Folding her arms, she narrowed her eyes. If she only had on a purple velvet robe, she could impersonate an angry monarch, behind her antique French Provincial desk. Adrian had confided that piece had cost north of four thousand dollars.

"I know this is about the flowers—"

"*You think?*" Diana pointed to the chair across from her desk. "Sit!"

Feeling like a scolded mutt, Ginny slid into the chair. "I'd like to explain."

"I'd like to hear your explanation"—Diana held up a hand—"when hell freezes over! What I want to know right now is what did you do with Rebecca's wedding flowers?"

"Well, I told you about rescheduling the Bremmer party and you said—"

"*What happened to Rebecca's floral arrangements?*"

"When I rescheduled the Bremmer—"

"Enough about the Bremmers!" Diana slammed both hands

on the desktop. "Vivian is furious! Rebecca was heartbroken and—"

"Heartbroken? *Seriously?*"

"You dare question me?" Diana's eyes became angry blue flames, and Ginny fully expected smoke to shoot out of her flared nostrils.

"Well, heartbroken?" Ginny frowned. "That seems an over-statement. After all, it was her wedding day, she should've—"

"She should've had her own flowers at her reception!"

"I agree, but the Bremmers thought—"

"I do not want to hear that name again! I know you gave your church friends Rebecca's flowers."

"I did not *give* them the flowers. They assumed they were—"

Diana leaned back with a slightly bored expression. "I know, I know. . . . The staff told me the anniversary people assumed the flowers were theirs to take home. But that was *your* responsibility, Genevieve."

"Yes, I realize that. But it was all such a mess and I—"

"I blame *you* for that mess, Genevieve."

"I'm aware of that." Ginny sat up straighter. "But you told me to do *whatever* it took to change the Bremmer party to a different—"

"The Bremmers again? Your nice little church friends, Genevieve, are a bunch of petty thieves. But that is not the point."

"What is the point?" Ginny had to bite her tongue to keep from defending the Bremmers again. Really, what difference did it make?

"The point is, once again, you have blown it, Genevieve."

"I'm sorry. If it makes you feel any better, I felt horrible when I realized what happened. I went to great lengths to replace the pilfered arrangements, but there wasn't much time and—"

"You honestly thought those clownish bouquets could replace the beautiful ones Vivian had ordered?"

"I did the best I—"

"Vivian threatened to sue me!"

"Your best friend?" Ginny blinked.

"My *ex*–best friend."

"I'm sorry."

"Spare me your pity." Diana stood with pursed lips. "I have agreed to cover all the expenses for the wedding reception."

"That seems unfair."

"Tell me about it. What I want to know is what are you going to do about it?"

Ginny stood too. "What do you expect me to do?"

"I could take it out of your salary." Diana drummed her fingertips on the desk.

"You could. Or I could just quit."

Diana made a feeble-sounding laugh. "And how would that help?"

"Look, Diana, you always seem to have it out for me. No matter how hard I work, it's never good enough. I'll admit that last night's fiasco was unfortunate, and I'm very sorry, but—"

"And you think quitting would fix everything? Leave me at the start of our busiest season to train a new manager? That would help?"

"I don't know." Ginny, clutching her notepad and close to tears, controlled herself from telling Diana she was the most self-centered person on the planet.

Diana turned away from her, facing the big window to one of the most spectacular views in Seattle, although Ginny wondered if her boss could even see it. "I hired you as manager when you didn't even have credentials, Genevieve. I have trained you and put up with your mistakes every step of the way." She let out a dramatic sigh.

Ginny wanted to defend herself, to point out all the good things she'd done for this hotel, helping to transform it from a run-down, lackluster, college kids' dive to the celebrated boutique hotel it was today. But she knew her words would be lost on Diana.

Really, it was probably time to step away. She put her notepad under her arm, started to turn around, then stopped.

"I have an idea," Ginny said abruptly.

"I'm sure you do." Diana sounded bored and weary. "Spare me."

"You might like this idea, Diana. A way to be rid of me for a while. And you might even discover a great new manager at the same time."

"Sounds too good to be true."

Ginny ignored her sarcasm. "I signed up with a website called JobSwap.com. They have a hospitality section." She opened her notepad. "And there's a lovely young woman in Idaho running a recreational resort . . . she's willing to trade jobs with me this summer. She has a degree in hospitality management and six or seven years of hotel management experience." Ginny opened up the best photo of Jacqueline and went over to show it to Diana. "Meet Jacqueline Potter. She's eager to trade jobs and would love to live in Seattle. It could be for a month or two this summer or, if it works out, you might want her here permanently." Ginny felt a rush of uncertainty. Was she burning a bridge? Or was it simply time to go?

Diana, rolling her eyes, turned to stare down at the face shot. After a moment, Ginny showed her the full-length photo, and the last one with the Hollywood smile.

"Pretty girl," Diana conceded.

"And unlike me she has a college degree," Ginny reminded her.

"And this website is legitimate?"

"Based on everything I've read, they are. They seem to check out their applicants very carefully. They've gotten excellent reviews. Even the Better Business Bureau had a good report."

"And this woman really wants to trade jobs with you?" Diana tapped the smiling photo of the beautiful blond.

"She seems to." Ginny wondered if Jacqueline would regret making this swap when she met her new boss. Or perhaps she and Diana would hit it off.

Diana's brows arched with interest. "Same salary?"

"That's part of the contract. I mean, if she agrees."

"And she's genuinely interested?"

"Definitely. The good news is, if we do this swap thing, I won't be leaving you without a manager," she said lightly. "Because I do think it's for the best that I go. At least for a while. We both need a break."

Diana turned to look at Ginny, her brow still creased. "I actually agree with you, Genevieve. I do think it is best." She pointed to Ginny's still opened notepad. "You work out the details with this woman. The sooner the better as far as I'm concerned." Once again, she turned her back to Ginny. "That's all."

Yes, Ginny thought, as she left the luxurious suite. *That is all.* If Jacqueline Potter was still interested, she could have this job. Maybe forever.

# seven

Jacqueline could hardly believe it when G. E. Masters sent an email asking to talk by phone. They scheduled an appointment for noon, but when the phone call came through, Jacqueline was surprised to discover that G. E. was actually a woman named Genevieve—or Ginny, she said, for short.

"I'd like to arrange a job swap," she told her.

"You're kidding?" Jacqueline anxiously paced back and forth on the front porch of the lodge, trying to calm herself. "I mean, when were you thinking you'd like to do this?"

"Actually, as soon as possible."

"You're kidding?" Jacqueline slapped her hand across her mouth, vowing not to keep saying *you're kidding*. "Well, that's very interesting. How soon would that be?"

"I suppose that depends on you. When is it practical for you to facilitate this?"

Jacqueline glanced at her watch. "Is tomorrow too soon?"

Ginny laughed. "Well, I'll admit that sounds tempting. But that might be a bit too hasty."

"Oh." Jacqueline sat down in a rocker.

"I'll need to get some things organized. And I'm sure you need to discuss this with your boss."

"Oh, that won't be a problem." Jacqueline refrained from admitting Grandpa Jack was her boss, or that he was about to kick her to the curb. "But, seriously, you're really down with this?"

"Absolutely. I'm ripe for a change. And your river lodge looks delightful."

"Oh, yeah." Jacqueline watched as the Brower party threw some of their gear into the back of a pickup while Mr. Brower noisily dumped ice into their smelly fish cooler. At least they were about to go home. "Delightful."

"So realistically. Do you know when you'll be ready to make this job swap?"

"You name the time." Jacqueline laughed nervously. "I wasn't completely kidding about tomorrow."

"Well, I think I'll need a full week to get everything sorted out. I want you to be able to hit the ground running. I'm sure you'd like to do the same for me."

"Of course." Jacqueline examined the nail she'd broken this morning while loading breakfast dishes in the dishwasher. She'd need to get that fixed.

"And in your application, you said you wanted to trade accommodations too. I live in an apartment with a roommate. I hope—"

"That's fine. I'd like having a roommate. And you'll be staying in my cabin."

"A whole cabin to myself?" Ginny sounded impressed.

"Oh, yes. Completely private." Jacqueline didn't care to mention it was also small and rather rustic. Ginny would find out soon enough.

"So how about if we do this next week?" Ginny suggested. "Although that's right before Mother's Day weekend. We have a special package, and the hotel gets busy that weekend. Are you okay with that?"

"Busy sounds wonderful to me."

"And you're certain you want to do this?" Ginny asked again.

"Absolutely. I've already started to pack."

"Really?"

"Yes. One way or another, I was ready to move on." Jacqueline paused, not wanting to sour this deal. She nervously glanced at the river. "I mean, this is a pretty place. You saw the photos."

"Yes, it looked beautiful."

"It is. But I'm ready for some city living. I can't wait to have some fun."

"And I'm ready for something quieter."

They talked a bit longer about the details, then, after agreeing to connect again later in the day, they settled on next Tuesday to accommodate the swap. They both agreed on a sixty-day swap, but Jacqueline would've gladly agreed to more. Ginny felt midweek was best since Hotel Jackson was the least busy then. Jacqueline had to agree that made sense, but if Ginny had said "tomorrow," Jacqueline would've been all in.

As she hung up the phone, Jacqueline couldn't help but do a Snoopy happy dance down the porch steps. "I'm so outta here, outta here, outta here," she sang to the fishermen as she scurried past them to her cabin. Her plan was to use the remainder of her lunch break to continue packing. After that, she'd go through the reception area and look over their bookings to make sure that Frederickson's Fishing Lodge was in as good a shape as possible. Like that was possible when they were running the place at 50 percent occupancy. No doubt, Ginny would have her work cut out for her when she arrived. But Jacqueline didn't want to think about that. Hopefully Hotel Jackson would run more efficiently and seamlessly than Grandpa's Podunk fishing lodge.

As Jacqueline opened her closet, she paused to admire her stylish wardrobe tightly packed into the tiny space. She extracted a pale-gray Ralph Lauren suit, still wrapped in its original garment bag. She'd gotten the jacket and skirt after graduating because it looked perfect for hotel job interviews. Not that it had landed her anything. And naturally, that expensive suit, as well as all the other fabulous pieces she'd acquired in hopes of a fancy career, had been completely useless out here in the sticks.

As she laid clothes on her bed, she held some up to her in front of the full-length mirror. "Note to self," she said as she noticed her messy ponytail. "Make another hair appointment." Maybe another mani-pedi too. She sighed happily to imagine the city people she'd soon be crossing paths with. The handsome suits and ties, fashionable women in pretty shoes, chic guests coming and going at the fancy Seattle hotel, driving expensive vehicles—something beyond old pickups and crusty SUVs. What fun it would be. And such a relief to finally mix with those who appreciated the finer things in life. It would probably feel just like a sophisticated working vacation. Who knew, she might even find romance in the city. Life was about to begin!

# eight

Ginny put all her energy into making everything about her job as clear and straightforward as possible. She wanted this transition to go smoothly for Jacqueline. And for the hotel. Despite her feelings about Diana, Ginny cared about Hotel Jackson. She felt personally invested in it—regardless of how her boss felt. And she planned to invest the same kind of enthusiasm in her new job at the recreation resort.

By now she knew, despite Jacqueline's glowing descriptions, that Frederickson's Fishing Lodge was a rather simple owner-operator resort that catered to outdoorsy guests. Not that it changed her interest in this swap. The idea of managing fishing cabins that accommodated only thirty to forty guests and an old-fashioned lodge that served "family style" dinners was hugely appealing. Even if for only a couple months of summer. During her time there, Ginny would do a larger job search and hopefully locate something suitable for the long term. Maybe a tropical resort in some far-off place.

Besides Diana, no one was supposed to know that Ginny was leaving until next week. Diana felt that would be easier on everyone. But somehow Adrian got wind of what was coming. And he was not happy.

"You can't leave us," he told her for the umpteenth time on the day she was scheduled to go.

"I already explained it to you," she reminded him. "Your mother and I both agree it will be for the best. For everyone."

"And it's really just a temporary trade? You'll be back in sixty days?"

Ginny closed the file drawer with a thud. "The agreement is that we swap for two months, but Jacqueline offered to extend it for the full summer."

"The whole summer?" Adrian looked seriously upset. "You'd stay that long?"

"I don't know." She bit her bottom lip, avoiding his eyes.

"But you are coming back, aren't you, Ginny?"

"That's the agreement. But anything could happen by then. Your mom may fall in love with Jacqueline and not want me back. Who knows?" She attempted her best nonchalant expression.

"And you still refuse to tell me where you're going?" he pestered.

"Why do you want to know?" She put the last of her personal items in her oversized bag. Everything else was packed in a box and stored, along with a lot of her other things, in the apartment building's basement.

"Maybe I'll want to come visit you." He leaned forward on her desk. "I know I'm going to miss you."

She forced a laugh as she reached for her notepad. "Well, I wasn't going to show you this, Adrian, but maybe it'll help." She opened it up to Jacqueline's pretty photos. "This is the new manager."

"Not bad looking." He nodded.

"I thought you might think so."

He looked back at Ginny with fondness. "But I prefer brown-eyed brunettes with sincere, open smiles."

She couldn't help but smile. "You're sweet, Adrian. I think I'm going to miss you."

"Don't go," he pleaded.

"Sorry."

"Is it my mom?" he asked for what felt like the hundredth time.

"I told you, we both agreed on this. It's just time. I need a little change."

"Just for the summer."

"That's what Jacqueline and I agreed upon." She picked up her bag. "I have to go, Adrian. Jacqueline is supposed to meet me here."

"She's already here?"

"Yes. We're meeting in the lobby. I'll help her get settled, then bring her back here for a quick tour." She looked hopefully at Adrian. "Maybe you'd like to help."

"Help?"

"Well, I could show her my office and a few things. Then perhaps you could give her the full grand tour of the hotel."

"I could do that. I'm supposed to have dinner with Mom at seven-thirty so I plan to hang around."

"Maybe you should invite Jacqueline to join you for dinner."

He shrugged. "I guess I could ask Mom."

Ginny actually hugged him. "Thanks so much, Adrian. You're a great guy."

"Do you really think you'll miss me?"

"I said so, didn't I? And, really, you should be happy for me. You're always telling me I'm all work and no play. Maybe I'll get a little time to play at the river lodge. Maybe I'll actually have some fun for a change."

He rolled his eyes. "Yeah, right. I bet you'll work harder than ever, Ginny. You'll probably try to reinvent the place like you've done here. You're a hopeless workaholic and you know it."

"Thanks a lot."

"Sorry." He put his hand on her shoulder. "I hope you do have some fun. You need to learn how to play a little, Ginny."

"I'll keep that in mind." She went for the door. "Anyway, Jacqueline and I should be back here around six. I'll shoot you a text to meet us."

"Can't wait." His tone belied his words, confirming to her that it really was time for her to go. Hopefully for good.

Her phone pinged. "That's Jacqueline. In the lobby. See you soon," she said cheerfully as she opened the office door to go out. She hadn't expected to feel emotional about leaving, but there was definitely a lump in her throat. She was about to give up a position she'd held for most of her adult life. This was it. She was done.

# nine

Jacqueline asked the taxi to wait while she looked for Ginny. The plan was to head for Ginny's apartment and drop off her things, but this hotel was so absolutely stunning, Jacqueline hated to leave. Was she dreaming? She was actually going to manage this place? It didn't look like a very big hotel—which was a relief—but from the luxurious lobby with its gleaming wood floors and expensive carpets, the elegant furnishings comfortably set around a marble-trimmed fireplace, a few well-placed antiques and paintings, and the enormous arrangement of fresh flowers on the front table, she felt like she'd been transported to a different world.

"Jacqueline," a tall, dark-haired woman said in a friendly tone.

"Ginny?"

"Yes." Ginny shook her hand. "Welcome to Hotel Jackson."

"It's absolutely gorgeous." Jacqueline stood straighter as she smoothed the front of her pale-gray blazer. First impressions were important.

"I'm glad you like it." Ginny nodded toward the front entrance. "Is that your taxi waiting?"

"Yes. With my bags and things."

"Well, let's get them to the apartment, then we'll come back here for the full tour."

"Great. I can't wait to see everything."

As they got in the taxi, waiting for traffic to move, Ginny told her more about the owner, Diana Jackson, as well as her son, Adrian. "It's possible you'll be joining them for dinner tonight. I asked Adrian to check with his mother."

"That'd be awesome."

Ginny's expression got serious. "I didn't really mention this before, but Diana can be, well, a little difficult at times. I tend to think it's just me. Probably because Adrian wanted us to date, and Diana didn't approve. Hopefully, you won't have that problem."

"Meaning, don't date her son?" Jacqueline asked.

Ginny nodded somberly. "That seems to aggravate Diana."

"Well, I'll watch my step then." Jacqueline smiled.

Ginny directed the driver to the apartment, which was only a few blocks away, but thanks to traffic the ride probably took longer than if they'd gone by foot.

"It's nothing fancy, but handy for walking to work," Ginny explained as they unloaded the bags. "Saves you a few bucks."

Jacqueline looked up at the lackluster building with disappointment. But since this was part of the swap, she didn't think she should complain. Besides, most of her time would be spent in that fabulous hotel anyway.

As they went up, Ginny told Jacqueline a bit about her roommate. "She's younger than me. Probably your age. She recently went from working nights to days. So you'll probably see a bit of each other in the evenings. When you're not working, anyway. But she's a sweet girl. I think you'll like her."

Inside the apartment was almost as disappointing as the exterior of the building, but again Jacqueline reminded herself she wouldn't be spending much time here. And who knew what new opportunities might arise before long. She dumped her bags on the floor of the tiny bedroom, then turned to Ginny with a bright smile. "I can unpack later. Right now, I just want to see Hotel Jackson and meet the owners."

"You got it."

Before long, they were in what had been Ginny's office but now belonged to Jacqueline. It wasn't as fancy as she'd imagined but was quite a few steps up from the fishing lodge. Ginny was showing her the computer and a few other things. Nothing too complicated. "This is the employee handbook," Ginny told her. "I tried to keep it relatively simple. More usable that way."

"You wrote it?" Jacqueline asked.

"Yes. I worked in several departments before becoming manager. So I sort of knew the ins and outs of the hotel."

Jacqueline wanted to know how Ginny could possibly leave such a delightful place—especially if she knew what she was getting in the swap. But Jacqueline had no intention of bringing any of that up. "Well, my grandpa, Jack Frederickson, is eager to meet you. They all are," Jacqueline told her.

"So they're all okay with the swap?"

"Oh, yeah. I mean, Grandpa was a little sad to see me go, but he understands."

Ginny handed Jacqueline a telephone directory for the hotel. "I know you'll get these numbers on your phone, but I think it's always handy to have a hard copy too. Plus, some of these are the landlines."

"Thanks." Jacqueline set it on the handbook just as someone knocked on the door. Ginny introduced a nice-looking man with sandy hair as Adrian Jackson.

"I'm very pleased to meet you." Jacqueline flashed her brightest smile. "You have a beautiful hotel here."

"Adrian is the CFO," Ginny explained. "His mother is the owner."

"Right." Jacqueline kept her eyes on Adrian. "Our resort is a family-owned business too. I like that."

"Adrian has kindly offered to give you the full hotel tour," Ginny told her. "That will allow me more time to get to the airport. And traffic gets gnarly this time of day."

"You're sure you don't want me to drive you?" Adrian offered.

"No. The hotel limo is already booked. Jeff's probably loading my bags right now."

Adrian nodded with what seemed a genuinely sad expression. "Well, stay in touch, Ginny."

"You too," she told him, then turned to Jacqueline. "You stay in touch too. If you have any questions, feel free to contact me."

"Same back at you," Jacqueline said.

"Well, I better go." Ginny gave her office one last long look, suggesting that perhaps she was having last-minute regrets.

"My grandpa plans to pick you up at the airport this evening," Jacqueline told her. "But you've got his phone number just in case, right?"

"Yes." Ginny held up her phone. "Well, this is goodbye." She reached out to shake Adrian's hand and then Jacqueline's. "Good luck." And then, with glistening eyes, she hurried out.

Now just Jacqueline and Adrian were standing inside the office. "Ginny seems really nice," Jacqueline said absently.

"She is. And a hard worker too. She'll be missed."

"Okay then, how about that tour?" she brightly asked him.

"Yes. Of course." He nodded politely.

"And Ginny mentioned something about dinner?" She flashed him her flirtiest smile. "That would be lovely. I haven't eaten since breakfast."

"Yes, my mother looks forward to meeting you."

"And I look forward to meeting her. The owner of such a marvelous hotel must be amazing."

"Amazing . . ." He frowned slightly. "Yes, that's one word for her."

AS THE COMMUTER JET flew to Idaho Falls, Ginny tried to suppress her doubts. No, this wasn't a mistake. And, yes, Adrian was a sweet guy, but he was not the guy for her. And she would not miss working at Hotel Jackson. Okay, she might miss it a little. She thought of the sweet farewell party her staff threw for her that morning. She would definitely miss them. But she would not miss Diana.

Expecting an elderly man with a gray beard to meet her at the airport, Ginny skimmed the people milling about the baggage claim and was about to check her phone when she saw a placard with her name on it. But the tall man holding it wasn't old and gray. She waved and, laden down with her luggage, walked toward him.

"Genevieve?" he asked.

"Yes." She nodded.

"Here, let me help you."

"Thanks." She paused as he took her more cumbersome bag and a duffel, leaving her with the wheeled case. "You can't possibly be Jacqueline's grandfather."

He chuckled. "No. I'm Ben Tanninger. I work for Jack Frederickson. He doesn't enjoy driving after dark. He asked me to get you. Hope you don't mind."

"Not at all." She smiled shyly at him. "Thank you."

"I assume Jacqueline made it to Seattle okay." He led the way out the door.

"Yes. We got her settled into my apartment, and she's probably just finishing up dinner with my boss by now."

"Hopefully having the time of her life." He chuckled as they crossed over to the parking lot.

"She seemed pretty thrilled with the hotel."

"I hope you'll be just as thrilled about the lodge." He glanced at her with what looked like curiosity, reminding her that, compared to his denim, khakis, and boots, she looked very citified.

"From what I've seen on the website and photos Jacqueline sent, I think I'll like Frederickson's Fishing Lodge."

"It's very outdoorsy and rustic."

"I observed that." As Ginny adjusted the shoulder strap on her purse, she wished she'd worn more sensible shoes. For a while, they both walked without speaking. But something about the silence felt awkward. Had she done something wrong? Finally, he paused by a dusty green SUV and began to load her luggage in the back. Then he went around to open the passenger door for her, waiting as she got in. A rustic gentleman?

As he drove out of the parking lot, the sun was dipping low into the treetops, but the sky looked clear and blue. "It must've been a pretty day here," she said absently.

"Not bad. We get a lot more sunshine here than Seattle."

"Yes, I've heard that. Must be nice."

For a while they drove without speaking and, once again, it felt awkward. Did Ben resent her coming here? Perhaps he, like Adrian, had been unhappy to see the manager go.

"What do you do at the lodge?" she asked. "I mean, your job?"

"Oh, I'm a river guide and fishing guide. But I only work during the summers. And not every day. It's not too demanding. Mostly I do it for my own pleasure."

"Must be nice."

Another prolonged silence. She glanced at his profile, which was strikingly handsome, but the firm set of his jawline suggested he was stewing on something.

"Oh, wow, what a beautiful sunset." She suddenly noticed the bright-red-and-gold colors out the side window. "Look at all those colors."

"That's from a slash and burn over that way. Probably last one for the season. Little late too, if you ask me."

"Oh." She continued looking at the sky. Even if the colors were from something burning, it was still pretty.

"I don't mean to be intrusive, Genevieve," Ben said in a stiff tone. "But Jack Frederickson is a good buddy of mine. And I just have to say something about this job swap business. Do you mind?"

"No, of course not. And I must admit this job swap feels a little strange to me. But please, will you call me Ginny instead of Genevieve?" She almost admitted the sound of her proper name always made her feel like she was being scolded since Diana so frequently used it.

"Right. *Ginny*, then. I just have to say that this whole job switcheroo might be a fun lark for Jacqueline, but I'm concerned it could be stressful for Jack."

"Oh, I hope not."

"Well, he's already stressed about it. And the poor old guy already has high blood pressure. He doesn't really like change. And Jacqueline jumping ship like that has got him a little worked up."

"I'm sorry to hear that."

"So if you're just doing this for the fun of it—"

"I'm a very hard worker. And I've been employed by the same hotel for most of my adult life." She regretted the sharp tone she was using, but couldn't quell it. "And for your information, I care deeply about excellence in the workplace. I'm committed to hospitality and fine customer service. I assure you, Jack Frederickson should have nothing to worry about. Thank you very much."

"Okay, okay. Sorry, I probably shouldn't have said that."

She bristled, folding her arms in front of her.

"But like I said, I care about Jack. He's more than an employer, he's a good friend."

"I understand that. But if Jack finds my work unacceptable, I will not hold him to the terms of the swap contract. I will not stay where I'm not wanted." She'd already done that—and it was not worth it!

Now Ben began to talk about the country and the river and other things, obviously trying to fill the air in hopes that whatever had just transpired would be neatly wiped away. Except that she was on the defensive now. She felt the need to prove herself. Not only with Jack, but with his river guide too.

# ten

Jacqueline was in seventh heaven as she dined with Diana and Adrian. Seated at the best table in a restaurant that overlooked the beautiful Puget Sound at sunset, being treated like a VIP, feeling like a celebrity, she resisted the urge to pinch herself.

"Your hotel is so amazing," she told Diana. "You must be so proud of all that you've accomplished—and you're so young too."

Diana looked amused. "Well, thank you, Jacqueline, but I am *his* mother." She pointed to Adrian. "So I can't be all that young."

"You could've fooled me." Jacqueline looked around the restaurant. "Everything about Hotel Jackson seems absolutely perfect. I'm so honored to be working for you. Even if it's only temporary."

"Who knows?" Diana waved to a waiter, who scurried right over. "I'd like a bottle of the Leonetti Reserve, the Bordeaux Blend. Served with the dessert cheese board, please."

"Perfection, Mrs. Jackson," he politely told her.

"Are you familiar with Seattle?" Diana asked.

"I wouldn't say I'm familiar. I've been here a few times. It's a delightful city."

"Well, perhaps Adrian can make time to show you around some. When you're not working, of course."

"Of course."

"When you're working, you're working." Diana narrowed her eyes slightly, then partially smiled.

"Yes." Jacqueline nodded. "Absolutely."

"Speaking of work, I assume Genevieve got you all set up in her office and walked you through things. I hope all is in order."

"Yes. Everything seems fine. And your staff seems very capable and enthusiastic."

"We do have good luck with employees. But you still need to let them know who's boss. I assume you know all about that though."

The waiter returned with an attractive cheese board and with a flourish uncorked the wine. Jacqueline tried not to giggle, thinking, *Toto, we are not in Frederickson's Fishing Lodge anymore.*

Jacqueline continued to effuse praise—she was almost worshipful—as they enjoyed the dessert cheeses and wine. She could tell that Diana liked being adored. And Jacqueline's admiration was 100 percent genuine. Diana was the kind of woman Jacqueline hoped to become someday. Perhaps she would rub off on her while she was here, under this amazing woman's wings, so to speak. Not that Jacqueline would say something that silly. Not aloud, anyway.

"Excuse me." Diana paused from telling Jacqueline about the hotel's history when her phone pinged. "I need to take this." She stood. "In fact, if you'll excuse me, I think I'll call it a night."

"Yes, of course." Jacqueline tipped her head as if addressing the queen. "It's been a pleasure getting to know you. Good night."

With Diana gone, Jacqueline turned her full attention to Adrian. "You're such a lucky man," she said, "to have grown up with all this."

"Lucky?" He frowned slightly. "Never heard it put quite like that."

"Maybe because you're used to it. To me it would feel like being a princess, growing up in a castle. Like in here." She waved a hand. "They treat you like royalty."

"At least to your face." He wrinkled his nose.

"Oh, well, that's just normal. I know my employees talked behind my back. But I just ignored it."

"Seemed like you and my mom hit it off okay."

"She's so wonderful." Jacqueline sighed. "I really look up to her."

"That's good. She'll appreciate that."

Jacqueline studied him closely. "You seem to have a little chip on your shoulder, Adrian. Something wrong?"

"No. Nothing I'm not used to. I'll just say this—everything is not always as it seems."

"Meaning?"

"Me, for instance. You assume I'm like the prince of the castle. But it's just a job. I don't own any part of this place."

"But your mom does."

He reached for the check. "It's getting late, Jacqueline. And I have an early appointment tomorrow."

"And I still need to unpack." Jacqueline stood, then glanced out the window. "That view is spectacular. And the sunset. So romantic. I bet you get lots of proposal dinners up here."

"Huh?" Adrian paused from signing the check.

"You know, couples getting engaged. This would be a great proposal restaurant."

"Oh, yeah. I guess so."

Jacqueline laughed. "Oh, Adrian. You're such an interesting character."

"Interesting character?" He frowned.

She playfully poked him in the side. "Okay then, maybe you're just a character."

This actually evoked a smile from him. Now that was progress! At this rate, who knew where she might get before this swap was finished?

# eleven

Ginny was relieved when they pulled into the lodge parking lot. By now it was too dark to really see much of anything. And the largest building, which she assumed was the main lodge, had no lights in the windows. "Looks like everyone's gone to bed," she said as she reached for her roller bag.

"Fishermen usually want to get up early." Ben pulled out her biggest bag. "I'm sure Jack's turned in by now. I'll see you to your cabin."

"Thank you."

Carrying her luggage, they trudged down a trail and past another building almost as large as the main lodge. "That's the Riverside Cabin. Large enough for groups. In fact, a group of ten will be checking in there tomorrow."

"That's nice." She knew her voice sounded flat. She felt flat.

"And these little cabins can house up to four guests, well, if two of them are kids. Otherwise, it'd be pretty tight."

"Uh-huh." She nodded woodenly as he turned up toward one of the small cabins.

"This one is yours." He set her bags on the porch, pulled a key from his pocket, unlocked and opened the door, then turned on the exterior light. "Here's your key."

"Thank you." She just stood there staring at him in the porch light. He still looked handsome, but harder somehow. Maybe because she suspected he didn't want her here. Well, there was nothing she could do about that. "Good night."

"Good night." He stayed on the porch. "I hope you're not one of those fearful types."

"What do you mean?" She tossed a bag inside.

"Well, sometimes we get guests up here who freak out over every little noise." He waved a hand. "We live in the woods."

"Yes, I know." She planted her fists on her hips. "And?"

"And we live by the river."

"So?"

"So animals live here too."

"Oh, really?" She heard the sarcasm in her tone. She wasn't usually like this.

"You know, bears and cougars and wolves. They live around here. The river draws their prey, and as predators, they follow. You need to respect that this is their home too."

"Are you trying to intimidate me?" She stood taller.

"No. Just saying. It's a fact."

"Fine. It's a fact." She tossed her duffel into the cabin with a loud thud.

"And sometimes we get raccoons or squirrels or other critters that can go bump in the night. But for city girls, well, it can all be a little unnerving."

"Okay. I get that. Don't worry, I won't be screaming my head off if I hear something. I don't scare that easily." She picked up the last bag from the porch and stepped into the cabin. "Thank you for your help. Good night." She firmly closed and locked the door, controlling the urge to let out a fierce growl of her own. All that talk of bears and cougars and wolves! Had he been intentionally trying to frighten her? Well, she would give him no satisfaction with that.

She turned on more lights and looked around her new home.

It was definitely small, but unlike the log exterior, it didn't look the least bit rustic. She turned on another light and studied the living room. The wood-paneled walls had been whitewashed, the pastel-colored shabby chic furnishings were actually more chic than shabby, and the small sofa and club chair looked comfortable. Not exactly her style, but not unattractive either. She wasn't so sure about the big-screen TV mounted to the wall. It just didn't fit with shabby chic or fishing cabin decor.

The bedroom was similar to the living area. The bed, with its white iron frame and soft pastel linens, looked inviting. And another not-so-big TV was in there too. Jacqueline obviously enjoyed watching TV. Like the living room, it was a little too cutesy for Ginny, but she couldn't complain. She opened a door to reveal a small but adequate closet. And another door led to a compact bathroom that was also light and bright, and even had a claw-foot tub. Much nicer than the old tub in her Seattle apartment.

The tiny kitchen had vintage-style aqua-blue appliances. Cute, but a little too tight for any serious cooking. Although the stove looked new, there was a layer of dust on it. She peeked in the fridge to see a few aging condiments, some moldy cheese and expired yogurts, and several bottles of water. And the musty smell suggested the shelves needed a good wipe down. Ginny surmised that Jacqueline hadn't eaten in her cabin very much. Probably easier to take her meals at the lodge.

Still, all in all, Ginny was pleasantly surprised. Even though the cabin was small, it was a little nicer than her Seattle apartment. She wondered what Jacqueline would think of her new accommodations . . . and her roommate.

As Ginny unpacked and put her things away, blowing away dust and brushing off a few cobwebs, she realized that Jacqueline hadn't been much of a housekeeper. But it would be fun to deep-clean a space that she would get to occupy all by herself. No roommate. It was heaven. Let the bears and cougars and wolves howl and growl and scratch down her door—she was staying!

# twelve

Jacqueline felt almost like floating on air when she walked up to Hotel Jackson in the morning. And she was wearing heels! The big flowerpots flanking the doors overflowed with succulent blooms and ivy, and as the sliding doors opened, she noticed how the glass gleamed in the morning sunlight. Entering the hotel felt like a dream, or perhaps the opening of a wonderful movie.

Everything inside looked even more elegant than she remembered from yesterday. She paused to take it all in. Everything looked orderly and peaceful. Nothing like Grandpa's somewhat chaotic fishing lodge! Even the music playing in the lobby sounded soothing and sophisticated. What a fabulously run place! And she hadn't even lifted a finger.

Apparently Genevieve—not Ginny, since Diana didn't call her that—anyway, *Genevieve* had the hotel working "like well-oiled machinery," as Grandpa Jack would say. Not that such a phrase would ever cross Jacqueline's lips. Not here, anyway.

"Good morning," the front desk clerk politely said.

"Good morning," Jacqueline replied, pausing to introduce herself. She read the woman's brass name tag, reminding herself that a good manager knows the names of all her staff. "So how are things going, Melinda?"

"Just fine, Miss Potter. All is quiet. How are you doing?"

"I'm doing quite well, thanks." Jacqueline ran a finger over the cool marble-topped counter, then smiled. "Have a good morning."

Melinda thanked her, then, turning toward a gentleman emerging from the elevator with a roller bag, she pleasantly greeted him. "I hope you enjoyed your stay, Mr. Renton. We look forward to seeing you again." *Sweet perfection*, Jacqueline thought as she strolled down the hallway to her office. Even the staff were perfectly trained. Heavenly!

In her office, Jacqueline went through the morning steps Genevieve had shown her yesterday. She reviewed the suggested to-do list and then checked the oversized calendar of events that Genevieve kept on the wall. "Naturally, I have all this in my notepad and desktop too," Genevieve had explained, "but I like a hard copy to refer to, just in case. It's my backup plan."

Jacqueline had agreed this was a wise practice. In fact, she kept the same sort of thing at the fishing lodge. Not as well done as this Genevieve, but it was there. As she sorted through some mail, she wondered how her replacement at the lodge was faring. Was Genevieve having any regrets yet? Fortunately, their signed contract would prohibit any changes of mind. Not that Jacqueline would blame her. But it would take armed guards to pry her out of this sweet place.

As she listened to voice mail messages, jotting down specifics from the concierge and housekeeping, she made a mental note to go speak to them directly. *Personal interaction between management and staff is vital to a well-run hotel*, she mentally quoted to herself. Last night before going to sleep she'd reread some sections in her favorite hotel management book, even highlighting some helpful tips. She looked up at the sound of a quiet tap on her door.

"Good morning." Adrian stuck his head in.

"Oh, hello, Adrian." She waved him into her office.

"How's it going?" He came in, leaning comfortably against the console.

"So far, so good." She stood. "Do you always come to work this early?"

"Not always. But I was hoping to leave early today."

"So you keep your own hours?"

"Kind of. CFOs don't need to be on-site as much as managers."

"So big plans tonight?"

"Not big. Just the Mariners game."

"Mariners? Is that hockey?" She moved out from behind the desk, hoping he'd notice how stylish she looked, or how this sky-blue suit brought out the color in her eyes.

He was clearly amused. "Baseball."

"Yes, baseball, of course." She nodded as if she knew this. "I adore baseball."

"You do?" He looked skeptical.

"Sure. My grandpa and I used to watch all those baseball games. On TV, of course. I mean, I've never seen a *live* game." She tilted her head to one side. "I assume that's what you meant. Or are you going home to watch it?"

"No, the game's at T-Mobile."

"T-Mobile?" She felt even more confused. "You mean you watch the game on your phone? Wouldn't it be better on a big-screen TV?"

Now he laughed. "T-Mobile is the stadium where the Mariners play their home games."

"Silly me." She moved closer to him with a sheepish smile, hoping he'd get a whiff of her spendy Coco Chanel perfume. "I just haven't seen enough of Seattle to get all these details figured out yet. You'll have to be patient with me."

"Well, you should probably ask the concierge for some help with that. Just in case a guest asks you." He stood up straighter, moving toward the door.

"Is the baseball stadium nearby?" she asked. "I might want to take in a game sometime . . . well, if I had someone to help me figure out how to get there and all. I assume there's a transit here. I mean, I don't even have a car." She reached over to pick a piece of imaginary lint off his sleeve. "To be honest, I feel a little lost out there."

He studied her for a brief moment, then smiled. "Well, as it happens, I have a spare ticket. Maybe you'd like to take in the game with me."

"I'd love to," she exclaimed.

"I don't want to interfere with your work." His brow creased slightly.

"Do you think your mother would mind? I mean, she did tell me that you might help me to get acquainted with the city. Going to a ball game is sort of like work."

"Can you be ready to leave by five?"

"Absolutely."

He looked down at her suit. "Do you have anything more casual to wear?"

"Of course. I'll grab something on my lunch break."

"Then it's a date."

She smiled. "I like the sound of that."

He looked a bit uncertain, but making a nervous smile, he backed out the door. Hopefully she hadn't come on too fast or too strong. She didn't want to overwhelm him. Then, as she watched him walking away, she remembered Genevieve's warning about Diana. Would she disapprove? After all, it was Diana who suggested Adrian show her around. Well, this might be a good test.

# thirteen

After a somewhat restless night of sleep, which Ginny attributed to the strange silence, she felt groggy when she woke up at seven. She had seen no coffee maker in the cabin's kitchen, but this provided her with a good excuse to pop into the lodge. Hopefully she'd get to meet Jack and some of the staff. Jacqueline had told Ginny that dress was casual here, but Ginny wasn't sure what that meant. She put on a neat khaki skirt, white shirt, and sandals. For Hotel Jackson, that would be way too casual.

As she walked toward the lodge, she noticed a pair of men down by the dock. Outfitted for fishing, they were loading a cooler into a riverboat. Curious to see more, she wandered down for a better look. "Going fishing?" she called out in a friendly tone.

"Nah, going duck hunting," the stout guy shouted over his shoulder in what sounded like a cynical tone.

"Aw, Brad, be nice," the taller man told him.

"Well, Jackie should know better than—"

"It's *not* Jackie." The taller man smiled at Ginny.

The other guy turned around. "Hey, you're right."

"Jacqueline did a job trade with me," Ginny said as she went down to the dock. "I'm Ginny. I start work here today."

"Welcome," the tall man said. "I'm Scott Woods and this is my brother Brad. We just got in last night. We'll be here through this coming weekend."

"A full week of fishing," Brad declared.

"Great. Then I'll probably see more of you." She pointed to the wooden boat. "That's a good-looking boat. Does it belong to the lodge?"

"Nah, it's Scott's," Brad said. "The lodge boats are already out. We got a late start."

"Well, good luck fishing." She waved to them, then took the path on up to the big lodge. She paused on the path to check it out more closely. It looked bigger in the daylight than it had last night. A handsome, rustic two-story log building, it had a substantial air about it. The generous porch ran the full length of the building. Several rockers and Adirondack chairs looked inviting. A nice place for a cup of coffee.

She went up the steps, then turned to look back. The view from the porch was gorgeous. Tall evergreen trees, a bright-blue river, snowcapped mountains, and a clear, clean sky. The front door was open and boasted an old-fashioned screen door that was painted dark green but was peeling a little. As she opened the screen door, she noticed a tear in the screen.

"Hello?" she called quietly as she went inside, although no one appeared to be about. She stood in the center of the large open room with well-worn wood-plank pine floors and a few area rugs. On one end of the room was a massive stone fireplace with comfortable-looking and slightly shabby furnishings. The walls, like the floors, were wood planks, but a darker brown and adorned with wildlife paintings and trophy fish. Everything had a manly, slightly worn look. But she liked it.

After walking through the room, she entered a large dining room with a number of wooden tables and chairs—including a couple tables that hadn't been cleared of what looked like breakfast dishes. Thinking to make herself useful, she gathered and stacked the plates and carried them toward a swinging door that she assumed was the kitchen.

"Hello?" she called as she went into the kitchen.

An older woman with flushed cheeks and a long gray braid wrapped around her head like a crown looked up from the sink with a surprised expression. "Can I help you?"

Ginny set the dishes near another stack and smiled. "I'd love a cup of coffee."

"Go ahead and take a chair out in the dining room. I'll get one out to you."

Ginny spied the coffeepot. "I can help myself if you don't mind. I'm not a guest. I'm Ginny." She stuck out her hand. "The new manager here. Jacqueline and I did that job swap."

"Oh, *Ginny.*" The woman wiped her damp hands on a stained apron. "I'm Margie, the cook. Jackie said you'd be here today. Good to meet you."

"Thanks." Ginny reached for a heavy cream–colored coffee mug, examining the faded, green logo. FFL, she assumed, was for Frederickson's Fishing Lodge, with a pair of crossed fishing poles beneath. Inside were old coffee stains. "Interesting mug."

"Yep, those are the old-timers. Been around the lodge since I was a youngin'. Only a few survivors. We keep 'em in here for the workers to use."

"Does that include me?"

"Sure, if you want. Jacqueline wouldn't touch 'em with a ten-foot pole."

"I like them." Ginny filled the mug with coffee, then stirred in some cream. "What kind of mugs do you use for guests now?"

"Just these." Margie removed a plain white mug from the dishwasher. "Boring."

Ginny nodded. "Yeah, a little. Too bad you couldn't get some more of these." She held up the clunky retro mug. "They're pretty cute."

"You hungry?" Margie asked. "I doubt there was anything edible in Jacqueline's cabin."

"I am a little hungry." Ginny went over to the big industrial stove, opening a lid to see some strips of bacon and slightly dry-looking scrambled eggs. "Is this up for grabs?"

"Sure, if you want. Should be warm still. And I just took them cinnamon buns out of the oven."

"They look yummy. Thanks." Ginny dished up a plate, then pulled a kitchen stool to the counter opposite where Margie was working. "Smells delicious." She forked into the eggs.

"Jacqueline never settled for leftovers." Margie rinsed a pot.

"For leftovers, this is really good." Ginny took another bite.

"We start serving breakfast at five thirty in the summer."

"Wow, that's early."

"Fishermen. They think they gotta be on the river by sunrise." Margie chuckled. "You know how them fish don't like to sleep in."

Ginny laughed. "So you must get up super early, then."

She nodded. "Before the chickens."

"Do you serve lunch here too?"

"Not exactly. I just make up a bunch of sandwiches and a few other things. I package 'em up and put 'em in the dining room fridge. Most go out with the fishermen, but there are always extras in case someone comes back early or forgets. You be sure and help yourself to 'em."

"Thanks. That's a great idea."

"Yeah, it gives me time for my midday nap."

"So, you're the only cook?"

"That's right." She pushed a strand of gray hair out of her eyes.

"Seven days a week?"

"During the peak season. Thankfully, my job slows down when the season slows down."

"Do you live here year-round?" Ginny sipped her coffee, which even with cream was still pretty strong.

"Oh, yeah. Otherwise, Jack would probably starve himself to death."

"Do you have any help in here?"

"Oh, sure. There's Cassie. She's the housekeeper. But there's not all that much to keeping house in fishing cabins. Change the linens, take out the trash, give it a wipe down and sweep up. Don't take that long. I used to do it back when I was younger."

"Sounds like a lot for just one housekeeper."

"Well, that's the way it is. And we're not usually full up. So when Cassie has spare time, she helps in here. And if I'm really desperate and ready to put up with some complaining, I put Jacqueline on KP. Well, I used to anyway."

"I'd be happy to help in here."

"Happy?" Margie looked doubtful.

"Really. I like cooking. I haven't had much opportunity lately. But I do enjoy it."

"Good to know." Margie scrubbed a baking pan. "So, you feeling at home in Jacqueline's cabin?"

"I'll say." Ginny tore off a piece of a cinnamon roll. "That bed was super comfortable. And I can't wait to try out that bathtub. Are all the cabins that swanky?"

Margie snickered. "Hardly. Everything's pretty rustic 'round here. The menfolk seem to like it that way."

"So Jacqueline must've fixed up her cabin herself?"

"Not exactly *herself*. She pressured Jack into them upgrades. Threatened to quit if he didn't give in."

"Oh?" She sipped her coffee.

"Yep. You're staying in the fanciest digs on the whole property."

Ginny felt a little guilty. "Well, it's a lot nicer than my apartment in Seattle. I hope Jacqueline isn't too disappointed."

Margie laughed. "Might be good for her."

Now Ginny felt even more guilty—and worried. What if Jacqueline was already regretting the swap? Maybe Ginny shouldn't be getting too comfortable here. Still, there was that contract. And this was only the first full day.

"You crossed paths with Jack yet?"

"No. I was hoping to meet him this morning. Is he around? Or did he go out with the fishermen already?"

"He would've liked to have gone out, but he hurt his ankle a week or so ago and it's healing up slowly. Makes him pretty cantankerous too."

"So where would I find him?"

"His office is on the south end of the building. It was added on back in the eighties, and the only entrance is on the exterior."

"Should I call him first? Make an appointment?" Suddenly Ginny felt intimidated. A cantankerous boss reminded her of Diana. And what if he was upset about losing his granddaughter to a city hotel?

Margie chuckled. "No, of course not. No one makes appointments with Jack. Just go knock on his door."

"Okay." She bit into a piece of crispy bacon.

"And don't pay him no mind if he seems grumpy. Jack hates being laid up . . . almost as much as he hates getting old."

"How old is he?"

Margie paused to think. "Well, let me see. I guess he's about seventy-five. No, maybe not. He's seven years older than me. I guess that only makes him seventy-four. Not that we talk about our age much around here. We like to think we're young for our age." She shook her head. "But eventually it catches up with you."

"How long have you worked here, Margie?"

"Goodness, forever." She wiped her hands with a thoughtful expression. "I guess it's been more'n thirty years. I came here after my marriage fell apart. Back in the early nineties."

"Wow, that's a long time at one job."

"Well, it's not just a job to me. Jack's like family."

"How did you meet Jack?"

"Through my best friend, Sandie. We went to school together in Idaho Falls. She married Jack about . . . oh, let's see." Margie counted on her fingers. "About forty years ago."

"Does Sandie work here too?"

"No . . . not anymore. Sandie passed away about seven years ago. Cancer."

"Oh, I'm sorry."

"Yeah, I still miss her . . . every day. We had such fun working together here. She had a delightful sense of humor. And she was a marvelous baker. Even when she was sick, she insisted on doing her part in the kitchen. At first I thought I'd leave—I mean, after she died. I was so lonesome for her. But then I wondered . . . where would I go? What would I do? And what would Jack do? He was already lost enough without Sandie around . . . I hated to leave him high and dry. So I stuck around. I thought for a while." She held up her hands. "But here I am still."

Ginny carried her dish to the sink to rinse, but Margie took it from her. "You better go meet Jack." She nodded to the counter behind her. "Take him one of those cinnamon rolls. They weren't out yet when he had his breakfast. But he loves 'em. Might sweeten his disposition."

"Good idea." Ginny put a good-sized roll on a plate. "Should I take coffee too?"

"Nah, he's got a crusty old pot in his office."

"Thanks." Ginny smiled as she pushed open the swinging door. "It's been a pleasure to meet you, Margie."

"You too. Already I think you're a better fit here than Miss Jacqueline. Just don't you repeat that." Margie winked.

"Don't worry, I won't."

As Ginny walked through the dining and main room, the morning sunlight highlighted a fair amount of dust on the wood surfaces. She ran a finger over the table by the front door, leaving a dark trail through the dust, and wondered when it had last been cleaned. She opened the screen door and decided, before the day was done, she would give this room some attention. Even if it was just a dusting.

She was still trying to wrap her head around the fact that Cassie was the only housekeeper for all those cabins. Plus, she did all the laundry? Well, it was no wonder the lodge looked neglected. Ginny wondered if their budget could afford another housekeeper, or even a cook's helper. But if summers were the busiest, why not hire students on summer break? They'd be looking for work.

The wheels in her head began to spin as she walked around the exterior of the lodge, taking mental notes about things that appeared overlooked. The porch and steps and railing were all in need of some attention. Weeds needed pulling. These were the things a responsible manager would've overseen. Had Jacqueline been negligent? Or was this simply a matter of budget?

# fourteen

Ginny braced herself as she walked up to the door with a carved wooden sign above that read THE BOSS STOPS HERE. This had to be Jack's office. She knocked firmly and, hearing a gruff "come in," opened the door. A grizzled old man looked up groggily from where he appeared to have been snoozing in a leather recliner.

"Who are you?" He scratched his head with a puzzled expression.

"I'm Ginny Masters. Your new lodge manager." She smiled stiffly and handed him the cinnamon roll. "Margie sent this for you. She told me I'd find you here."

"Oh, yeah. The city gal who traded jobs with my granddaughter—even though I told her I wanted no part of this tomfoolery." He set the roll on a cluttered side table, then pushed his chair to a sitting position. "I'd get up, but I'm a—"

"No, please, stay put." Had he really just said *tomfoolery*? "In fact, you should probably keep that sore ankle elevated."

"Ding-dong-dang foot." He reached for the cinnamon roll, pulling off a big chunk and biting into it.

She knelt down to peer at his foot, resisting the urge to touch

73

it, which she felt certain he would not appreciate. "Looks pretty swollen. How'd you do it?"

"Slippery rocks in the river," he mumbled. "Should've known better."

"Did you get it x-rayed?"

He waved a dismissive hand. "No need for that. Just a sprain."

"Did your doctor tell you that?"

"Don't need a doctor for a dang sprain."

"How long ago did you do it?"

"You a doctor?" he demanded as he chewed.

"No . . . but my baby sister is."

"Your *baby* sister is a doctor?" His tone dripped with skepticism.

"Well, she's not really a baby." Ginny pulled up a chair and briefly explained that Gillian had just finished med school and was now in Boston working in a research clinic. "To be an oncologist."

He set down his half-eaten cinnamon roll, wiping his sticky fingers on his corduroy trousers. "A cancer doctor?"

She nodded, and standing up, she glanced around his messy office for a napkin or paper towel for Jack but didn't see any.

"Not sure those cancer doctors do much good, but they sure get paid enough."

Ginny paused by his crusty-looking coffeepot, remembering that his wife had died from cancer. "Uh, do you want some coffee to go with that cinnamon roll?"

"Sure," he said gruffly. "I take it black. Help yourself if you like."

"No thanks. I already had some." She filled a mug, then seeing the pot nearly empty, turned off the burner.

"Well, have you seen the place?" he asked as she handed him the mug. "Frederickson's Fishing Lodge in all its glory?"

"Some of it."

"So . . . whaddya think?" He took a sip.

"I think it's beautiful."

He blinked, then opened his eyes wide. *"Beautiful?"*

"The river and the trees and the clear blue sky—and the mountains in the distance. It's all amazing. Even this lodge and the log cabins are charming. The whole place is really very beautiful."

He brightened ever so slightly. "So you're not sorry, then? That you traded jobs with Jacqueline?"

"Well, it's probably too soon to be certain, but I think I'll be happy here."

"After managing that fancy, citified hotel?" His brow creased. "Wait'll you been here awhile. *Stuck out in the sticks*, as my dear granddaughter liked to say. Give you a week or two and we'll see what you have to say about it."

"Okay." She folded her arms in front of her. "Unless you have anything I can do here to help . . . or other instructions you'd like to give me, I think I'll go check out the manager's office and see what needs to be done in there today."

"Fine. You do that." He set his mug aside to bend over for a fishing magazine that must've slipped from his lap, huffing loudly as he reached for it. But Ginny picked it up first, smiling as she handed it to him. He accepted it, grunting with a half-hearted thanks.

*Okay*, she thought, as she went outside, *that could've gone better*. Or it could've gone worse. She could tell he resented her presence here. Or maybe he was missing his granddaughter. Perhaps he was just unhappy in general. Or simply in pain. That ankle had looked very swollen through his thin sock. She was no medical expert, but she thought Jack should see a doctor.

After an hour in the manager's office, Ginny realized organization was not Jacqueline's strong suit. Or maybe she just hadn't cared. Ginny listened to phone messages, some from almost a week ago, and read emails that were even older. She jotted down notes and requests for bookings, and checking with the calendar she realized many of them were asking for days with vacancies. Being this hands-on with bookings was a little new to her, but she quickly got the hang of it and even devised a little make-do system in a separate notepad to streamline things.

It was actually fun talking to guests personally. Some were excited to return to a beloved retreat. Others had never been to the lodge before. But she could see that, although the lodge had visitors steadily throughout the summer, there was still plenty of room for more bookings. She wondered why a place this beautiful wasn't busier. Perhaps that was the way Jack liked it. Besides, she reminded herself, they didn't even have adequate staff to be fully booked. Poor Cassie and Margie would be run ragged. But on the other hand, if they were more fully booked, they could probably afford more staff.

During the quieter part of the day, when Margie was probably enjoying a much-needed nap, Ginny decided to attack the main room in the lodge. She'd located a storage closet with cleaning items, and after changing into old jeans and a T-shirt, she jumped in with Murphy's Wood Soap, a bucket of warm water, a mop, and some rags. She was just finishing up by the fireplace when a young woman wearing overalls and a ball cap came into the room.

"What're you doing in here?" the young woman demanded. She pulled off her cap to reveal shoulder-length, wavy red hair, and frowned at Ginny like she'd just caught her stealing the silver.

"Excuse me?" Ginny dropped her damp rag into the bucket and stood up.

"Who *are* you?"

"I'm Ginny, the manager of this lodge." Ginny wiped her damp hands on her jeans and forced a smile. "Just doing a little cleaning. Are you a guest here?"

"*You're* the manager?" She looked uneasy. "Why are you cleaning this room?"

"Because it needed doing."

"But that's *my* job."

Ginny's smile grew more genuine. "Then you must be Cassie.

I was hoping to cross paths with you today." She went over to shake her hand.

"Uh, nice to meet you, Ginny. But why are *you* doing this?" Cassie frowned down at the bucket.

"Like I just said, it needed doing." Ginny put a hand on Cassie's shoulder. "Look, I know you're the only housekeeper here. And I honestly don't know how you do it. You clean all the cabins, do all the laundry, and even help Margie in the kitchen?"

"Yeah." Cassie nodded.

"Well, I think you could use a little help. And I was done with the office work and thought it'd be fun to clean up this room."

"Fun?" Her pale brows arched.

"It's a beautiful room." Ginny pointed to the wood mantel she had just cleaned. "Look how this golden wood just gleams. Isn't it handsome?"

Cassie studied the mantel. "Well, yeah, I guess so."

"And after I do the tables and things, I'm going to mop the whole floor."

Cassie frowned. "Want me to help?"

"I'm sure you have plenty of other things to do." Ginny picked the rag from the bucket, wringing it out.

"Yeah, I need to start another load of laundry and get clean towels out to the cabins."

"See." Ginny started to wipe down the big rustic coffee table. "You have your work and I have mine."

"And you really don't mind doing this?" Cassie still looked doubtful.

"Not a bit. Before I became a hotel manager, I worked in house-keeping."

Cassie's eyes grew wide. "You did?"

"And I waited tables and a few other hotel jobs too. Those experiences made me a better manager." She grinned. "I jokingly tell people that I graduated from the Hotel Managerial School of Hard Knocks."

"That kinda makes sense." Cassie nodded. "Think there's hope for me? Could I manage a hotel?"

"Why not? Put your mind to it and get some additional training, and I'm sure you could work your way up into management."

"Well, I better get those towels out before the fishermen come home."

"Right. Nice to meet you, Cassie." Ginny returned to scrubbing the table.

"Yeah, uh, nice to meet you too." Cassie still looked slightly bewildered as she headed out. Did she really think Ginny's work in here threatened her job in any way? The poor girl was overworked and didn't even know it. Something needed to be done!

With the wood furnishings all gleaming, Ginny turned her attention to the pine floors. She was just finishing up the last of it when Margie came in with a basket of produce.

"Hello there." Margie set her basket on the table by the door and looked at the rolled-up entry rug. "What is going on here?"

"Not much." Ginny came over to peer in the basket. "What's this?"

"Some things I just picked from the garden."

"There's a garden?"

"Sure. But to be honest, the garden's not coming on too good yet. Too cold. But the greenhouse is full of fun. You should see my tomato plants." She picked up a small tomato and sniffed it. "Can't wait to get 'em transplanted outside."

"Need any help with that?"

Margie laughed. "Are you kidding?" She pointed to the mop and bucket. "So, really, what's going on? Looks like the cleaning fairy's been here."

Ginny just smiled.

"And here I thought she'd lost our address." Margie pointed to the mantel clock. "Almost time for me to start prepping for supper."

"Supper? Is that the same as dinner?"

"Of course it is." Margie looked amused as she picked up the basket. "I must say it's been a while since I've seen this room this clean. Even smells good." She frowned. "But does Cassie know?"

"Yes. I had to explain that I just wanted to do it. No reflection on her work. Honestly, I don't even know how you can keep up this lodge with so little help. You and Cassie must get pretty tired."

Margie sighed. "I'll admit, we get a little worn out. Especially toward the end of summer when we get real busy. By then, we're looking forward to the offseason, our chance to slow things down and get rested up."

Ginny had lots of questions but knew Margie had a schedule to keep. "I'll let you get to your kitchen. After I clean up some, I'll come give you a hand."

"I'd like that." Margie smiled. "Even if just for the company. You may not have noticed yet, but there's not a lot of gals around here."

"Don't women fish?"

"Of course," Margie called over her shoulder. "I like to fish myself, when I get the chance. But our lodge seems to attract more men than women. Like Jack says, it's a man's world here."

Ginny wondered about this as she gathered her bucket and cleaning things. Was that the intent? That Frederickson's Fishing Lodge remain a *man's world*? That might explain the worn, dusty furnishings and casual, unkempt feeling here. Maybe men liked it that way. Maybe Jack liked it. But it seemed a waste. With some well-planned improvements and upgrades and maintenance, this could be an amazing river retreat. And it could appeal to more than just fishermen. She closed the storage closet, then turned to look around the big room. It did look better, but there was still so much more that could be done. But not today. And not without Jack's blessing.

Ginny, feeling grubby from her housekeeping venture, was headed for her little luxury cabin when she noticed Ben strolling up from the docks. Unless she ran or took a different route, they were about to literally cross paths. Bracing herself for what she feared would be an awkward confrontation, she kept her eyes downward as she walked.

"Ginny?"

She glanced up to see him just a few feet away, frowning curiously at her. Suddenly aware of her dirty white T-shirt, slightly damp jeans, and dusty Keds, she felt embarrassed. Not exactly the picture of a respectable hotel manager.

"Hi." She shoved her hands in her pockets.

"Have you been fishing?" he asked.

"No." She forced a smile. "Just doing some cleaning."

"Part of your job description?" He looked amused. "Don't recall Jacqueline ever doing any cleaning."

"I sort of guessed as much." She nodded to her cabin. "Anyway, I need to get changed."

"Don't let me keep you from it." His tone sounded a little sharp.

"Right." She turned and continued on her way. It was hard to read that guy. Sometimes he acted kind of sweet. Then, he'd say something off-putting. But there was no denying that Ben was strikingly handsome. And he probably knew it too!

# fifteen

Jacqueline studied Adrian as he drove them to the baseball stadium. He wasn't nearly as handsome as Ben, but unlike Ben, he was giving her the time of day. And even if she did sort of talk him into taking her to the ball game, he was being quite nice about it. He'd even complimented her on her casual attire. She didn't admit that she'd spent almost a hundred dollars, on her credit card, for a new pair of jeans. But only because she'd left her "river" clothes in storage at the lodge. But these beauties fit perfectly and the Mariners T-shirt was, she thought, a nice touch.

"So how was your first day at Hotel Jackson?" Adrian asked as he waited in traffic that was trying to get into the stadium.

"It was wonderful." She sighed. "The hotel almost seems to run itself."

"Thanks to Ginny."

"You give Genevieve the credit for everything? I'd think your mother deserves some too, don't you?"

"I guess."

"How long has she owned the hotel?"

"Actually, it's my dad's family that owns it," he said as the traffic started to move. "But after the divorce, he let Mom run it." He glanced her way. "And I'd appreciate it if you didn't repeat that. Mom likes to think she owns it."

"Oh, yes, of course."

"She's been running it since I was a kid. But it was a real mess then."

"A real mess?"

"Oh, yeah." He made a face. "It stunk. Literally. The rooms were nasty. My grandfather Jackson was kind of a slum lord. He rented the rooms by the week. As a kid I thought the place was haunted. Sometimes I still wonder." He laughed.

"Wow, and she turned it around like that?"

"A lot of the credit goes to Ginny."

"Seriously?" Jacqueline had a hard time believing that. "How long has Genevieve worked there?"

"Since she was in high school. She worked in the laundry at first. Her mom worked there too. Until she died."

"Genevieve's mom died?"

"Yeah. Ginny was in college. She had to quit school to raise her little sister. She went to work full-time at the hotel then. Housekeeping. Then, she managed the restaurant. She helped figure out so many things that Mom eventually made her manager. All the while she was taking care of her sister. Ginny even helped put her through med school."

"Wow, maybe you should call her *Saint* Genevieve."

He laughed. "Yeah, maybe."

Jacqueline changed the subject by telling him about her grandfather's fishing lodge. Of course, she made it sound much nicer than it really was, but Adrian didn't have to know that. "Maybe I can take you there sometime," she said as he drove through the stadium parking area, looking for a place to park. "Do you like to fish?"

"Fish?" He pursed his lips as he parked. "That's something I've never done. Not even sure I'd want to. Do you fish?"

"No." She laughed. "I can't stand that stinky, fishy smell. I won't even eat fish anymore."

"Oh, I don't mind eating fish. Salmon, halibut, even swordfish from time to time. But I don't know about catching one myself."

"Well, then, we have that in common," she proclaimed as they got out. She continued to make small talk as they walked toward the stadium, getting into the back of a long line. "It's so strange to be out among so many people," she said.

"You mean compared to the river lodge?"

"Yes. It's pretty amazing." She studied a young couple ahead of them, thinking how cute the woman looked with her blond ponytail out the back of her dark-blue Mariners ball cap. Maybe Jacqueline would have to try that next time. Hopefully there'd be a next time. Because she'd already decided that even if the ball game was the most boring thing she'd ever seen in her life, she would pretend to love it. She would pretend to love everything about Adrian too. Even his plain white SUV, which she'd hoped would've been a convertible. But that could always come later.

IT WAS FUN HELPING MARGIE in the kitchen, but even more fun serving the hungry fishermen, listening to snippets of conversation, and trying to learn what it was that drew them to this lodge. Mostly it seemed to be the river and the "good fishing."

There were more than twenty guests in the dining room, but only two were women—middle-aged wives who'd come here with their husbands but didn't look overly happy about it. After dinner, as the men gathered here and there, in the main room and on the porch, or in camp chairs out by a firepit, the two women remained drinking coffee in the dining room.

"More?" Ginny held the coffeepot toward them.

"Not for me." The petite blond waved a hand. "I've had too much already."

"Half a cup." The other one pointed to the empty creamer. "And more cream, please." She smiled. "If it's not too much trouble, dear."

"Not at all." Ginny nodded. "By the way, I'm Ginny."

"I'm Becky," the blond told her. "This is Gayle."

"This is my first day of managing the lodge." Ginny got a creamer from another table, then asked how the women were enjoying their visit.

"Not as much as our husbands," Becky said a bit sharply.

"What happened to that other woman who worked here?" Gayle asked. "That beautiful young thing with the bad attitude. Did she get fired?"

Ginny couldn't help but laugh. "No. We actually did a job swap. She went to Seattle to manage my hotel, and I came here."

"Want to join us?" Becky offered.

"Sure, if you don't mind." Ginny filled a mug for herself and sat down. "I'd like to hear your thoughts about this lodge."

Gayle actually rolled her eyes. "You won't rat on us to our husbands?"

"Because we won't give them the satisfaction of knowing they were right." Becky scowled toward the main room where the fishing tales and after-dinner beer were flowing freely.

"They told us we'd hate it here," Gayle confessed.

"You can speak freely. This is off the record," Ginny assured them. "I'm just curious. This doesn't seem to be a very female-friendly place. Do you go fishing with your husbands?"

"That was the plan," Gayle said.

"We thought we'd give it a try." Becky scratched what looked like a bug bite on her elbow. "Our guys always go on and on about how great it is up here. They plan this big trip with a bunch of their old college buddies every year. Always in May. So this time, we thought, hey, why not join them?"

"Big mistake." Gayle set down her mug with a clunk. "Huge."

"We got ourselves fishing gear and vests and hats and everything." Becky wrinkled her nose. "What a waste of money that was."

"Our husbands warned us we wouldn't like it." Gayle slowly shook her head. "We didn't believe them."

"But they were right."

"So you don't like fishing?"

Becky's brow creased. "I don't know. I mean, I think I could learn to like it."

"The river is really pretty," Gayle conceded.

"But . . . ?" Ginny waited.

"They called this place a *resort*," Becky told her.

"A *last* resort." Gayle laughed.

"How long have you been here?" Ginny asked.

"Three days."

"Four more to go."

"So tell me about your accommodations," Ginny pressed.

"Accommodations? You'd really call them that?"

"I just got here last night," Ginny explained. "I haven't even seen the inside of one cabin yet. I mean, besides my own cabin."

"And?" Gayle waited with arched brows. "You *like* your cabin?"

"Well, I have to admit my cabin has been fixed up rather comfortably."

"Wanna invite us over for drinks?" Becky teased.

Ginny considered this. "Sure. How about tomorrow? Unless you're going fishing."

"I'm done with fishing." Becky pointed out several more bug bites. "Our husbands parked us on an island today. For the whole day. Fly-fishing. But the only thing biting was the bugs."

"It was torture."

"Jim and Clark liked it," Becky conceded.

"We told them no deal tomorrow. I think they were pleased." Gayle sighed.

Ginny stood. "Well, I need to go help in the kitchen, but tomorrow I'm officially inviting you to my cabin for lunch. Do you want to come?"

"Beats any other offers," Gayle said.

"And if you don't mind, I'd like to pick your brains," Ginny confessed.

"I don't think there's much left there to pick," Gayle told her.

Ginny laughed. "We'll see about that. But as the new manager, even if it's only temporary, I'm interested in what guests—especially female guests—think about Frederickson's Fishing Lodge."

"Well, if you're seeking positive reviews, you better—"

"No. Just honesty and suggestions. And I'll make sure you get a good lunch," Ginny promised.

"With drinks?" Gayle's eyes lit up. "Besides beer."

"I'll see what I can do." Ginny picked up the coffeepot and, with a wave, headed back into the kitchen to help Margie. Despite her reassuring Cassie, the girl's nose was still a little out of joint. Somehow she actually believed that Ginny wanted to replace her. Like that was even possible. But as a result, Ginny knew Margie was shorthanded.

"I'll get those." Ginny carried a tub of dirty dishes to the sink and began rinsing them, handing them to Margie to load in the big dishwasher.

"Were you visiting with the guests?" Margie asked.

"Yeah. It was pretty interesting."

"Interesting?" Margie frowned.

"Yeah. I'm curious about this lodge. Can you tell me, Margie, why do women feel unwelcome here?"

"Ask Jack."

"You think he'd even tell me?"

"No. He'd just say the lodge is a man's world. Fishing is for the fellows."

"But you said *you* like fishing."

"That's right."

"Did Sandie like fishing?"

"She sure did." Margie wiped her hands on her apron. "She and I used to go out together sometimes. We had a ball."

"Did more women come to the lodge back then?"

Margie got a thoughtful expression. "We did get more couples back then. And families. And sometimes women would come for a girls' trip."

"So what happened?" Ginny asked.

Margie held up her hands. "I don't know. Sandie died. Maybe Jack's interest in luring women here died too."

Ginny simply nodded. Maybe Margie was onto something. "Speaking of Jack, I'm worried about that ankle of his. It seems quite swollen. And it sounds like he hasn't seen a doctor."

"Tell me about it. I've been nagging him for a week."

"Does he have a doctor?"

"Not really. His doc retired a few years ago."

"We could take him to urgent care," Ginny suggested.

Margie laughed. "I'd like to see you try."

"Maybe I will." Ginny thought of Gillian. What would she suggest? Maybe it was time to give her baby sister a call and seek some medical advice.

As Ginny left the lodge, she noticed Cassie sweeping the front porch. "Nice work," Ginny told her.

"Yeah, the guys' shoes were extra dirty today. I started to sweep inside, but there's still a few in there. So I thought I'd get this."

"I can get inside later." Ginny smiled at her. "But I appreciate you doing this."

Cassie leaned on her broom handle with a skeptical expression. "If I'm not doing things the way you want, just let me know."

Ginny looked into her eyes. "I think you're doing a wonderful job."

"Really?" Cassie's brow furrowed. "You're not just saying that?"

"Not at all. But I am concerned you're doing the work of two people."

"It's okay. I'm used to it."

"Maybe, but I do want to talk Jack into hiring more house-keeping help."

Cassie shook her head. "Jack'll think I'm not pulling my weight. Already you're doing some of my chores. He might can me. And I really need this job."

"Don't worry. I'll make sure he understands." Ginny put her hand on her shoulder. "And just think, Cassie, if we hire another housekeeper, it will make you the *head* housekeeper. And that's like the first stage of management."

"Really?"

"Yes. And if things improve around here, and we get more guests, we'll need more help. And we should be able to afford it too. Who knows, maybe you'll be managing several housekeepers before long. How would you like that?"

"I'd love it." Cassie brightened, then shook her head again. "But . . . Jack will never agree to it."

"Give him time and he might."

"Like by the time I'm as old as Margie?" Cassie returned to sweeping.

Ginny just crossed her fingers and grinned. "We'll see about that." But as she walked to her cabin, she wondered . . . Jack was definitely a hard nut to crack, but it didn't mean she should quit trying.

AFTER THE MARINERS GAME, for which Jacqueline should've gotten an Oscar for her performance, Adrian drove her home. To Genevieve's apartment. He knew right where it was without even asking. She wished it was the kind of apartment where you could invite a guy up for a drink, but knowing that her roommate was probably parked on the sagging sofa in her grungy sweats kind of killed that idea.

"Thank you for the super fun evening." She smiled brightly. "Those Mariners are really amazing."

"They lost," he reminded her dourly.

"Yes, but they gave it their best effort." She waved her bright-blue foam finger beneath his nose. "And I enjoyed it."

"Well, you're a good sport, Jacqueline." He smiled.

"Thank you." She reached for the door handle, wondering if he might be going to go around and open the door for her. But since he just sat there, she opened it herself. "I'd love to see a Mariners game where they win. That would be so awesome."

He laughed. "Yes, I'll try to arrange that."

"Thanks, Adrian." She flashed her best Hollywood smile at him. "See ya tomorrow." And she blew a kiss. Hopefully he'd take the hint.

As she went inside, she wondered if he was really worth the effort. After all, he admitted that his mother didn't actually own the hotel. Although hadn't he insinuated that his grandfather did? Maybe that meant that Adrian would inherit it someday. That was worth even more!

As she entered her apartment, she got a text. She looked to see it was Genevieve—or Ginny, as she called herself. Worried that Genevieve was regretting the job swap, Jacqueline was reluctant to read it.

"Hey you," Rhonda called from where she was parked on the sofa with a remote. Jacqueline glanced at the unimpressive TV to see she was watching another true crime show. Not Jacqueline's cup of tea.

"Hello," Jacqueline said crisply. "And good night." Without another word, she disappeared into her room and sat down on the twin bed. Even with the bed against the wall, she barely had enough floor space to change her clothes. And Jacqueline had thought her tiny cabin was small. Compared to this jail cell, her cabin was a palace. However, that did not matter. The potential to have a great life in Seattle, meet interesting people, manage a gorgeous hotel . . . it made up for everything. And someday, hopefully in the not-so-distant future, she'd ditch this crummy apartment. She wondered how Genevieve had been able to stand it. Surely, she didn't want it back.

So she read her text message from Genevieve. To her relief, it was just a brief inquiry about how her day went. Jacqueline texted back that all was well here and asked about Genevieve's day. A similar reply came back and Jacqueline, convinced that Genevieve was having no regrets, started getting ready for bed. But before she turned off her light, she pulled out tomorrow's outfit, taking a few minutes to remove some wrinkles with her travel steamer. She believed in "dressing for success." And Diana, so far, seemed impressed with her new manager's chic sense of style. Jacqueline planned to keep it that way!

# sixteen

Breakfast was finished and cleared up, and Ginny had completed what few tasks needed doing in the office, when Margie offered to give her the "two-bit tour" of Frederickson's Fishing Lodge. "In all its glory." Her tone was tinged with sarcasm.

"I thought I'd already seen most of it." Ginny followed her to the back door.

"There's more to this place than meets the eye," Margie explained as they went outside. "Jack's grandpa bought the land back in the 1920s. He used it for a cattle ranch. About five hundred acres back then."

"So it's not that big now?"

"After Jack's grandpa passed, Jack's father sold off all but thirty acres of the best river frontage. That was in the late 1940s." Margie led the way down a trail that snaked out around the trees behind the main lodge. "While Jack's dad was in the Pacific, he'd had this dream of building a fishing retreat here when the war was over. He used the money from the sale to build the lodge and Riverside Cabin." She pointed to a cabin tucked into a thicket of fir trees behind the lodge. "That's where Jack and his parents lived when he was growing up, and where Jack lives now."

"It looks bigger than the fishing cabins."

"It is bigger. Not as big as Riverside Cabin, but good for a family."

"Nice." Ginny nodded. "Where do you live?"

"I have my own room. Upstairs in the lodge."

"Just one room?"

"It's a nice, big room. All I need. And it makes my commute to work a snap." She chuckled. "Not only that, but it's the warmest, coziest spot on the entire property in winter. I'm snug as a bug in a rug up there."

"Do you get any guests during the winter?"

"Not like we used to. It was better when Sandie was alive. But we still get a few. Folks that enjoy winter sports and activities nearby."

"I bet this place looks charming in winter." Ginny could imagine the little log cabins surrounded with snow.

"Sandie loved Christmastime here. She was always full of ideas. We used to put lights on that big spruce tree outside of the lodge. We'd all gather 'round with cocoa and caroling. And when the pond froze hard, there'd be ice skating with bonfires and big pots of chili simmering."

"That sounds amazing."

"It was." Margie's sigh was wistful.

"Is there still a pond?"

"That's right where we're headed." Margie led the way through a small aspen grove, and there on the other side was a fairly large pond, complete with cattails.

"How picturesque. Not as stunning as the river, but it's certainly pretty."

"It's a man-made pond. Jack's grandpa had it dug for cattle. But then, Jack's dad turned it into a trout pond. Stocked it with rainbows."

"Does it still have fish?" Ginny looked across the water's reflective surface.

"Of course." Margie led her out onto a slightly rickety-looking dock.

Ginny knelt down to peer more closely. "Oh, I see a fish! And there's a couple more. Do people actually fish here?"

"Used to. Back when this was a family place. Back when Sandie was still alive. Women and kids would come over here to fish and play and picnic . . . while the menfolk braved the river."

"And now?"

"Well, we don't get many women and children these days."

"Because you cater more to men?"

"I guess." Margie shrugged, then headed back down the rickety dock toward the shore.

As Ginny followed Margie down another trail, she got a better look at the back of Jack's cabin. It was somewhat overgrown but appeared to have once had a nice backyard. "So Jack and Sandie lived in that cabin too?"

"That's right. Jack added on to it after he and Sandie got married. It's got three bedrooms and two baths and its own laundry room."

"And they had children?"

"A daughter, Laurie." She paused to gaze at the cabin. "And they had a son too. Jack Junior, but they called him JJ."

"Jack's namesake. Is he Jacqueline's father?"

"No. Laurie is Jacqueline's mom."

"Oh. So is JJ involved with—"

"No." Margie sadly shook her head. "They lost JJ to the river."

"Really?" Ginny turned to look at her.

Margie's lips were pursed as if she was considering her words. "I might as well tell you about it . . . 'cause I know for sure Jack won't."

"What happened?"

"Well, let's see." Margie rubbed her chin. "Laurie was about six years older than JJ. In fact, Sandie had pretty much given up on having any more children by then. They were so happy when

JJ came along. He was the apple of his daddy's eye. Everybody's really."

"And he drowned?"

Margie led Ginny into a clearing where what appeared to be a garden was planted, then she pointed to a wooden bench. "I might need to sit down to tell this story proper."

"Of course." Ginny waited for her to sit, then sat beside her.

"Well, JJ was ten years old. He was a sturdy boy and old for his age. He'd already spent plenty of time on the river with his dad, helping with excursions and fishing and gear and the like. He was a real good swimmer. Jack made sure of that. And he knew the rules of the river. Jack made sure of that too. Jack never let JJ go out in a boat or a raft alone. That was a strict rule."

"Yes, ten seems young to be out there alone. I've seen riverboats going over the rapids from the lodge's porch. They look pretty scary to me."

"They can be . . . if you don't know them. Anyway, Laurie was a teenager. She never much liked being on the river, but she didn't mind helping out in the lodge. Anyway, it was late fall and the busy season had slowed down. Jack and Sandie had gone to town for supplies and left the kids at home. That wasn't unusual. Laurie was sixteen and used to watching JJ. Anyway, as the story goes, JJ somehow talked Laurie into taking out a river raft with him. No one could ever really figure that one out, and Laurie wouldn't talk about it. But the two took the raft out and hit some rough water. The raft flipped. Laurie barely made it out and JJ drowned."

"Oh my goodness." Ginny's hand covered her mouth. "So tragic."

"Devastating."

"Laurie must've felt terrible."

Margie just nodded. "Everyone thinks that's why she married so young. To get away from the whole thing."

"And Laurie is Jacqueline's mother?"

"That's right. She got married straight out of high school, and they moved off to Southern California. That's where Jacqueline was born."

"Did she grow up there?"

"Yep." Margie bent down to tug at a tall weed growing by the leg of the bench. "Laurie's first marriage fizzled when Jacqueline was young, but then she married again. Laurie was a real pretty girl—she snagged a wealthy older man second time 'round. They all came up to visit once. Then again for Sandie's funeral."

"So Sandie never really got to know her granddaughter?"

"Only through letters and packages and an occasional phone call. But you're right. Sandie never really knew her."

"Too bad."

"Not long after Sandie passed, Jacqueline got her fancy college degree and came up here to manage the place. Supposedly for a year or two. Her stepdad thought it'd be good job experience— you know, to help her to get into a bigger hotel. But Jacqueline ... well, she might not be cut out for this kind of work." Margie stood up and stretched her back. "Although it seems to have worked out for her, now that she's at your fancy Seattle hotel and you are here." She grinned. "At least for the time being."

Now Margie walked Ginny through the garden, pointing out what was growing or would soon be growing in the various raised beds. And then they walked through the greenhouse where the plants were further along.

"I like having fresh produce right here. Saves money and trips to town. Plus, it tastes better." She rubbed the small of her back. "Although the older I get, the more it plays havoc on my old bones."

"I'd love to help out here as much as I can."

"I'll be glad to take you up on that offer." Margie pointed to the rear of some nearby cabins. "Now if you'd like a little peek into one of the unoccupied cabins, I just happen to have some keys on me." She jingled her cardigan pocket.

"Great. I know they're nothing like Jacqueline's. I'm really curious."

"Right this way." Margie pushed back some brush growing up around the little front porch. "We really need to do some thinning, but with Jack laid up, well, some things just have to wait." She unlocked the door, swinging it open. "There you go. I'll warn you. The cabins on this end haven't been used since last fall. You never know what you might find after a long winter."

"Do animals move in?" Ginny poked her head into the dimly lit and musty-smelling space. Did she really want to go inside?

"Jack's worked hard to keep pack rats out, but you can never tell."

Ginny reached in to flick the light switch, then cautiously entered with Margie behind her.

"Smells okay-ish." Margie pulled a cord on some raggedy blinds, letting more light in to reveal very ratty furnishings. "If pack rats took over, it'd stink to high heaven. But might still be a few field mice hiding about. I keep telling Jack we need to get us a couple mouser cats."

Ginny noticed that one arm of the sagging sleeper sofa appeared to have been gnawed by a critter. And a scurrying sound made her jump and feel extra grateful for Jacqueline's shabby chic cabin. Because this one was downright shabby. She peeked into the kitchen. It was laid out like Jacqueline's but looked like circa 1980. Or maybe it just hadn't been cleaned since 1980. The single bedroom, with a pair of bunk beds and stained mattresses, didn't look any better than the rest of the place.

"This is even worse than I remember." Margie grimly shook her head.

"Why hasn't it been kept up?" Ginny asked. "Or is it just never used?"

"We're never fully booked anymore so the cabins down on this end don't see much use, if any. I think Jacqueline discounts them when we're full up, which is hardly ever. But be assured the other cabins are in a little better shape."

Ginny thought about the two women she'd met last night.

She couldn't imagine them spending more than five minutes in a cabin like this. In fact, she felt embarrassed to be the manager of such a dirty, decrepit place. It reminded her of how awful Hotel Jackson was when she'd first gone to work there in the laundry. But then they'd brought it back. It took time and work, and a boatload of money. But Diana's ex-husband's family had seen it as a good investment—whether or not it made money—because losses were considered valuable by people as rich as the Jacksons.

"Well, it's about time for my midday rest." Margie feigned a yawn as they stepped outside. She relocked the front door. "Gotta get my beauty sleep."

"Thanks for the tour. I should probably get my little luncheon ready for our female guests."

"You really gonna entertain them gals in *your* cabin?"

"I thought they might feel more open about sharing in there." Mostly she wanted to pick their brains without concerns that Jack might show up and overhear them.

"When they see Jacqueline's fancy cabin, they might throw you out and move in," Margie teased.

Ginny laughed. "I wouldn't be surprised." Especially if their cabins weren't much better than the one she'd just seen. No wonder Frederickson's Fishing Lodge had gotten a handful of one-star reviews. She'd researched some websites last night and wasn't terribly surprised at the stinker reviews FFL had received in the past few years. But for the short time she was supposed to be here . . . was it even possible to change anything?

BECKY AND GAYLE WERE SURPRISED to see the cabin Ginny was occupying. Of course, she'd primped it up a bit with a thorough cleaning, some furniture rearranging, fresh flowers, and a tempting light lunch prettily arranged on the coffee table. But after the women saw everything in her cabin, they were both impressed and irked.

"Why don't our cabins look like this?" Gayle asked Ginny as she flopped down on the white sofa. "You have a TV in the living room and the bedroom."

"We don't even have one." Becky sat next to Gayle with a frown. "I feel seriously cheated now."

"I'm truly sorry." As Ginny opened a bottle of Chablis that Margie had given her earlier, she explained about Jacqueline. "I guess she felt like the manager deserved the best. So she renovated her personal living quarters. To be honest, I feel a little guilty for getting the use of it."

"Feel free to hand it over to us," Gayle teased. "We won't feel guilty."

Ginny laughed.

"As manager, why didn't Jacqueline fix up the other cabins like she did this one?" Becky asked.

"I've wondered the same thing." Ginny filled their wineglasses as the women helped themselves to the food.

"Well, it is nice to be someplace a little less rustic than our crummy digs." Becky picked up her wineglass. "Too bad the whole place isn't run like this. That might entice me back."

"Really?" Ginny sat in the chair opposite the sofa, taking out a small notepad that she planned to use to record their thoughts and suggestions.

"If all the cabins were this comfy, I might invite other women to come up here too." Gayle put some salad on her plate.

"Do you think they'd come?" Ginny asked. "I mean, this is such a man's world."

"It doesn't have to be." Gayle waved her hand. "This cabin proves that."

"Why shouldn't women enjoy this place?" Becky pointed out the front window. "The river and everything outside of the cabins is so naturally beautiful. When we first got here, before I saw that lousy cabin, I thought I was in heaven."

"If only the accommodations matched the outdoors," Gayle said glumly.

"I agree," Ginny said. "This place could be amazing."

Suddenly they were all three talking about what it would take to transform the fishing retreat into a tempting vacation getaway. Besides the interior luxuries, they suggested flower boxes and comfortable outdoor seating areas overlooking the river.

"I actually thought I was coming to a romantic getaway," Becky confessed.

Gayle laughed. "Yeah, and don't those bunk beds just scream romance? And that bathroom—it could be used in a Stephen King movie."

"Especially with that flickering fluorescent light above the mirror," Becky added.

"The lighting in there makes me look dead. I could star in that Stephen King movie." Gayle made a face with creepy sound effects.

"I get it. The cabins are horrible," Ginny said. "But do you have any more suggestions for the exterior?"

"It's mostly pretty good. I love the look of the little log cabins and the big lodge. Even the Riverside Cabin looks good on the outside," Becky said. "But according to my husband, it's no better on the inside than our cabin. Just bigger."

"So we agree the property's exterior has a lot going for it." Ginny made a note.

"Well, other than a few maintenance things." Becky's expression grew thoughtful. "It's pretty weedy in places. Is there a groundskeeper?"

"I think the owner likes to do that himself, but Jack's a little laid up," Ginny told them.

"Yeah, we've seen him hobbling around."

"Any other thoughts or suggestions for improvements?" Ginny held up her notepad.

"The railing around our cabin's porch is a little rickety," Gayle said.

"Yeah, ours is too," Becky added.

"And the lodge building seems pretty good . . . until you look closer. Like that porch. It could use some upkeep." Gayle picked up a sandwich.

"And flowerpots would be nice on the porch."

"And more comfortable chairs. Maybe some blankets and pillows for evenings."

"And you should serve wine out there." Gayle refilled her glass.

"And hire a masseuse to work on our sore shoulders after a day of fishing."

Ginny laughed as she jotted that down. "That sounds lovely but might be pushing things too much. Still, we can dream."

"It might not take all that much to make this place dreamy," Becky said.

"It's such a departure from the city." Gayle sighed. "I was so happy when we first got here."

"Until you went into your cabin." Becky shook her head.

"That was a letdown."

"But there are good things here. I do like walking the river trail, and I did hope I'd learn to fish," Becky explained. "But fishing for hours on end and getting eaten by bugs. Well, it's not my cup of tea."

"The guys sure love it," Gayle said, "and I wanted to love it too."

"Because, honestly, I wouldn't mind a rustic experience," Becky added, "if there's a little luxury involved. You know, like this."

"And like that gorgeous bathtub in there." Gayle nodded toward the bedroom. "I'd pay you good money to soak in that thing."

"You don't have to pay me," Ginny told her. "You can soak in it for free."

"Seriously?"

"Absolutely. Just say when and it's all yours."

"Me too?" Becky asked hopefully.

"I guess you could take turns."

"I'd say tonight, but our hubbies have planned some sort of surprise." Gayle laughed. "I can only imagine."

"Probably fishing by moonlight," Becky added.

"I think that's illegal," Ginny told them.

"How about tomorrow night?" Gayle asked. "After dinner."

"That's fine." Ginny nodded.

"Me too?" Becky asked.

"Sure. Whatever." Ginny vaguely wondered if her cabin was about to turn into a bathhouse.

"That sounds heavenly." Becky sighed.

Gayle pointed to the big-screen TV. "Maybe we could watch a chick flick too."

"Why not?" Ginny said. "And there are lots of good bath salts and things in the bathroom. I'll be sure to put out some extra towels tomorrow. It can be like a spa night."

"I can't wait." Becky rubbed her hands together. "Imagine feeling clean."

"Have you seen the showers in the cabins?" Gayle asked Ginny. She held her hands about two feet apart. "So narrow you can barely turn around."

"And they smell moldy." Becky wrinkled her nose.

Ginny just shook her head. "I'll see what can be done about that."

"I asked Jim to complain to housekeeping." Becky shook her head.

"Our husbands couldn't care less," Gayle said.

"And they make fun of us if we complain."

"Or they say, 'We told you so.'" Gayle rolled her eyes.

"A real lose-lose situation." Becky helped herself to more salad. Ginny knew she couldn't possibly fix everything that was wrong with Frederickson's Fishing Lodge, but it might be fun to implement a few improvements. Like mildew-free showers? Surely that wasn't too much to ask. Even if Ginny had to do it herself, she was determined that by tomorrow night, the mildew would be eliminated from these two women's cabins!

# seventeen

The next day, Ginny took her notepad to Jack's office. Once again, he was asleep in his leather recliner. She apologized for waking him, and he pretended that he hadn't been asleep.

"Whaddya want?" he asked in a gravelly voice.

She held up her notepad. "I've been talking to some of the guests, getting ideas for ways to improve the fishing lodge."

"Huh?" He sat up straight in his recliner, giving a little moan as his feet landed on the floor. "Why are you doing that?"

"Because that's what a good manager does," she told him as she sat down.

"Why?"

"Because a good manager wants the guests to have the best experience they possibly can. Don't you agree?"

"Yeah, and that means good boats, good fishing, good food."

"And that's all?"

He shrugged. "Look, Ginny, you aren't going to be here very long, and things are just fine the way they are. If it ain't broke, why fix it?"

"What if something really is broke?" She looked at things she'd starred on her list. "Rickety handrails on porches can be dangerous. A guest could fall and break a leg, and you could get sued."

"Aw, pishposh."

She pointed to his foot. "Think how you'd feel if you hurt your foot just because someone had been negligent on their property. Would you blame them for your injury?"

"I dunno."

"Speaking of your foot, I asked my sister about it and—"

"The baby sister who's barely out of med school?"

"Yes. And she said you should get it x-rayed and that it might be broken, which is why it's not getting better. A sprain would heal more quickly."

"That's her professional opinion?" He pointed to her pad. "What else you got on that list?"

She knew he was trying to distract her. "Well, I was trying to focus on the simpler things first. Things that don't cost too much."

"Such as?"

"Well, the grounds are neglected. I've been pulling weeds around the lodge, but they seem to be—"

"Well, that's my job."

"And you are laid up."

"I can sit in a camp chair and pull a few weeds."

"Good. But what about the lodge porch? It really needs to be refinished before the wood starts to rot. Can you do that from a camp chair too?"

He glared at her.

"You need to get that foot looked at, Jack. I called the urgent care center in Idaho Falls. They said you don't need an appointment. You can just walk in and get an X-ray and—"

"And how much does that cost?" he growled.

"Don't you have insurance?"

He shrugged.

"Medicare?" she asked.

He shrugged again, avoiding her eyes.

"So you want to sit there being stubborn about your foot? Don't care if it gets any better? Meanwhile your wonderful property goes to rack and ruin?"

"Rack and ruin?" He scowled.

She looked at her list, reading off more neglected chores until he waved his hands for her to stop. "Are you always this much trouble?" he demanded.

"Trouble?" She made an innocent expression. "Trying to help improve your property is trouble? Trying to get you help for your ankle is trouble? Just how do you define *trouble*, Jack?"

He almost smiled.

She pointed to his foot with resolve. "You need to get that looked at. You want me to drive you to town or would you prefer Margie take you?"

"You mean right now?"

"Why not?"

"It'll be after five by the time we get to Idaho Falls."

"The urgent care place stays open until eight. Now you want me to drive or Margie?"

"Margie's got to fix supper." He narrowed his eyes. "That is, unless you can cook. Ready to take that on too, Miss Ginny?"

"Not exactly. I'm learning some tricks from Margie, but I don't think our guests would enjoy my cooking attempts just yet." Besides, she wanted to add, she looked forward to having his captive attention during the drive back and forth—but she didn't think he'd appreciate it.

"You know how to drive a stick?"

"A stick?" She frowned. "I know how to drive a car."

"Never mind. Tell Margie we'll be taking the van. See if she needs anything in town while we're out. No sense wasting gas."

"Good point." She stood. "I'll go talk to Margie. Can you be ready in a few minutes?"

"I was born ready."

She gave him a sideways glance, holding back on a retort as

she reached for the doorknob—then, hearing him groan as he stood, she felt sympathetic. "I'll be back with the van in a few minutes," she told him.

After explaining the plan to Margie, jotting down a short grocery list, and leaving her cabin key for Becky and Gayle, Ginny drove the van around to pick up Jack. She'd gotten her license years ago while driving the hotel van for guests and errands, but she hadn't driven much in recent years. Still, she felt fairly competent. Hopefully she wouldn't make too many driving mistakes with Jack watching. Although he'd probably enjoy ribbing her for it.

After a few minutes of riding in silence, Jack cleared his throat. "So, Miss Ginny Masters, tell me a little about yourself."

Ginny hid her surprise. "What would you like to know?"

"Well, so far I know you have a younger sister who's a doctor and you used to manage a fancy-schmancy city hotel." He folded his arms in front of him. "And I know you're a bossy gal. But not much more'n that."

She smiled. "A bossy gal? Not sure I've been called that before. But thank you."

"Thank me for what?"

"Oh, nothing." She turned onto the main road. "Well, let's see. There isn't really much to tell you about me . . . I was born in Seattle, lived there my whole life. I've worked at Hotel Jackson for most of my adult life." She sighed. "I guess I'm pretty boring."

"You didn't go to college? You seem like a bright gal."

"I went for a couple years . . . and had planned to finish . . ."

"Why didn't you?"

"My mom died when I was twenty-one. My little sister was only ten. So I quit school in order to take care of her."

"What about your dad?"

"He left when Gillian was still a baby." She bit her lip. "Probably a good thing too. One less person for my mom to support."

"Your dad didn't support her?"

"He didn't exactly believe in work."

"Huh? So what did he believe in?"

"Freedom, I guess."

"So he never helped support you and your sister? Even after your mom died?"

"Nope. I haven't seen him since I was a kid."

"And you took care of your sister? And supported her? When you were only twenty-one?"

She nodded. "I'd been working part-time at the hotel where my mom worked. She managed housekeeping. And I'd been working weekends in the laundry since I was sixteen. To help out my mom. Especially when she got sick."

"How did she die?"

"Cancer," she said quietly.

"I'm sorry."

For a while, neither of them spoke. Ginny was relieved he didn't want her to talk about when her mom had died. Those were years she didn't like to remember. Sometimes she still felt guilty for being too caught up in college and not paying attention to how sick her mother really had been, not urging her to get medical treatments. And then it had been too late.

Ginny pointed to a ridge of mountains. "Are those the Sawtooth Mountains?"

"Nah, those are the Blackfoots. The Sawtooths are a lot taller, and more jaggedy looking. Like a sawtooth."

"I guess that makes sense. Anyway, the mountains are pretty."

"So back to your life, Miss Ginny. Were you ever married?"

She grimaced. Here she'd been wanting to ask him about the lodge—instead he was grilling her. Well, maybe if she cooperated on this leg of the trip, he might cooperate on the way home. "No, I've never been married." She pursed her lips.

"Engaged?"

Her grip on the steering wheel tightened as she nodded grimly. "But it didn't work out."

"Why not?"

She considered this. Carson had been wealthy and nice-looking and intelligent . . . a dream guy really. Just not her dream. "Probably because he was all wrong for me."

"How long ago was that?"

She tapped the steering wheel with her fingers, trying to remember. "I guess it was about ten years ago. Gillian was almost done with high school."

"Hmm. And no beaus since then. You're a real pretty girl, Miss Ginny. And smart too. I'd think they'd be lining up at your door."

She controlled herself from laughing. "Not exactly lining up. There's a guy back at Hotel Jackson. The CFO. His family owns the hotel. He's asked me to marry him a time or two."

"Sounds like a catch. But you passed him up too?"

"He's a nice guy . . . but I'm not in love with him."

"Mighty picky, ain't ya, Miss Ginny?"

"I guess so." She laughed and considered telling him the "miss" part of her name was unnecessary, except that she sort of liked it.

"How old are ya anyway? I been trying to do the math in my head based on what you told me, but I can't figure it. When I first met you, I thought you were Jacqueline's age. But now I realize you gotta be older."

"How old is Jacqueline?"

"Old enough that I keep telling her she might end up an old maid if she don't get busy. I think she's north of twenty-seven."

"Well, I'm ten years ahead of her. I suppose that makes me an old maid." She pointed to her phone resting in the console's cup holder. "Can you turn on my GPS?"

He laughed. "You're talking to the wrong man. I don't know nothing about them things and got no plans to learn."

Keeping her eyes on the interstate traffic, she didn't see any place to pull over. "Well, it's already set, Jack. Just pick up my phone." She told him her passcode, and after several attempts he got it on. "Now click on the GPS app."

"What's an app?"

"Those little square icons on your phone are called *apps*."

"Not on my phone," he snapped.

She remembered Margie telling her Jack still used an old flip phone and it was usually dead. "Okay, look for the little square that looks like a tiny map and click on it."

It took a few tries and lots of coaching, but he eventually got it working. It was almost five when she pulled into the nearly empty parking lot. "They don't look very busy," she pointed out as she helped him hobble up to the entrance.

"Well, if they're like a truck stop, not being busy is a bad sign." He paused to catch his breath. "Maybe we better just forget the whole—"

"No way, Jack. We're here and we're going to get an X-ray." She held the door open, allowing him to go in ahead of her into the mostly empty waiting area. "You sit down and wait." She approached the reception desk, explaining the situation, then taking a clipboard back. "You need to fill this questionnaire out."

Jack squinted at the paper. "Not without my glasses."

"Then I'll fill it out for you." She sat down and began peppering him with questions. To her surprise, he sounded like a fairly healthy old guy. He didn't even take any prescriptions. She returned it to the receptionist and after a few minutes, Jack's name was called.

"Want me to go with you?" she offered.

"Wanna hold my hand too?" He growled like a grumpy old bear.

She wrinkled her nose. "Not particularly. If you don't mind, I'll go get Margie's groceries. I noticed a Safeway down the road."

"Fine." He pulled out a worn billfold, extracting a credit card. "Get gas too. I noticed the gauge was low." He handed her the card with a furrowed brow. "Just don't head off on a peanut whiz, that card's gotta limit."

She laughed. "Right. And if you get done before I get back, just wait—"

"Whaddya think I'll do," he growled, "walk home?"

"His exam and X-ray will probably take at least an hour or more," the receptionist told Ginny as Jack limped toward the door. "You should have plenty of time for your errands."

Ginny wished Jack good luck, then gave the receptionist her phone number. Just in case. The kind woman assured her that Jack was in good hands, and Ginny, trying not to feel like a negligent mother, left the clinic. After all, Jack was a grown man. And he didn't even want her there. Still, as she drove to Safeway, she prayed for him.

After gathering everything on Margie's list, Ginny got a few things for herself, then called Margie. "I don't think we'll be home until well after supper," she explained.

"Figured as much," Margie said quickly, probably because her hands were full. "Stop an' get a bite in town. Jack likes Sizzler."

Ginny told her they'd do that, then she checked out and went to get gas. By the time she got back to the clinic, the waiting room was empty. Even the receptionist was missing. Hoping nothing was wrong, she sat down and waited . . . and waited.

# eighteen

If Jack had acted like a grumpy old bear when Ginny left him behind at the clinic, he was a cantankerous grizzly when he finally came out. But at least his foot looked properly wrapped in some kind of bright-blue bandage. Seemed like an improvement. The receptionist handed Ginny some paperwork as Jack struggled with a pair of aluminum crutches, clumsily making his way to the door.

"And these too." She handed Ginny a little white bag. "The doctor prescribed pain pills for Mr. Frederickson, and I ran next door to the pharmacy to get them before they closed."

"Thank you." Ginny took the bag, then raced ahead of Jack to open the door.

"How are you doing?" she asked as he hobbled ahead of her.

"Dad-burned doctor," he growled as he worked his way toward the parked van.

"What happened?" She hurried ahead and opened the passenger door, waiting for him to fumble with the awkward crutches before he simply shoved them her way, making them crash down on the asphalt. As she scrambled to pick them up, he let out a loud groan getting into the seat.

"What happened?" she asked for the second time. "Why are you so angry?"

"Darn fool doctor," he grumbled as she tossed the crutches into the back.

She hurried around to the driver's seat. "What did the darn fool doctor do to you?" She put in the key but didn't start the engine.

"She broke my foot!"

"Broke your foot?" Ginny turned to stare at him. "What do you mean?"

"I mean she broke my dad-burned foot!" he spat at her. "And if I thought it hurt before, it hurts like the dickens now."

"Why on earth would she break your foot?" Ginny demanded.

"Just what I wanted to know!" he sputtered. "Hurt like the dickens. Still does. Crazy fool doctor!"

Ginny grabbed the bag and, removing the prescription bottle, she held it up. "Care for a pain pill?"

"I hate pills."

She shrugged. "Okay. But if you're really in pain . . . you know the road to the lodge has some bumpy sections."

"Fine." He snatched the bottle from her. While he struggled to remove the childproof cap, she reached into the back for a water bottle, handing it to him and waiting as he slogged down a pill.

"Margie suggested we get dinner in town." Ginny turned the key. "She says you like Sizzler." She picked up her phone—she'd already set her GPS for the restaurant. "Want to go have a steak?"

He firmly shook his head, then took another swig of water.

"You don't want a steak?" She pulled out of the parking lot.

"Don't want nothing to eat." He leaned back with another moan. "Just take me home."

"Yes, of course." She felt concerned now, but focusing on the traffic and how to get back on the freeway, she didn't say anything. Finally, sure that they were going the right direction, she glanced at Jack, relieved to see he looked a bit calmer. "Feeling a little better?"

He just grunted.

"I'm still confused," she said gently. "Why would a doctor break your foot?"

He let out a long, loud sigh. "The X-ray showed that my foot was broken."

"Oh?"

"According to Dr. Dreadful, it was healing up wrong."

"Uh-oh." Ginny thought she knew where this was going.

"That durned doctor. I think she got her medical experience in the Army. Anyway, she told me I needed to see a specialist—maybe even a surgeon." He took another sip of water.

"That makes sense."

"I told her in no uncertain terms that I had no plans to go see another doctor of any kind and that I was going home, and my foot could just keep on healing on its own. Even if it was healing up all wrong."

"Really? You don't want it to get better?"

"That's right. But Dr. Dreadful warned me I'd probably walk with a limp for the rest of my life."

"That doesn't sound good."

"So I told her I was an old man. It's about time I started to use a cane."

"And?"

"She told me I wasn't that old. And then she offered to reset my foot. Told me she'd done it before, and if I could take it, she could dish it out."

"So she reset it?"

"She broke it! I heard the bones snap."

"Oh dear."

"So I yelled at her, I told her she broke it, and even threatened to sue her."

"Oh no." Ginny felt terrible. Was this all her fault? Why had she interfered?

"So then, while I'm still suffering from Dr. Dreadful's treatment, the sadist forces me to get another X-ray. She wants to prove that she fixed it."

"And?"

"Well, according to the second X-ray, the bones are supposedly in the right place now. But according to the pain I'm feeling . . ." He paused to catch his breath. "I dunno."

"I, uh, noticed your blue bandages. Is that a cast?"

"Oh, yeah. And let me tell you that was no picnic either. Dr. Dreadful claims I should be able to walk on it—with some special kind of boot—by late June."

"Well, that's good news."

He harrumphed, then leaned back. She glanced over to see his eyes were closed. Maybe the pain pill was kicking in. After a few more minutes of quiet driving, she could hear him snoring. Hopefully, he'd keep that up for the rest of the trip. As much as she'd hoped to get better acquainted with him tonight, she knew this was not the right time. She even felt grateful for "Dr. Dreadful" getting the blame for all his pain. At least he wasn't blaming Ginny. Not yet, anyway.

AFTER PARKING THE VAN back by Jack's private cabin, she managed to help him get into the house. And, despite his protests, she got him settled in his recliner, where he insisted he planned to sleep. She read the directions for his pain pills, then wrote a note explicitly telling him when he could take the next one and, leaving it with a glass of water, set it on the end table by his chair.

"How about a little food?" she asked for the second time, but he just shook his head and waved her away.

As she walked back to the lodge, Ginny noticed the lights still on in her cabin's bathroom window and the flickering of the TV in the living room, suggesting that Becky and Gayle were still enjoying themselves there. She would've liked to have joined them but didn't want to intrude. So she went into the kitchen, and while helping Margie finish cleaning up, Ginny told her the whole story of Jack and Dr. Dreadful.

"Oh, for goodness' sake. Poor Jack. This will make him hate doctors and medicine more than ever." Margie hung the dish towel by the sink.

"I tried to get him to eat something, but he refused."

"I can make him eat." Margie opened the big fridge and foraged around. "How about you? Hungry?" She pulled out a plate of leftover fried chicken.

"Thanks." Ginny took a piece, then helped herself to some potato salad too.

Margie soon had a tempting plate ready to take to Jack. "You turn the lights out in here when you're done," she called over her shoulder as she left.

Feeling like Jack was in good hands, Ginny finished her late dinner. Hearing men's voices in the front room, she ventured out to see a pair of men sitting in front of the fireplace where a cheerful fire was crackling.

"Come on and join us," a middle-aged man called out to her. "Aren't you the new manager? The one who replaced Jacqueline?"

"Yes, but I don't want to intrude." Smiling, she kept her distance.

"No intrusion," the younger man said. "Andy was just lying to me about the *trophy-size* rainbow he caught and released today."

"It was—"

"Yeah, sure, Andy. But with no photo, no witness"—the younger man shrugged—"who will believe you?"

"Come on, Sully, you know I'm a man of my word."

"So how big would a trophy fish be?" Ginny hoped to quell the argument. "I mean, this is all new to me. As the lodge manager, I should probably start learning how these things work, right?"

The men were both talking and showing her with their hands the sizes of various fish when Ben entered the room with an armful of firewood. "Should we keep this going?" he asked as he stacked the birch logs on the hearth. Ginny could tell he hadn't seen her and considered slipping away before he did, but the two men were still talking to her.

"Sure," Andy called to Ben. "The night is still young and now we got a young lady to entertain too."

Ben turned to see Ginny. His smile looked curious as he stood. "Good evening, Ginny. To what do we owe this pleasure?"

She gave him a smirk. "I'm loaning Becky and Gayle my cabin tonight. They were feeling deprived of the simple pleasures."

"Simple pleasures?" Ben asked.

"You know, a bathtub, a TV, the basic luxuries that don't seem to exist here."

"Aw, no one expects luxury in a fishing cabin," Andy told her.

"Maybe fisher*men* don't, but fisher*women* might feel differently."

"Yeah, but that's exactly why we don't bring our wives up here," Andy protested.

Sully laughed. "Your wife wouldn't be caught dead here, Andy."

"And that's just how I like it." Andy popped open another beer, then held it out to Ginny.

"No thanks."

"Still on the clock, eh?" Andy teased.

"Maybe she doesn't like beer." Sully elbowed him.

"I was thinking I might get coffee instead." Ginny went back to the dining room to see the pot was still half-full, but cold. She filled a mug anyway, then warmed it in the microwave and added cream.

"Enough for one more?" Ben asked.

"Sure. I can't guarantee it's any good." She held up the pot of very dark brew.

"I'm used to lodge coffee."

"Cream or sugar?"

"Black."

"Brave man." She filled a mug, then put it in the microwave.

"Margie said you took Jack to urgent care."

"Yeah." She cringed. "Hope that wasn't a mistake."

"A mistake? I was giving you kudos for getting him to go. Jack hates doctors."

"I know. And he probably hates them more than ever now."

"That bad?" His dark brows arched as the microwave dinged.

As he took out his coffee, she briefly told him the story. He took a slow sip, then shook his head. "I was worried it could turn out that way. I tried to get him to go in right after it happened. But he was so certain it was just a sprain."

"I know."

"So he's really in a lot of pain?" Ben frowned. "Poor Jack."

She told him about the pain pills. "I had to convince him to take one."

"And he did?"

"Reluctantly." She glanced back toward the fire in the living room. The other men had left by now. "That's a nice fire you got going."

"Maybe we should go enjoy it." He waved his hand that direction.

She turned off the dining room lights, then went over to the fireplace. After warming herself for a few minutes, she sat in one of the big armchairs and, pulling her knees up and tucking her feet under her, cradled the mug in both hands. She watched Ben pick up a large birch log with one hand, using the fire poker with the other to rearrange the burning logs. His broad shoulders easily filled out his gray sweatshirt, and she suspected he kept himself in shape year-round, not just while working on the river. He tossed the log in, then turned around to look at her.

"You seem troubled." Ben sat down across from her, studying her with an intensity that was both disturbing and delightful. "Something wrong?"

"To be honest, I'm a little worried Jack will be seriously mad at me for forcing him to go to that doctor today." She smiled sheepishly. "He called her Dr. Dreadful."

"First of all, no one forces Jack Frederickson to do anything he doesn't want to do. Second of all, he'll probably thank you for it . . . *someday*."

While it was a relief to see Ben acting more civilly toward her, she still couldn't forget his accusing tone a couple days ago. "I hope you're right." She glanced at the clock to see it was past nine. "Isn't it getting a little late for you? I'll bet you have to be up early tomorrow."

"It's okay." He leaned back, casually sipping his coffee. "I don't mind keeping you company. How long did you say the ladies could use your cabin?"

"I didn't really say."

"Oh?" He smiled. "You might have to go pry them out of there."

"I think I'll give them until ten. But please don't feel you need to stay up for my—"

"Like I said, I don't mind."

She thought for a moment. "Then would you mind if I asked you a few questions?"

"Questions?" His brow creased with what looked like suspicion. "About what?"

She realized he might assume she meant *personal* questions. Although she had a few, that wasn't her intent. "Questions about the lodge, you know—the way it's been run and why certain things seem run-down and neglected. I'd hoped to gently probe Jack on our trip back home. And after the way he grilled me all the way to the clinic, I thought I'd earned the right."

"What'd he grill you about?"

She looked down at her nearly empty coffee mug. "My life."

"Jack doesn't usually show much interest in anyone's personal life."

"Guess he wanted to know more about who was managing

his lodge." She shrugged. "But on the trip home, the pain pill knocked him out. So I didn't really get any answers."

"Even without the pill, you might not have gotten the answers you wanted. Jack's pretty stubborn about his lodge. For years Jacqueline's tried to get him to modernize, but he doesn't like change."

"That's kind of what I thought." She downed the last of her coffee, then looked directly at Ben. "Can you explain why—if Jack loves this lodge as much as you've told me—why doesn't he take better care of it? Why is he letting it run down? Why doesn't he want to improve the cabins? Doesn't he want all his guests to have an enjoyable visit? Or is fishing the only thing that matters?"

Ben held up his hands. "Hey, that's a lot of questions."

"Sorry."

"But they probably boil down to just a couple of answers." He set his mug on the coffee table and leaned forward. "Do you know about Sandie?"

"Yes. Margie's filled me in. I realize that was really hard on Jack. But it's been about seven years. Seems he'd have moved on."

"Seems like it. But Sandie was sort of the heart of this place. She's the one who would've pushed for improvements and up-keep. When Sandie was around, the cabins were nicer. She liked good linens and attractive bedding. Even the toiletries were nicer when Sandie was managing things. She'd put little bouquets, picked from her own garden, in the guest rooms. And she'd put bigger arrangements in here and the dining room too." He pointed above the fireplace. "And her favorite painting used to hang there. A friend of hers painted it. She always said it was Jack in the riverboat, casting a line into the river. It looked great up there."

Ginny looked at the mounted trophy fish. It was still coated with dust since she'd been afraid to clean it and accidentally wipe off its scales. "What happened to Sandie's painting?"

"I don't know."

"Okay, so I get it. Sandie was the heart here. But if Jack loved

Sandie like I believe he did, wouldn't it be more honoring to her memory to maintain the lodge in the same way she did?"

"You'd think so. But that was never Jack's forte. His focus was always on the river experience—the fishing, the rafts, the boats, the equipment. If you check that out, you'll find everything is in pretty good shape down there."

"I'm sure that's important. And the men seem to appreciate it. But it's a shame the rest of the lodge doesn't measure up to the river. It's such a beautiful place. But it's not exactly female friendly. Which brings me to the big question—is it Jack's intention to keep women away from here?"

Ben laughed. "I don't think so."

"Well, you should've heard Becky and Gayle complaining about their accommodations here. Unless things improve, they will not be return customers."

He rubbed his chin. "Yeah, I'm pretty sure Jack's lost a lot of return customers. Couples and families, mostly. I know I've noticed the change over the years. Of course, the true fishermen put up with the less-than-pristine cabins."

"Less than pristine?" She frowned.

"Okay, downright crummy." He smiled. "But fishermen come home dirty and tired. They like to kick off their boots and throw their fishing junk on the floor. A little grime doesn't bother them."

She slowly nodded. "Okay, I get that."

"But there's more to it."

"More?"

"Jack's been steadily losing money on this place. Even though he hasn't increased his prices, his cabins are never full anymore."

"What did Jacqueline think about that?"

Ben looked uncertain. "I think she cared early on. She tried to reason with Jack. But Jack, as you know, is pretty stubborn. Jacqueline eventually just gave up. She focused on fixing up her own cabin and seemed to enjoy doing less and less."

"She was probably frustrated. I know I am. In fact, I'm surprised she hasn't found a better place to manage."

"I thought she had."

Ginny smiled. "Well, yes, but it's supposed to be temporary. Remember?"

"I wouldn't be too sure about that."

"Well, if she likes my job at Hotel Jackson, she can have it." Ginny blew out a sigh.

"Meaning you won't be going back to it?"

"I told my boss before I left that she should start looking for a new manager. Maybe it will be Jacqueline. She seemed quite charmed with the hotel."

"I'm sure it felt like a real departure from here." Ben tipped his head to one side. "I'll bet you're missing it by now."

Ginny considered this. "I definitely do miss some things." She thought of her fine staff, the cleanliness and order, the attractive amenities. She even missed Adrian's smiling face at times.

Ben stretched his arms, letting out a yawn, and Ginny stood up. "I'm going to take a peek at my cabin," she told him as she went to the window, trying to peer out.

"You can probably see it better from outside." He opened the front door that led to the porch.

She went to the end of the porch to see her front window. "Looks like the TV is off. That's probably a good sign."

"Want me to turn the lights off in the lodge?"

"Thanks." She watched him secure the fireplace screen and turn off the lights. Standing in the cool night air, she gazed up at the starry sky. She'd never known there were so many stars before coming here.

"It's so quiet and beautiful," she said as she heard his footsteps returning.

"Magical," he said quietly.

"And chilly." She shivered in the cold night air, wrapping her arms around herself to stay warmer. "The stars are so amazing. I never saw stars like this before." She felt something on her shoulders and for a brief instant thought he was putting his arm around her. But then she realized it was just one of the worn wool porch blankets. "Thanks," she told him.

"These clear nights are great for stargazing, but they can get pretty cold." He pointed to her cabin. "Hey, look, the two women are leaving now."

"You're right." She removed the blanket and set it on the chair behind her. "I don't have to be up as early as you, but I'm ready to call it a night."

"Me too." He pulled out his phone and used the flashlight to illuminate the path that led from the porch.

"Thanks for hanging out with me," she said as they walked together, parting at the fork that led to her cabin.

"My pleasure," he said in what sounded like a genuine tone. "Good night."

She told him good night, then hurried up to her cabin, thinking, *Yes, it has been a good night.* It gave her hope.

# nineteen

Although Jack was keeping a very low profile, Ginny tried not to worry about him for the next few days. According to Margie, who was keeping close tabs on him, his foot was starting to feel better. "But he hasn't left his house yet," she told Ginny as they washed up after breakfast. "He still hasn't got the hang of those crutches. But at least his appetite has improved." She pointed to the cleaned-off breakfast tray that Cassie had just brought back from Jack's cabin.

"Well, I've been taking advantage of his absence," Ginny confessed.

"So I've noticed."

"I'm trying to do all I can to improve things around here—without spending a penny."

"And I'm impressed. I particularly love the flower arrangements you've been putting here and there. So do the guests."

"Thanks to Sandie's picking garden. It's been so fun getting it back into shape."

"You've done a wonderful job out there. And I wanted to tell you that there's a bunch of old planter pots behind the greenhouse. Feel free to put them to use if you like."

"I like!"

"And I got to thinking." Margie rinsed a pan. "There's a bunch of old furnishings, antiques, linens, and all sorts of things up in the attic. Some that Sandie had collected and planned to use here and there, as well as some pieces Jacqueline stashed away because she didn't think they fit in here. But you might unearth something useful up there."

"Do you think Jack would mind?"

"I already asked him, and he didn't seem to think there was anything worth anything up there. He actually thought Jacqueline had cleared it all out and donated it to Goodwill."

"Did she?"

"No." Margie hung a saucepan on the pot rack. "I took a peek up there just this morning. It's full of hidden treasures."

"How exciting." Ginny dried a platter. "I'd love to see it."

"What's keeping you?" Margie nudged her with an elbow. "I can finish up in here." She told her where to find the attic staircase. "You're burning daylight, girl!"

"I'm on my way." Ginny removed her apron. Feeling like a kid setting off on a treasure hunt, she headed for the stairs.

When she got to the attic, she was amazed. Not only were there all sorts of interesting furniture pieces, there were also boxes of antique linens and unopened packages of new linens. She found charming framed prints of wildlife and nature. Old lamps, vases, mason jars . . . Perhaps the best treasure of all was a cardboard box full of woolen blankets with Native American designs. She shook one out, noticing the dust motes sparkling in the sunlight that streamed through the high window, as well as a few moth holes. But the blankets were beautiful, and she knew exactly what she would do with them. She couldn't believe that Jacqueline had ignored all of these delicious items—they were so absolutely perfect for the lodge and cabins. She couldn't wait to put them to use.

BY THE THIRD WEEK OF THE JOB SWAP, Jacqueline was completely disillusioned with her dingy, frumpy apartment. And she didn't know what to make of the strange woman sharing it with her. How did Genevieve ever put up with Rhonda? It wasn't that Rhonda was unattractive. With a complete makeover, she'd be rather nice-looking. And she was about the same age as Jacqueline . . . but she just wasn't the type of person Jacqueline would've chosen for a housemate. Or a friend.

For one thing, Rhonda worked at a restaurant. Not even a nice restaurant. Sure, it was a popular spot, but it was more like a greasy-spoon diner. When Rhonda came home from work, she smelled like onions. Or sweat. Maybe both. It was extremely unpleasant, and it permeated the whole shabby apartment.

To add to that, Rhonda had absolutely zero fashion sense. Oh, she thought she did, but her "thrift store rags," which Rhonda liked to boast about whenever she got the chance, looked like they should've remained on the rack. In fact, when Rhonda wasn't home, Jacqueline had hidden a few hideous items in the back of the coat closet in the living room area. Rhonda was such a slob she hadn't even noticed. And really, Jacqueline told herself, she was doing the girl a favor. No one in their right mind should wear a crop top with fringe! And hot-pink paisley leggings—really? She justified burying them in the trash because they had a run going right up the backside. Indecent!

Not that these feeble attempts at style direction had made any difference to Rhonda. In fact, Jacqueline's attempt at a serious fashion intervention had been misinterpreted as a girl-to-girl chat about *sharing* clothes. Rhonda had actually wanted Jacqueline to borrow her faux fur–trimmed *pleather* jacket—which, of course, smelled just like onions. Although Jacqueline had politely declined, Rhonda was not about to give up. If anything, she was more determined than ever to get Jacqueline into something more "creative and fun."

"Clothes should be an expression of our personalities," Rhonda told Jacqueline as she held out a large, rumpled paper bag.

"I agree," Jacqueline crisply told her. "But I'm not into wearing a brown paper sack, thank you."

Rhonda just laughed as she reached into the bag. "I found these little beauties on my lunch break." She produced a pair of well-worn black leather pants. "But when I finally tried them on, they were too long and too tight. But I bet they'd fit you, Jackie."

"I don't think so." Jacqueline controlled herself from telling Rhonda, for the umpteenth time, that she didn't go by *Jackie*. Not that Rhonda ever listened.

"No, really, I bet they'd fit you. I mean, they might be a little tight around your hips. But they're real leather and will stretch if you get 'em wet." Rhonda tipped her head to one side as she held the despicable trousers up to Jacqueline's waist. "And you can have 'em for only ten bucks."

"No, that's okay."

"Fine. I'll give 'em to you for six. That's half price. They cost me twelve, and the thrift shop has a strict no-refund policy. So you might as well—"

"No. I mean, I don't *want* them." Jacqueline stepped back with a frown. "Looks like the motorcycle mama who gave them away didn't want them either."

"Oh? Well, okay. Maybe I can sell them to Martie. She's a cook too, and she really likes my taste in clothes."

"Great." Jacqueline continued backing away, going into her room and shutting the door. How did someone like Genevieve put up with a roommate like Rhonda? Or a room like this one? And, according to Rhonda, Genevieve had lived here for quite a long time. Genevieve felt like a mystery to Jacqueline. Nothing made sense. But thinking of the woman now managing Grandpa's fishing lodge only made Jacqueline feel more frustrated. Not that she wanted her job there back. She did not! But after another difficult week at Hotel Jackson, she knew she was in way over her head.

Jacqueline picked up her phone and dialed, waiting impatiently as it rang. "Hello, Genevieve?" she said eagerly. "This is Jacqueline. Are you too busy to talk?"

"No, this is a good time. I just finished helping Margie clean up the supper things. What's up?"

"Oh, Genevieve, I really need your input."

"First off, please, call me Ginny. The only one who calls me Genevieve is Diana."

"Yes, well, Diana is part of my problem." Jacqueline sat on the edge of the bed.

"What happened?"

Not wanting to appear unprofessional, Jacqueline considered her answer. How much to disclose? "Diana and I seemed to hit it off . . . at first. But the last couple of days . . . well, I'm not sure what to think."

"About what?"

"About Diana. I mean she's a wonderful person, but she can be so . . . so unreasonable at times. I was wondering, is it just me? Or is she a prickly sort of person?"

To Jacqueline's surprise, Ginny actually laughed. "Diana can be rather prickly."

Jacqueline felt a glimmer of hope. "So maybe it's not just me?"

"Do you want to tell me what happened?"

"Well, it wasn't just one thing. I mean, I understand Diana's impatience with me. She is such a perfectionist, and I'm still figuring things out."

"Have you been following the protocol I laid out for you?"

"I've been trying. But sometimes I forget something and Diana can get so angry. I actually thought she wanted to fire me today."

"Oh, she used to threaten to fire me too. But then she'd cool off."

"That makes me feel better."

"How are you getting along with the other employees?"

"Okay . . . I guess. I mean, they still seem to miss you." Jacqueline couldn't admit that several had quit. But it was important for a manager to hire congenial staff.

"That's sweet. I miss them too. Please tell them hello for me." Ginny listed some names. "I sure could use a couple of them out here."

"I know it! I used to nag Grandpa to hire more help. But did he ever listen?"

"I think he might be starting to listen now. Have you spoken with him lately?"

"No . . ." Jacqueline felt a little guilty. "I've been pretty busy here."

"Then you might not know his foot was broken, not sprained." Ginny shared that she'd taken him to urgent care in Idaho Falls. "He was pretty grumpy about it for a while, but he's better now."

"That's good. I wish something would make Diana less grumpy."

"She likes being flattered and admired. I think she has a pretty big ego."

"That's an understatement! But sometimes even a really good compliment can set her off. She gets mad so easily. She totally lost it yesterday. I'm surprised you didn't hear her yelling in Idaho."

Ginny laughed. "What happened?"

"We'd been super busy thanks to a couple other events. And I was a little late in getting the ballroom all set for a little family reunion. Just half an hour. The family were waiting down in the lobby and didn't even complain." Well, not to Jacqueline anyway. Apparently, someone had complained to Diana. But Ginny didn't need to know all the details. "Anyway, you'd think I'd set the hotel on fire."

"Well, problems with scheduling can really upset Diana. Especially if it's someone she knows personally."

"Yeah, unfortunately, that was the situation. I apologized all over myself and even got her a box of really nice chocolate truffles." Not that Diana had ever acknowledged the expensive gift.

"I'm sure she liked that." Something about Ginny's tone wasn't convincing.

"I'm also aware that she's not too pleased that I'm dating her son." Jacqueline knew that "dating" was an exaggeration. The Mariners game and meeting for drinks twice—because she'd asked him—probably didn't really count as "dating." But it was a beginning.

"You're dating Adrian?" Ginny sounded genuinely curious.

"Oh, yeah. Do you mind? I mean, I realize you and he used to—"

"We were only friends," Ginny interrupted. "I think it's great that you're dating him. Well, except you're right. It might aggravate Diana."

"Yes. Adrian warned me too. So we'll keep our relationship under wraps." She told Ginny about the baseball game, overblowing it some, but it was fun to imagine how it could've been.

"Oh, that must've been fun. I used to go to the games with Adrian. He's a huge Mariners fan."

"For sure. I think we'll go again on Thursday." Okay, that was a flat-out lie. But she didn't want Ginny to think she could come back and steal Adrian from her by simply attending a ball game with him. "So, I'm going on and on about my life, Ginny. How are things on the river?"

"Interesting."

"Interesting?" Jacqueline blinked. "How so?"

"Well, I've gotten Jack to agree to a few small improvements."

"Small improvements?" Jacqueline felt indignation rising. "What kind of improvements?"

"Nothing that costs much money, of course."

"Of course. Grandpa is such a tightwad."

"Well, the lodge has been underperforming financially. But you already know about that. Anyway, I've convinced Jack to allow me to work on things that don't require any capital."

"Really? What can you possibly do that doesn't cost anything?"

"Not a lot." Ginny sighed. "But I have been doing some minor repairs and some deep cleaning and even some landscaping up-keep. Stuff that requires more elbow grease than funds. Small projects."

"And you do these small projects yourself?"

"Sure. It's not that busy in the office. And it's been fun seeing small things getting better. Jack's still a little laid up with his foot. Hopefully he'll get a walking boot soon."

"Yeah, I guess. So what exactly have you been doing? What kind of small projects?" Jacqueline leaned back on her bed, trying to imagine why a manager would want to deep clean or landscape.

"Well, yesterday, Margie let me use some old flowerpots and I transplanted things from your grandmother's overgrown flower garden. I've been picking flowers for bouquets. Just simple arrangements in mason jars. I put in wildflowers and branches and grasses and things. No big deal. But it's free decor that dresses the place up a little. Plus, it's just fun. And the guests seem to like it."

"Oh?" Jacqueline suddenly remembered she hadn't ordered floral arrangements for the upcoming weekend. She'd meant to do it first thing this morning. Now it was too late. Hopefully tomorrow would be soon enough. She realized Ginny was still talking about things she'd done at the lodge.

"And I've been going through the attic. Margie asked Jack and he gave the okay. Anyway, I've found some pretty cool things that I've been trying to put to good use."

"Cool things? Like what?" Jacqueline had meant to get some of that old junk cleared out and sent to Goodwill but had never gotten around to it.

"All sorts of treasures. Old furniture that I've cleaned up and put to use. You know, a table here or a chair there. And some charming linens and quilts. And these blankets that are amazing."

"Amazing blankets?" Jacqueline laughed.

"Well, they were pretty dusty. But I've been cleaning them and mending moth holes. And the old linens have great potential."

"Potential for what?" Jacqueline thought Genevieve must be losing it.

"They'd be perfect for making curtains and accents for the cabins. You know, for a softer touch."

"Seriously? Lacy curtains in the fishing cabins?" Jacqueline snickered—wouldn't those tough old fishermen just love that!

"You know, sort of shabby chic." Ginny's tone was apologetic.

"With an emphasis on the *shabby*?"

"I guess so . . ." Ginny sounded discouraged now. And for some reason that made Jacqueline feel better. Who did Ginny think she was—making all these changes?

"Face it, Ginny." She tried to sound sympathetic. "The fishing lodge will never be chic or stylish or even comfortable. Grandpa doesn't give a hill of beans about any of that. Fishermen come to the lodge for cheap beds, good food, and great fishing. How many times have I heard that before?"

"I know. I hear it a lot too."

"And you have to be careful with Grandpa, Ginny. You push him too far or too hard and he'll let you know."

"I'm sure he will."

"He can be super territorial about his little old lodge. But, hey, if you're having fun with it, why not enjoy yourself?" Jacqueline made her voice lighter. "Because I'm sure enjoying your gorgeous, luxurious hotel." She looked around the crowded bedroom. "Your apartment, well, not so much."

"Sorry about that. It was my way to save money. I'd planned to be out of it by now. Oh, yeah, I am."

"Right. And I keep telling myself it's just temporary digs." Jacqueline kicked a high-heeled boot into the tiny closet that was overly packed and cluttered with her clothing and bags and shoes.

"Well, if you do find something better, Rhonda is eager to take over the lease. She has a couple friends looking for cheap housing. You wouldn't even have to give her notice."

"You don't mind letting it go?"

"Not at all."

"Good to know." Jacqueline wasn't surprised. Why would Ginny put up with Rhonda or want to stay in this awful place if she didn't have to?

"I'm going to have to hang up," Ginny told her. "I promised to help Ben with the campfire tonight."

"Help Ben with a campfire? What, is his arm broken?"

"No, of course not. He's fine."

"Well, he's always been able to handle the firepit unassisted." Jacqueline bristled to think of Ginny getting friendly with Ben. Didn't she know the man was a confirmed bachelor? Maybe she should inform her.

"I know, but tonight we're doing something new."

"Something new?" Jacqueline didn't like all this newness and change. What was wrong with Ginny anyway? Couldn't she leave well enough alone?

"We're going to set out the makings for s'mores and a few other kid-friendly things."

"Kid friendly?"

"Well, we have some guests with kids visiting. Kind of unusual, I hear."

"Oh, yeah, I remember booking those families last spring. These two women are sisters and wanted to give their husbands a special treat. I explained how the place was pretty rustic, but they didn't seem too concerned since the price was right." Meaning cheap! "But speaking of Ben. How is the old boy anyway?"

"Ben's just fine. And he's been so supportive in getting Jack on board with my little improvements. He and Margie both. I think you'll be pleasantly surprised when you come back, Jacqueline. But I really do need to go now. The kids are dancing around the campfire like they mean to throw someone in, and I hear Ben calling for me."

"Right. Have fun." Jacqueline could hear the flatness in her own voice as she said goodbye. She didn't like the sound of any of that. She really didn't want Ginny to have fun. And especially not with Ben!

# twenty

Ginny carried out the tray she'd set up earlier with chocolate bars, marshmallows, and graham crackers. She was halfway to the firepit when the children raced toward her with shrieks of delight. As if s'mores were better than gold. And maybe they were.

She set the tray on the picnic table she and Ben had moved over here earlier. As he handed out roasting sticks, she realized it made a charming picture.

"I think I'll take some photos." She pulled out her phone. "Might be nice to have some of these on the website if the parents give permission."

"Good idea," Ben told her. "It's all very photogenic."

Ginny stepped back, taking candid shots of the kids by the campfire as Emmy, the oldest girl, tore open the marshmallow bag. Emmy had bragged to Ginny earlier, saying she knew "all about making s'mores." While Emmy handed out each white powdery puff, explaining the steps to the kids with the authority of a know-it-all twelve-year-old, Ginny snapped more shots.

"Now, you all be careful with those sticks," Ben warned the kids.

"And remember those marshmallows can get hot," Emmy added. "Watch your fingers."

"And your tongues," Ben teased.

Ginny paused from picture taking to adjust the mason jar filled with wildflowers, centering it on the old red-and-white-checked tablecloth she'd found in the linen closet.

"That looks nice," Ben told her as she snapped a shot.

"I'm sure the kids don't care about the decor, but it makes me happy." She lowered her voice. "Cheap thrills."

"I like it too." Ben pointed to the nearby Adirondack chairs. "Care to sit?"

"Thanks. It does feel like I've been running all day."

"You've accomplished a lot this past week. Even Jack's impressed." He presented a thermos and a pair of the vintage mugs from the kitchen. "Coffee?"

"I'd love some."

"I even added cream." He opened the thermos.

"Wow, thanks." Ginny pocketed her phone. "You'll never guess who just called me."

"Anyone I know?" He filled a mug, handing it to her.

She nodded. "She even asked about you."

His brows arched. "Jacqueline?"

"That's right."

"Interesting." He filled his mug, then sat beside her.

She took a sip of coffee and smiled. "Wow, this is *really* good, Ben. It can't be from the dining room."

He chuckled as he replaced the thermos lid. "It's my own coffee. I don't want to hurt Margie's feelings, but I'm not a big fan of the dining room coffee. I bring my own beans every summer. I grind them fresh every day and make coffee in my cabin."

She sniffed the aromatic brew. "Well, this is just lovely. Thanks so much."

"Don't let it out that I'm a coffee snob." He pointed to the thermos. "I take that out on the river with me every morning. Makes for a good day."

"I might need to set something like that up in my cabin." She took another sip, and for a few minutes, they both just quietly enjoyed their coffee and the kids making s'mores.

"So how's ole Jacqueline doing?" Ben asked in a tentative tone.

"That's funny. She said the same thing."

"Huh?"

"I mean, she asked how *ole Ben* was doing."

He chuckled. "Well, I guess that one makes sense. I'm a lot older than her."

She wondered how old that was exactly but didn't want to ask. "To be honest, Jacqueline sounded a little frustrated at the beginning of our call." Ginny didn't want to admit she'd felt slightly frustrated at the end of it.

"Frustrated in that beautiful, luxurious Seattle hotel? I'm surprised. Jacqueline seemed certain she was landing in heaven."

"You're right, it is a beautiful, luxurious hotel, but I'm afraid my old boss is making poor Jacqueline pretty miserable."

"I hope Jacqueline's not threatening to come back here." Ben looked genuinely concerned.

"Oh, I don't think so. I tried to assure her that Diana—that's my old boss—is . . . well, a hard taskmaster. I speak from experience. She can be incredibly difficult."

"More difficult than Jack?"

She smiled. "Compared to Diana, Jack is as kind as a kitten."

He laughed. "Don't let him hear you say that."

"Don't worry. I'm working hard to win him over."

"I didn't think it could be done, but you really do seem to be making progress. I actually overheard Jack saying something nice to a guest that was complimenting those flowerpots you put on the porch. Like it was his idea." Ben chuckled.

"Maybe it's because I told him that I'd transplanted the herbs—you know, the rosemary and mint and oregano—in order to save Margie the walk to the garden. I thought he'd appreciate it, but at the time he just grunted and told me the walk was good for her." She laughed.

"Sounds about right."

"But he did confess that he wouldn't be such an old grouch if he could just go out on a fishing boat." She gazed out toward the dock.

"Yeah, I think that's really been eating at him."

"I asked him why he couldn't fish from the riverbank, and he just gave me that look." Ginny frowned. "But I've seen other men fishing from the bank."

"Not good enough for Jack."

"I did remind him he could probably go out in a boat once he gets that walking boot."

"Speaking of fishing, I heard you've encouraged the kids and their moms to try out the pond. How's that going?"

"It's more like pretend fishing. We have some old poles and gear that I scrounged out of the boathouse shed, but if a real fisherman saw us, he'd probably crack up. We really need someone to teach us. I asked Jack and he just laughed in my face. Literally! But it was nice to see him smiling. Margie's willing to help, since she does know how to fish, but she's got enough on her plate. I'd be happy to teach them, but I know zip about fishing."

"That is just wrong." He pointed to her. "Any fishing lodge manager worth her salt should know how to fish."

"Did Jacqueline?" she challenged.

He just rolled his eyes.

"So who will teach me to fish?" She looked hopefully at him.

He rubbed his chin. "Well, I'm booked throughout the weekend and even on Monday. But I'm available next Tuesday. How about I take you out then?"

"I'd love that. But I can't be gone for a whole day."

"How about a couple hours in the midday? The lodge is usually pretty quiet then. I doubt you'd be missed."

"Midday sounds perfect." The idea of being alone with Ben on a boat sounded perfect too. Hopefully she wasn't making too much of this. But it looked like Ben was warming to her.

JACQUELINE COULD HARDLY BELIEVE she made it through three days in a row without making any major mistakes. At least nothing that had hit Diana's radar. Of course, Diana had been a little preoccupied with a visit from her mother. According to Adrian, as he met with Jacqueline for coffee on Wednesday afternoon, his grandmother always expected to be fully entertained when she came to Seattle.

"Mom's already taken her to the ballet and the theater, and they're hitting some art galleries and then shopping later today," he told her.

"Wow, that's a lot to pack into a few days." Jacqueline wondered how much longer she'd get to enjoy this little break from being under Diana's critical spotlight. "Your grandmother must have some stamina."

"She does. Tomorrow they'll take a ferry to Victoria and stay there a few days."

Jacqueline smiled to think of more days sans Diana. "I've seen pictures of Victoria." She sighed dreamily. "Looks so romantic. I'd love to see it someday."

"I guess it's okay if you like rose gardens and tea parties."

"Hmm." She considered this as the barista arrived with their drinks. "Maybe it's not my cup of tea after all."

"Tea?" The young barista frowned.

Jacqueline grinned. "No. Mocha here and latte for him."

The barista set their coffees down and left.

"Victoria is actually better than I made it sound," Adrian told her. "I haven't been there since my mom took me for my twelfth birthday. I probably didn't appreciate it much, since I would've preferred a ball game."

"Of course." She nodded. "But Diana isn't much of a Mariners fan."

"Yeah. She just wanted to give me some culture."

"Trying to be a good mom." She sipped her mocha.

"Yeah. And I'd probably like Victoria more now. The architecture is very old-world. Kind of like being in Great Britain. And I've heard the whale watching can be great up there."

She brightened. "That'd be fun. And going by ferry would be fun too. I wonder if I'll ever get the chance to see Victoria . . . someday . . . and before I'm as old as your grandmother." She studied him as she sipped her drink. Could he take a hint?

"You could plan a day trip. Sometime when it's slow at the hotel. Leave early and come back late."

She arched her brows with a flirty smile. "It'd be lots more fun to see it with someone who's already been there. You know, to sort of show me the ropes."

He stirred his latte. "I guess I could take you . . . someday."

"Oh, that'd be fabulous. I'm going to hold you to this, Adrian."

"Maybe later this summer." He checked his watch.

"Are you in a hurry?" she asked.

"No. Just habit. My mom usually checks on me this time of day."

"Yes, me too. It's when she makes her three o'clock rounds."

"Well, I'm glad she's with Grandma."

"I got to meet your grandmother yesterday. She seems very sweet."

"Sweet and tough. She and my grandpa have a small farm in Eastern Washington. You should see her vegetable garden. She grows all kinds of things and then she cans them herself. Kind of like a real pioneer. My grandpa too. He can fix almost anything. I used to love visiting them when I was a kid. But I haven't been there in years."

"Why not?"

"Too busy I guess." He shrugged. "Guess I should plan a visit. Who knows how long they'll be around . . ."

"Yeah." She sighed. "What you said about your grandmother reminds me of mine. I didn't get to visit my grandparents much. When I finally did, my grandma had just passed away. I still regret that . . . not spending more time with her."

He slowly nodded with a thoughtful expression. "My grand-parents are good people. Real hardworking, salt-of-the-earth sort of folks. I really should get some time with them while I still can. I had breakfast with my grandma this morning . . ." He frowned. "She said Grandpa is having some health problems."

"Then you better not put your visit off."

"I guess so."

She thought about her grandfather and how she'd sort of taken him for granted in recent years. "At least I've had time with my grandpa. Did I tell you he's the one who owns the lodge where I worked?"

"I knew it was family owned but didn't realize it was your grandfather. Do you miss him?"

She considered this. "I guess I do. I mean, I've been so busy I haven't really given it much thought."

"I bet he misses you."

She frowned. "Probably so . . . and now you've got me feeling all gloomy." Okay, she was not feeling as bad as she wanted him to think. But she did feel a tinge of sadness. More due to her regrets over her grandmother than anything.

"Tell you what, Jacqueline, how about if I take you to dinner to cheer you up tonight? I know I promised to show you more of Seattle's scenic sights. And I just got an idea I think you'll like."

She perked up. "Oh, Adrian, that'd be awesome."

As they finished their coffee break, she thought she was making real progress with Adrian. And if that was true, it meant she had to be making real progress with his mother too!

A CRISP EVENING BREEZE blew off the river as Ginny shook out a blanket that a guest had been using on the porch. She carefully refolded it, laying it out attractively over the back of one of the Adirondack chairs. She was just reaching for another blanket when Jack, aided by crutches, hobbled out the lodge's front door.

"Guests all gone to bed?" he asked in his usual gruff voice.

"Yep." She smiled as she shook out the next blanket. "You know those fishermen. Early to bed, early to rise, to catch the fish before they get wise."

"Heh-heh." He took the blanket from her and sat on a chair, laying it over his lap. "You make that one up yourself?"

She shrugged, then sat in the chair by his. "I'm not much of a poet."

"Well, you are a pretty good manager."

"Really?" She turned to look at him.

He just nodded.

"So you don't mind the little changes I've been making." She studied his profile in the golden porch light, his eyes looking out toward the river and darkening sky.

He pointed to the blanket in his lap. "Do you know where these blankets came from?" he asked.

"You mean the attic?"

"Before that."

She flipped the blanket over to see a blue tag. "Pendleton?"

"Yep. Me and Sandie used to go to the Pendleton Round-Up sometimes."

"What's that?"

His gray brows arched. "You don't know about the Pendleton Round-Up? It's just one of the biggest rodeos in the world."

"Oh." She nodded.

"Anyway, Sandie grew up on a cattle ranch and was quite a cowgirl. She liked going to the round-up. And every time we went, we'd come home with some of these blankets. Sandie loved them."

"I'm not surprised. They're beautiful. I'm surprised you had them stashed away in the attic. They look so great out here on the porch. And they're really warm. I hope you don't mind."

"Not at all. I guess I forgot about 'em. I think maybe Jacqueline put 'em up there."

"They have a few moth holes, but Margie showed me how to fix them. She thought they should be put back into use. And you probably noticed I put a couple of the nicer ones in the lodge."

"Yep. Looks nice too." He smoothed his hand over the blanket. "I just wanted to tell you that I think you're doing a real good job, Ginny. Thank you."

She felt a rush of pleasure. "Well, thank you, Jack."

"Why thank me?"

"For telling me that. I've been worried I might've overstepped my bounds. Jacqueline called the other day . . . she sounded a little concerned."

"Concerned about what?"

"Oh, I told her about some of the things I was doing. It's been so much fun. Anyway, she seemed a little concerned. Like maybe I was trying to do too much."

He laughed. "Do too much?"

"So you don't mind?"

"I just told you, Ginny. I think you're doing just fine. I appreciate it." He blew out a sigh. "Kinda reminds me of the sort of things Sandie used to do. I can imagine her looking down with real approval."

"Wow, that really makes me feel good."

"Don't let anything Jacqueline says worry you. I love my granddaughter, but when it comes to managing this lodge, she has a lot to learn still." He pointed to Ginny. "Maybe you can teach her."

"I don't know about that."

"How's Jacqueline doing anyway? Have you heard from her?"

"Okay, I guess. She sounded happy when she texted me this afternoon." Ginny had been surprised to hear how much attention Adrian was paying to the new manager. But she was glad for Jacqueline's sake.

"That's good. About time she was happy." He slowly shook his head. "I sure know she wasn't too happy here."

"She needed a change of venue." Ginny smoothed her hand over a blanket.

"How about you, Ginny? You happy here?"

She smiled brightly. "You know the truth is, Jack, I don't remember ever being happier. I love being here. It doesn't even feel like work to me. I mean, I know I'm working hard because I'm so tired at the end of a day. And I really do sleep well. But the work is so fun and rewarding, I think I'd work here for free."

"Better watch out, I might hold you to that."

"Maybe not free." She chuckled. "Just room and board. And only until things pick up financially."

"Well, if your plan for luring more guests here works like you think it will, that could happen."

"It's already working. The photos I've added to the website and social media have garnered us some new reservations."

"That's great." He reached over to pat her hand. "And I want you to know that I'm ready to consider some of those other improvements you asked about. Why don't you make me an itemized list with your cost estimates and a timeline?"

"Sure. I can do that." She'd actually already done it, but she'd been afraid to present it to him.

He reached for his crutches and slowly stood. "Guess I'll hobble off to bed now. Gonna try fishing from the south bank tomorrow. Ben promised to set out a camp chair for me and a few things in my favorite spot."

"That's great, Jack."

"Yep, we'll see. Good night, Ginny."

She wanted to offer to help him, or even just walk him to his cabin, but she knew he wouldn't only reject her offer, he'd probably growl at her as well. So she simply told him good night, then returned to straightening the porch.

# twenty-one

Ginny changed into her fishing clothes, realizing she couldn't wait to go on the river with Ben again. They called it "fishing lessons," but she had that part pretty much down by now. She knew how to bait a hook, cast a line, and even how to remove a hook and release the fish when Ben explained it was necessary. Sometimes they kept a fish, most times not. But she did worry that a hooked fish might suffer from PTSD after being released. Ben assured her that fish had short memories, plus they'd probably use their frightening experience to their advantage by not allowing themselves to get caught again. But she had her doubts.

She picked up the thermal cooler that she'd packed with their lunch for on the river, as well as her windbreaker, and headed out to meet Ben by the dock. It was another gorgeous sunny day, already getting warmer. She was glad she'd worn her new fishing shorts—waterproof with lots of pockets.

"Hey there, Ginny," Ben called out, jogging up to her. "Let me take that." He exchanged the lunch pack for a life vest.

"Hey, is this new?" She sniffed the olive-green vest, surprised that it didn't smell fishy. It looked unusually clean.

"Yeah, I thought you deserved your own vest." He grinned. "Now that you've proved yourself as a real fisherwoman."

"Really?" She grinned as she slid it on. "Thanks!"

"Thanks for this." He held the lunch bag up. "Anything special today?"

She laughed. "Sorry to say it's just sandwiches and potato salad from the fridge today. But I did nab some oatmeal cookies fresh from the oven."

"Works for me." He loaded it into his boat, then reached for her hand.

She got into the boat, taking her seat in front as usual, waiting for him to start the motor. She listened to it quietly idling as Ben untied the rope from the dock and shoved off—so gracefully, it felt like poetry in motion. He guided the boat out onto the river, aimed at the current, and with motor running, waited there for a moment. The sleek riverboat rocked gently as Ben carefully surveyed up and down the river, like the experienced guide he was, before taking off. Then it was just the two of them, out on the river. And it was magical . . . just magical.

IT'D ONLY BEEN ABOUT A MONTH, but Ginny felt so at home at the fishing lodge that she really hoped to stay on indefinitely. And perhaps it could happen. Jacqueline had called earlier today, raving about what a wonderful time she was having in Seattle. Adrian seemed to have pulled out all the stops for her, showing her the highlights of Seattle.

"He took me to the top of the Space Needle the other night," Jacqueline had told her this morning.

"How fun." Ginny had continued folding towels while she listened to Jacqueline gushing. "I've been up there a few times. Amazing view."

"Well, have you ever eaten up there? In the Loupe Lounge?"

Ginny stopped folding. "Adrian took you to the Loupe Lounge?"

"Yes! It's the most amazingly beautiful restaurant in the world. You must've been there lots of times. Don't you love it?"

"I've never actually dined there." Ginny didn't mention that Adrian had asked her many a time. But, worried it was an "engagement" sort of restaurant, she had always declined. "I've heard it's quite expensive."

"I'll say. But it's so romantic. I think it's totally worth it. I can't believe you've never eaten there. You really should, Ginny."

"Yeah, right." She shook out a towel, carefully folding it. "I'm glad you enjoyed it, but I should get to work."

"You don't mind that I'm dating Adrian, do you?"

"Not at all. Like I told you, Jacqueline, Adrian and I are only friends." Ginny pulled more warm towels from the dryer, trying not to feel aggravated. Did Jacqueline really think Ginny was her rival?

"So if Adrian and I got serious, you'd be okay with that?"

"Of course. I'd be very happy for both of you," Ginny reassured her. "But I have a lot to do today. You know it's Saturday and extra busy with the summer season. I'm sure it must be for you too." And then she had told Jacqueline goodbye and hung up. It kind of irked her that Jacqueline felt the need to communicate all this to Ginny. Did she think Ginny would get jealous or feel bad to be missing out on all that big-city fun? Because she wasn't and didn't!

Still, as Ginny stayed super busy all day, more grateful than ever that Jack had given her the green light to hire another housekeeper—as soon as she had time—she couldn't help but feel a little annoyed at Jacqueline. And worried for Hotel Jackson. Jacqueline hadn't mentioned a word about Diana. That in itself was mysterious. But perhaps Jacqueline was doing such a wonderful job that things had smoothed over. And maybe Diana approved of Jacqueline as a potential daughter-in-law. If so, Ginny really would be happy for all of them. Still, it was puzzling.

Fortunately, Ginny had too much to get done to obsess over Jacqueline today. And by the end of the day, although she was exhausted, she was not ready to turn in. After the last of the fishermen cleared out of the lodge and off the porch, she went around straightening and tweaking, just like she always did in the evening. She liked for everything to be clean and attractive for the early risers. Besides that, she just enjoyed this time of the evening. All was quiet and calm, the sound of the river soothing, and the air was so fresh and clean, and not too cold. She wanted to take her time and soak it all in. She was just refolding the last of the porch blankets when she heard footsteps coming up the porch from behind. She turned to see Ben approaching with his thermos in hand.

"Coffee?" He held up a pair of mugs.

"You must be reading my mind." She reached for a mug. "But I'm surprised you're not in bed by now. Don't you have an early morning tomorrow?"

"Yeah, but it's so nice out. And the moon's about to rise. Thought I'd soak up a little ambiance before hitting the hay." He sat down and opened the thermos.

"I was just thinking that exact same thing." She sat by him, holding out her chunky vintage mug. "It's such a lovely evening."

He filled her mug. "I was hoping I'd catch you out here."

She took a sip. "You even added cream."

"You're getting me hooked on it too." He filled his own mug, and for a few moments they both just quietly sipped.

"This is so perfect after a long, busy day."

"Yeah, Jack said we have more guests this weekend than ever. Welcome to summertime."

"Cassie, Margie, and I have been running ourselves ragged. I can't wait to hire another housekeeper. And Jack said I might even get to hire a second one if we keep getting more bookings."

"He's already had to call in some of his backup river guides." He took a sip. "But that's a good thing."

"It's fun to see Jack acting almost happy," she confessed. "For a while I thought he was just a perennial grump."

"Jack told me something about you today . . ."

"Oh?" She looked at him, admiring his handsome profile in the porch light.

"He said having you here reminds him of when Sandie was alive."

"Really? He said that?"

"Yep. I don't think Jack could pay anyone a higher compliment."

"That's very touching . . . and very reassuring." She pulled the wool blanket around her bare shoulders, then wrapped her hands around the mug. She really did feel at home here. And Jack seemed to think so too!

"So . . . I wanted to talk to you about something tonight." His tone had changed slightly, capturing her full attention.

"What is it?"

"I realize I haven't told you much about myself, Ginny. To be honest, I'm not usually very forthcoming with anyone."

"Forthcoming?" She felt uneasy. Was he about to say he was involved with someone, or married, or in the witness protection program?

"I mean, I'm a rather private person. But I do consider you a good friend."

"Thanks," she said nervously. "I think of you as a good friend too."

"Well, you may have heard I'm divorced."

"Actually, no . . ."

"It's been seven years now. My ex, Misha, has been happily remarried for nearly that long."

"Oh?" She felt strangely relieved . . . and curious.

"Anyway, Misha and I have a daughter . . . Alexi."

This caught her by complete surprise. "You have a daughter?"

He nodded, then sipped his coffee. "Alexi just turned fifteen.

Misha has full custody, but I have visitation rights. Alexi used to visit me regularly. Every other weekend and some holidays and sometimes in the summer. But as she got older, and busier with school and friends and activities, I saw less and less of her. Her life has gotten pretty full."

"Where does Alexi live?"

"Boise. I still live there too, when I'm not here. It's where I have my practice."

"Practice?" She blinked. "You're a doctor?"

He chuckled. "No. Attorney."

"Oh?" She felt caught off guard as she realized how little she really knew about Ben.

"I spend summers here because I need the mental break . . . and also because I've been working on my novel. When I'm not on the river, I'm in my cabin writing."

"You're an author?" She stared at him.

"I wouldn't use the *A* word." He chuckled. "I'm more like a wannabe writer. I've had a few small pieces published, but I've been working on this novel for almost five years now."

"Here I thought I knew you, but turns out you're a real mystery man, Ben. A lawyer and a novelist. Kind of like Grisham, eh?"

"I wish." He chuckled. "And, really, it's not that I want to keep my lawyer identity a secret, it's just that when I'm up here at the lodge, I like to forget that part of my life. Although I occasionally have to leave for a day or two when a court case pops up. But Jack is very understanding."

"I'm sure he is." She smiled. "I've gone over the books. You don't take any salary for your work here. I'm sure Jack appreciates that."

"How could I take money for doing what I love? Plus, Jack doesn't expect me to work full-time. He understands taking time off to handle a court case or work on my novel."

"What's your novel about?"

"Well, you mentioned Grisham." He smiled sheepishly. "It's a legal thriller."

"Very cool. I'm a big Grisham fan. So how's your novel coming?"

"I'm actually on my third rewrite. I hope to get it as polished as possible before I look for an agent. I've heard that's the best way for a first timer to break into publishing."

"Sounds like a good plan. Not that I know much about that sort of thing."

"But you are a Grisham fan?"

She nodded. "I've probably read all his books."

Ben's brows arched. "That's a lot of books."

"Okay, I'm kind of a Grisham geek." She grimaced at her embarrassing admission. "I've never told anyone this, but I've read some of his books twice."

"Seriously?" He looked surprised and impressed. "Maybe I can ask you a favor, then."

"Of course."

"Think I could get you to read my manuscript?"

She didn't know what to say. "*Really?* You'd actually let me read it?"

"Yes! I'd be grateful to hear your thoughts."

"Well, I'd be honored to read it, Ben. Absolutely!"

"Great." He exhaled loudly. "You see, I've never been sure about this whole writing business. My ex used to call it a pipe dream. And I suppose maybe it was . . . back then, I used to talk about it more than do it. Probably because my legal practice isn't terribly thrilling. Mostly corporate law. My daily life isn't much like a Grisham character's."

"I doubt that many attorneys' are."

"So, after my divorce, I got serious about my writing. To be honest, it's been sort of therapeutic. Watching my wife leap straight into another marriage, not seeing my daughter as much I'd like—well, it's been tough. Writing was a great escape."

"I can understand that. I'm sorry for all you've gone through." She was surprised but grateful he was telling her all this. She just hoped she wasn't misinterpreting his motives—assuming his interest in her was anything more than just friendship.

"So anyway, Alexi has suddenly decided she wants to come visit me here. She just sent me a text saying she wished she was here with me instead of at Disneyland."

"Wow, that's a pretty cool compliment."

"It is. She texted me while waiting in line for the teacup ride."

"Isn't she a little old for the teacup ride?"

"Alexi has two younger half brothers. I suspect Disneyland was more about them."

"Right." Ginny felt sympathy for Alexi . . . and for Ben.

"Anyway, I've been inviting Alexi to visit me here for years, but she and Misha always have some excuse. Always some big summer plans going on. Camps, trips, whatever. I'd given up."

"That's wonderful she wants to come now, Ben."

He ran his fingers through his hair. "Yeah, I guess. But I'm not really sure how to handle it."

"What do you mean?"

"Well, I guess I'm worried. What if she hates it here?"

Ginny considered this. "Is she an outdoorsy girl?"

"Not exactly. She used to be. But her mom is more citified. Their idea of a good time has always been shopping, hairstyling, manicures . . . all that stuff." He kind of laughed. "In fact, I used to think if Alexi ever came to see me, she and Jacqueline would've hit it off. Similar tastes, you know?"

"Right . . . that does make sense." Ginny felt uneasy. "But Alexi does know this is a fishing lodge, right?"

"Absolutely."

"And she really wants to come." Ginny tried to sound optimistic. "So maybe she's ready for some outdoorsy activities. Maybe she'll get into fishing or rafting."

"Maybe . . ."

"When is she coming? How long will she be here?"

"Soon, but Misha didn't say how long she'd be here."

"So Misha is setting this up?" Ginny felt confused.

"Yes. Alexi reached out to me first, but Misha called me from Disneyland this evening to make the arrangements."

"You said 'soon,' but how soon?"

"They already booked Alexi a flight to Idaho Falls. It arrives tomorrow."

"Wow, that is soon. What time?"

"Midday."

"But you have a fishing trip to—"

"I know. I could cancel it, but I thought maybe you could pick her up for me."

"I guess so. Midday is the least busy time for me." She felt uncertain . . . Was she getting in over her head? But seeing the desperation in Ben's eyes made her want to do this for him. "So, she'll be okay with me picking her up?"

He shrugged. "Yeah, I guess."

"You said Misha made these arrangements. Is Alexi good with it?" Ginny didn't want to judge Misha, but the whole plan sounded a little abrupt.

"I guess." Ben scowled. "Misha sounded a little irked. She said Alexi wasn't enjoying Disneyland."

"So they're shipping her home." Ginny frowned.

"Misha also said Alexi needed a change of venue."

"A change of venue?"

"Those were her exact words. I suspect they're locking horns over something. Could be a showdown in Disneyland. I'm not sure, but something feels amiss. Misha also mentioned that Alexi's had a difficult year. She hinted that she made some bad friends, but it's the first I've heard of that."

"Well, she is fifteen. I remember that was kind of a tough time for my baby sister. Fortunately, she grew out of it."

"I've wondered if it might relate to her younger brothers."

"How old are they?"

"The older one is about ten years younger than Alexi—about

five—and the other one is barely a year younger. I get the impression the boys are a handful and require a lot of attention. Alexi was super helpful when they were babies, but maybe she's feeling resentful or even jealous now that they're older."

"Maybe she just needs some Dad time."

He slowly nodded. "Maybe . . ."

"So what else can I do to help?"

"Well, she'll probably stay in my cabin. Small as it is. I thought I'd give her the bedroom and I can sleep on the sofa bed. Do you think you could spruce up my cabin a little? I know there's not much time, but it's pretty bare-bones in there right now. And I like how you've fixed up some of the others. It might make Alexi feel more at home."

"I'd love to help with that." She'd actually wanted to ask him before but didn't want to overstep her bounds.

"And maybe you can sort of befriend her? You know this is such a boys' club up here. Might be easier for her to have a woman to hang with."

"I'm happy to do that too. When I have time." Ginny wondered if Alexi would want to be helpful. She sure could use some help right now. And she could even offer to pay her for some for it. "But I've never been that much of a girlie girl," she confessed. "Not like Jacqueline." She cringed to imagine what she'd do with a girl who wanted only to talk about fashion or hair or paint her fingernails. Besides not having the time, she had about zero interest.

"That's okay."

"Let's just hope Alexi will fall in love with the river." Ginny paused to listen to the sound of the ripples on the water. "I know I have."

Ben let out a slow sigh. "I feel better already." He pointed to the eastern sky. "Look, here comes the moon."

Ginny spied the shimmering golden globe between the branches of the tall pine trees. "It's so big. And so beautiful." They sat in silence, watching the moon slowly rise above the treetops.

Ginny wanted to stay in the moment, to savor the beauty, the sounds of the night, but her mind was racing ahead. So much information to absorb. Ben, a lawyer and author, was divorced and the father of a teenage girl. More importantly, that girl would be here soon. Tomorrow even! And Ginny was going to help with her. But how? And why did she suddenly feel so nervous about it . . . and about Ben?

# twenty-two

After several amazingly wonderful days with Adrian while Diana was distracted by entertaining her mother, Jacqueline felt like she'd finally started that fabulous life she'd always dreamed about. Then, as if the magic carpet had been jerked out from under her, she was slammed back down to earth with a dull, hard thud. It was Sunday morning and, cowering in her darkened office with the door closed and blinds down, she was ready to give up.

Or else come up with some sort of escape plan. Maybe it was the cowardly way out, but she knew she needed a way to get out of her job swap agreement. Or, if it was possible—which seemed unlikely—she needed a way to avoid Diana's wrath. Because she knew it was coming. And this time she probably deserved it. At least partially. She'd been racking her brain to come up with someone else to blame, but nothing quite worked.

After all, she'd been the idiot who'd booked the bachelorette party. But in all fairness, she'd done it only after Jeremy, the new reception clerk and night manager, had balked at making the reservation. Her nightmare had started a couple of weeks ago. She hadn't realized it was a nightmare then, but now she did.

At the time, she'd simply blamed Jeremy's reluctance to reserve rooms for this sweet pair of sisters as ineptness or inexperience. He'd never booked a group like that before. The Musgrove bridesmaid party of seven had requested two full suites on the same floor. Not a big deal, but it required a little shuffling. Somehow Jacqueline got it all figured out. So much so that she couldn't even pin the blame on Jeremy.

And really, Jeremy was her fault too. Beverly, the former evening reception clerk and night manager, had quit the first week Jacqueline started working here. They'd had quite the go-round, but Jacqueline had held her ground, determined to win, and Beverly had walked out. By the next day, Jacqueline had replaced her with Jeremy, a guy with more looks than brains. Or maybe he did have brains. For all she knew, Jeremy might be down there laughing at her right now. He probably wanted her job. She'd seen him playing up to Diana recently.

Diana! Just the thought of that woman sent chills down Jacqueline's spine. She knew Diana was out to get her. She'd already threatened to fire her twice. And when Diana discovered how the Musgrove party trashed the best suites in Hotel Jackson, Jacqueline would be toast. If only there was a way to fix this before Diana got back.

Jacqueline knew she was lucky. Diana had been in Victoria with her mother for the weekend. And Friday night had gone well enough with the Musgrove party. Only the bridesmaids had been up there and, according to Jeremy, it had been a quiet night.

But last night those irresponsibly reckless, wild bridesmaids had hosted a rip-snorting party. Jacqueline couldn't even imagine what might've happened if Diana had been in her own suite last night . . . or today. Maybe she'd have thrown them all out herself. More likely, she'd have called the police and had them all arrested. Perhaps that's what Jeremy should've done. Maybe she could pin it on him. According to Jeremy, there'd been dozens of noise complaints last night. The bachelorette party had gone on until 2:00 a.m., when Jeremy had finally sent up a security officer.

"Why didn't you send security sooner?" Jacqueline had demanded early this morning when he'd called her at home with his grim report.

"Because I called up there myself several times, and the girls kept assuring me they would quiet down."

"Then why are you calling me now?" she'd asked him.

"Because I think you, uh, you should come in. You need to see this for yourself."

And so, even though it was before seven on a Sunday, she'd thrown on clothes and come in. Jeremy was already on his way out, but the look he gave her suggested a serious problem. A problem he was neatly escaping. And when she got up to the deluxe suites, just a few doors down from Diana's swanky private quarters, she knew she was in trouble. Really big doo-doo.

The entire hallway was littered with the remains of what was obviously an out-of-control party. There was even a young man spread-eagled through the opened door of one of the suites. Fortunately, he was breathing. She peeked inside the suite and felt sick. Partly from the stench from someone else who'd lost their cookies. Probably numerous someones. The scene was so disgusting that, even wearing her old Adidas, she didn't care to step one toe into the contaminated, nauseating suite. Instead, she'd called Rosaria, the head housekeeper, and told her to check on both suites. "And get your best crew up there ASAP."

"I already looked in there. I just hope you charged those slobs a humongous deposit," Rosaria wryly told her.

"You need to start cleaning on both suites immediately," Jacqueline commanded.

"But it's not checkout time until—"

"It's checkout time for *those* guests." Jacqueline tried to imitate Diana's I-mean-business voice.

"I'll see if we can get the guests outta there, but my crew won't be able to clean the suites until later."

"When later?" Jacqueline demanded. "Why?"

"I checked the schedule. We have occupied rooms with *respect-able* guests staying into the week. As you know, that's top priority," Rosaria reminded her. "Those deluxe suites aren't reserved again until midweek and through the weekend. They can wait."

"I don't care about that! I want them cleaned today!" Jacqueline shouted into the phone.

"I'm sure you do. Maybe you should call in some hazmat abatement services." And Rosaria hung up. Jacqueline had called her back, but Rosaria didn't answer. And it was probably for the best because, although Ginny had sworn Rosaria was the best head housekeeper ever, Jacqueline would've fired her on the spot. But that would've just left her even more shorthanded.

Throughout the morning, Jacqueline had made several nervous trips to the top floor. It took until midafternoon for the "guests" to clear out—with the help of security. Before they left, Jacqueline had Melinda, the day reception clerk, photocopy all of their IDs, as well as warn the slovenly party girls that they would be billed for the damage.

"They didn't seem overly concerned," Melinda informed Jacqueline. "But then, they weren't overly coherent either."

The last visit Jacqueline paid to the disaster area was well after four o'clock. By then, she'd already called several abatement cleaning services, but had been able only to leave a message or put herself on a list. Housekeeping appeared to be steering clear of the ruined deluxe suites, motivating Jacqueline to fetch a trash bag and rubber gloves herself. She picked up most of the disgusting debris from the hallway before tossing the gross bag into one of the suites and closing the door. She even sprayed some aerosol about . . . just in case Diana came home early.

Feeling desperate and frustrated and angry, she tried to call housekeeping one more time. But just like the other times, her call went straight to voice mail. They were purposely ignoring her. She knew it! If they didn't get to those suites before five when the day shifts ended, it would be too late. They always were short-staffed on Sunday nights. And by the time the morning crew showed, it would be too late. According to Adrian, Diana was supposed to put her mother on the train and arrive back this evening, and it was certain that someone would spill the beans. Maybe even Jeremy!

So Jacqueline was still hiding out in her office. Pacing back and forth with the blinds down. She knew it was pointless and childish, but she didn't know what else to do as she watched time ticking by. She could just imagine Diana bursting in and exploding like a fire-breathing dragon. But holing up in here with her overactive imagination felt like torture in itself. What was wrong with her?

"You're a grown woman," Jacqueline said aloud. "Handle this yourself!" That's what Diana would do. And it was probably what Ginny would do . . . if she'd ever got herself into a mess like this. Had she? Well, at the very least, Jacqueline ought to be able to do some damage control. She could demand that the housekeepers stay late tonight. Maybe she would offer overtime. Somehow, she needed them to clean those suites!

With resolve and determination, she strode toward the elevators. As she pushed the button to go up, she heard giggles down the hall, and turned to see some of the housekeepers pointing her direction before they vanished. By the time she got down there, they'd disappeared into the service elevator. Suspecting they were headed to the employee rooms, she decided to follow. But when she got the next elevator down, she was casually informed by a restaurant worker that the housekeeping day shift had already gone home.

"It's not even five o'clock." She pointed to the employee punch clock. "It's only 4:48."

"Guess they finished early," the guy said lightly.

"You don't look too busy." She pointed at him. "I could use some help up—"

"Sorry, my shift ends at five." He reached for a windbreaker, pulling out a pack of cigarettes. "And I've been here since seven. That's ten hours."

Without even responding, she turned and headed back to her office to get her purse and lock up. What was the point of remaining here? If Diana showed up, it was Jacqueline's head that would roll. Why stick around to see that? It was over. She had lost.

With designer purse in hand, but still dressed in grubby sweats, Jacqueline had just started through the lobby when she saw Diana strolling in. Like the queen of her world, dressed in a sophisticated pale-blue pantsuit with a creamy silk scarf, she looked like a million bucks. She tossed a polite, businesslike greeting to the reception clerk and continued directly toward Jacqueline, where she stopped with raised brows.

"I didn't expect to see you here right now." Her lips were pursed as her eyes traveled up and down Jacqueline with suspicion. "Everything okay?"

"Yes. Sure." Jacqueline fumbled with her purse strap, suddenly remembering her casual attire. "I'm, uh, just leaving."

"Alright, then." Diana nodded to where the bellhop was carrying in her Louis Vuitton luggage. "I'll see you tomorrow."

Jacqueline barely nodded and, feeling she'd dodged a bullet—at least for the moment—said, "See ya!" and practically ran out.

She was only a few feet away from the hotel entrance when she called Adrian. She didn't know what he could do to help, but she needed to talk to someone. When he answered, she broke into tears. "Please, Adrian, I have to see you! It's urgent! Life or death! I desperately need a friend right now. And I honestly don't have anyone to call besides you."

"Well, I—"

"Please—don't make me beg."

"Okay, okay. But I'm just leaving a Mariners game and traffic's a—"

"That's fine. Just meet me at O'Hara's in about an hour."

"You buying?" he teased.

"Yes, yes, of course. See you soon!" She shoved her phone into her purse and hurried toward her apartment. Somehow she had to concoct a plan. She wasn't even sure what it would be, but she had to do something before her life went up in smoke.

WHILE GRABBING A SPEEDY SHOWER, Jacqueline went over plan A and plan B. Plan A was to get into grubby clothes and somehow convince Adrian to assist her in sneaking up the service elevator to do a fast cleanup of the two suites before Diana figured things out. But Jacqueline knew that was pointless. First off, Adrian would never agree to manual labor. Second, the suites were too bad to be rescued by a couple of amateurs. Third, thanks to some employee's big mouth, Diana probably knew already.

That left plan B—*the persuasion plan*. Jacqueline would get herself all dolled up for drinks with Adrian. She felt confident he liked her. They'd even kissed once. Well, she'd initiated the kiss, but he had complied. Tonight, she would turn on all the sweetness and light she could muster. Combine that with some helplessness and a few alcoholic beverages, and she knew she could win Adrian over. After all, he knew how unreasonable his mother could be. And once Jacqueline presented her very sad and desperate case, she would gain his sympathies.

Part two of plan B was for the two of them to go meet with his mother. There Adrian would calmly plead Jacqueline's case. Perhaps even beg for her mercy. He would explain how that silly bridal group had tricked Jacqueline, taking advantage of her kind heart and generous spirit. Somehow he would convince his mother that Jacqueline was the innocent victim here. It could happen!

Shoot, by the time Jacqueline was done charming Adrian, he might really come around. Sooner than she'd originally hoped. If he saw how badly she needed him right now, he would feel like the big, strong knight saving the beautiful princess from the fire-breathing dragon (his mother). He might even consider her marriage material. It wasn't impossible! Guys loved feeling like the hero.

As she applied a second coat of mascara, she thought about fishermen strategies. The way they enjoyed making special lures and flies and picking the perfect bait—all with the goal of catching the perfect fish. Maybe that's what she was doing. And Adrian would not be a bad catch!

As she styled her hair, she imagined the two of them making their happy announcement to Diana. Then, Jacqueline could apologize to Diana, admitting she wasn't the best manager, assuring her she would gladly give up her career in hotel management to be a good wife to Adrian. A great trophy wife! Maybe Diana would let them occupy one of the deluxe suites on the top floor. Well, after it was thoroughly cleaned and purged and detoxified . . . and tastefully redecorated and stylishly furnished. It could happen!

# twenty-three

Ginny had gotten up extra early on Sunday morning. First, she helped Margie and Cassie with breakfast. Once she saw they had things in hand, she quickly explained about Ben's daughter coming unexpectedly and excused herself to get some things ready for her visit. With a laundry basket loaded with items she thought would make Ben's cabin a bit more "female friendly," she went over and let herself inside. To her relief, his cabin was in better shape than some of the others she'd worked on. And it was surprisingly clean. But it was still fairly Spartan.

Seeing that he'd been using the kitchen as his writing space, she wondered if she could help with that. She'd seen a small desk in the attic and thought it would fit nicely under the side window in the living area. She moved some things around and then called Cassie, asking her to help get it down the stairs.

After a couple of hours, the desk was in place, and the cabin looked rather sweet. Not fancy like Jacqueline's cabin. But friendly and cozy. Hopefully Alexi would like it. Now Ginny had just enough time to check on a few things, clean herself up, and get over to the airport to pick up Ben's daughter. Jack already knew about the visit and fully approved, but when Ginny had invited him to go to the airport with her, he'd firmly declined. "I don't know how to talk to teenage girls," he'd brusquely told her. "Can't even talk to my own granddaughter, and she's a grown woman."

Feeling grateful that Jack was able to talk with her, Ginny didn't pressure him further. The only reason she'd asked him in the first place was because she was feeling pretty uneasy herself. What would this girl be like? What if Misha was just trying to unload her on Ben because Alexi had turned into an adolescent nightmare? That happened sometimes.

As Ginny drove to the airport, she actually prayed. She prayed for Alexi to feel welcomed and loved and at home on the river. And she prayed for herself to be understanding and to have words of encouragement for this slightly displaced young woman. Ginny remembered how she'd felt as a teenager. Her mom had been single and working hard at Hotel Jackson. Gillian had been young, and Ginny had to babysit and help out a lot. It hadn't been easy. But somehow she'd made it through. Alexi would too.

When she got to the airport, she texted the number Ben had given her, letting Alexi know her ride was here and to meet her outside of the baggage area. Ben had described Alexi. "She's tall and thin with dark-brown hair." He'd chuckled. "She looks kind of like you."

"Or maybe she looks like you," Ginny had teased back.

But when she saw a tall girl with long brown hair, standing outside baggage claim with a backpack and hot-pink roller bag, she felt relatively sure it was Alexi. And when she got close enough to see the rather sad countenance with downcast eyes glued to her phone, Ginny parked nearby, got out, and called to her. "Alexi?"

The girl looked up. "Yeah?"

"I'm Ginny." She waved. "I just texted you. Your dad sent me."

Alexi nodded and, pocketing her phone, came over. "It figures he couldn't meet me himself," she grumbled as Ginny helped load her bags into the back of the minivan.

"He would've, but it was such short notice." Ginny smiled at her after they got inside. "It's the start of the summer season. And the lodge is pretty busy this weekend. But he can't wait to see you."

"Yeah, leave it to Mom to dump me on him like this."

Ginny started the engine. "So you were at Disneyland?"

"Ugh, don't remind me."

"I bet it was busy there."

"Crawling with little kids. At least the places we went."

"I hear you have two little brothers."

"Little brats, you mean."

"Right . . . I'm guessing you get to babysit them sometimes."

"Too much of the time. I'm like their live-in nanny."

"I know how that goes." Ginny stopped for a traffic light.

"Seriously?" Alexi sounded skeptical.

"Well, I didn't have two little brothers. But my sister was ten years younger than me, and my mom had to work. So I got stuck watching her a lot."

"Who are you anyway?" Alexi asked.

"Huh?" Ginny glanced at her as the light turned green.

"I mean, how do you know my dad? Are you his girlfriend or something?"

"No." Ginny laughed. "I'm the manager of the fishing lodge. Your dad and I are just friends."

"Oh, good." She pulled out her phone. "How's reception at the fishing lodge."

"It can be spotty."

"Figures. Do they have internet?"

"Yes. Have you ever visited there before?"

"No. Dad's tried to get me to, but I'm not into fishing."

"Well, there's more than just fishing there. Have you ever gone white water rafting?"

"No." She dropped her phone into her lap. "I didn't even get to go on Splash Mountain!"

"Is that in Disneyland?"

"Yeah. Reggie and Raleigh were too small so, naturally, that meant I couldn't go either."

"I don't know how exciting Splash Mountain is, but I bet the rafting trips your dad leads are better. I've heard grown men admitting how scary it can be, and sometimes the raft flips and everyone falls out."

"That sounds a little too scary for me. Not sure I'd like that. I'm not such a great swimmer."

"You'd have on a life vest, of course. And nobody ever drowns out there." She paused to remember that Jack's son had drowned. Not that Alexi needed to hear about that.

"Have you ever been on a white water trip?" Alexi asked.

"No. I've gone fishing in a riverboat a few times. That's pretty fun. But we only go up the quieter forks. No white water."

"You're the manager and you never took a white water trip?" Alexi poked her in the arm. "You scared?"

"I don't think so. To be honest, I never really thought about it." She considered it now. "But if I got the chance, I think I'd like to try it. Sounds exciting."

"Are you a good swimmer?"

"Not particularly. But I'm okay . . . I can hold my own."

"Are you a good fisherman, or woman, or person . . . whatever they call it?"

"I wouldn't call myself *good*. I've seen ones who are. But I've had fun learning."

"Have you caught any fish?" Alexi asked.

"Yeah, a few. Some we had to release."

"Release?"

"Ones that are protected or too small or whatever. I can't even remember all the reasons we put them back. But I've caught ones that we brought home to cook. Well, Margie cooks them. She's the cook at the lodge. Do you like fish? I mean to eat?"

"Yeah, I do. My parents think I'm a picky eater, but I do eat fish."

"Margie knows some great ways to cook it. There will be plenty tonight."

"What's the lodge like?" Alexi asked.

Ginny loved that this girl was full of questions. "Well, I think it's quite handsome. But that might just be me. Some people think it's too rustic. The main lodge is made of logs. And some of the cabins are logs too. Your dad's cabin is logs."

"Cool. I like log cabins. At least, I like how they look. I never stayed in one before."

Ginny felt encouraged by that. "Well, it's all very campy and rustic. Have you done much camping?"

"Not really. Rolland, that's my stepdad, he rented a big, fancy RV once. But it was a disaster. Reggie and Raleigh were too young to enjoy it, and Mom hated it. I think maybe I would've liked it . . . if I'd been with a different family." She laughed, but there was a sad edge to her laughter.

"I didn't grow up with an outdoorsy family," Ginny said. "I didn't even know anyone like that. But when I came to manage the lodge, I almost instantly felt at home. Now I'm pretty much in love with all of it."

"How long have you been the manager there?"

"Not very long." Ginny explained about the job swap.

"Wow, that's wild. You actually left everything in Seattle and just traded places?"

"Pretty much."

"For the whole summer?"

"I wish. It's supposed to be for sixty days. We're about half-done now. But to be honest, I don't want to swap back."

"That's too bad. What about the lady you swapped with?"

"I actually think she'd be happier in Seattle."

"Then maybe you won't have to swap back."

"I'd be fine with that."

"I wonder if I could swap lives with someone . . ." Alexi sounded wistful.

"What would you swap for?"

"A normal family that wanted me."

"Is there such a thing?"

"Thanks a lot."

"No, that's not what I meant, Alexi. I'm sure anyone would want you. Including your parents. Especially your dad. But I meant, is there any such thing as a normal family? I've never known any."

"Yeah, I guess you could be right. I don't either."

Alexi's phone rang, and when she answered, Ginny could tell it was Misha. "Yeah, I made it here just fine, thank you. Not that you care." She paused to listen to what sounded like a rant. "*Whatever*, Mom! I know you and Rolland are glad to be rid of me. I hope you all have fun." This was followed by more ranting. "We're on our way to the lodge," she said finally. "The manager is driving me." Alexi made a face at Ginny. "Yeah, I'm probably being abducted, Mom. And it'll be all your fault." Then Alexi pretended to lose connection and hung up.

"Trying to get your mom worried?" Ginny asked.

"She doesn't care."

"She probably cares more than you realize."

"Ha."

"But you seem pretty mature for your age, Alexi. Your mom probably thinks you're capable of handling things. Maybe that makes it appear she doesn't care." When Alexi didn't respond to this, Ginny glanced over to see she'd put in earbuds and was doing something on her phone. Oh, well. The silence was actually kind of welcome.

Ginny wasn't totally sure what to make of this girl. Her first impression was actually pretty good. But she could tell there were a lot of layers here. There was hurt and bitterness, probably from her parents' divorce. But there was a layer of lostness too. And hopelessness. Oh, sure, all teenagers felt like that at times. But Alexi's layers went a little deeper. Hopefully Ben—and a father's unconditional love—would be good for her. She definitely needed someone.

# twenty-four

Jacqueline, finally ready to implement plan B, was dressed to the nines with every shimmering golden hair in place, her makeup pure perfection. And although her budget was stretched to the max and her meager savings steadily shrinking, she even splurged on a cab to O'Hara's. This was an investment . . . in her future.

The bar was busy, but she found a table in a corner. She was surprised Adrian hadn't made it there already, but she sat down and conspicuously crossed her legs, making sure they were visible to anyone entering the room. Her attractive legs were just one of her many assets. Taking on an air of confidence, she held her head high and ordered a cosmo. According to *Glamour*, this was still a popular drink with fashionable young women.

She toyed with her drink, pretending to sip it, but after nearly an hour, she felt certain she'd been stood up. Then, just as she was about to call it a night, she saw Adrian stroll into the bar. Still wearing a ball cap, T-shirt, and faded jeans, he approached her. As he got closer, his expression grew slightly suspicious. Just the same, she attempted a shaky smile. She knew this would be her big chance to win him over. Maybe her only chance.

She stood and grasped his hands desperately, hoping her eyes glistened with the hint of tears. "Oh, Adrian. Thank you so much for meeting me. I'm so upset. I don't know what to do, or who to turn to—" She blinked and made a choking sound that she hoped resembled a suppressed sob. Feeling his hand on her shoulder, she thought maybe it was working.

"Sit down," he said firmly. "Tell me what's wrong."

She sat down, clasping her hands around the thin stem of her cosmo glass. "I need a sip to calm myself." She took a tiny sip, then waved to the bartender. "You need a drink too. It's on me."

Adrian ordered a microbrew, then turned back to Jacqueline. "What is going on?"

So she began telling him about the Musgrove party. "It sounded like just a sweet gathering. You know, bridesmaids having a special evening with the bride-to-be the weekend before the wedding. The woman who booked the rooms was the bride's older sister. Her name's Michelle and she's a successful realtor. Their dad owns Musgrove Toyota."

"Yeah, yeah, but I still don't get it." He sipped his beer.

"I let the Musgrove party have the two deluxe suites on your mom's floor."

His brows arched. "Pretty pricey party."

She nodded. "And I had to rearrange some things just to accommodate them on the same floor."

"And?"

"And they totally trashed the place."

"What do you mean by *totally*?"

"I mean all sort of things are broken or missing, and people got sick all over the place, and the suites stink and—"

"Okay, okay. Well, that's happened before. Maybe not as bad as this time. And not in the deluxe suites. But it's probably all cleaned up by now and—"

"But it's not. The housekeepers didn't even get to it yet. I think they're trying to sabotage me—" She choked back a genuine sob.

"Your mom is already back, and she probably knows all about it and I'm sure she'll—"

"Did she call yet?"

Jacqueline grimly shook her head. "But I don't really know. I have my phone on silent."

"Well, look and see."

She tentatively removed her phone, then gasped. "Oh, yeah, she's called. Like eight times." She reached for his hand again, grasping it tightly.

"She obviously knows."

"I bet Jeremy told her. He's on duty by now."

"Well, whatever. She knows."

Jacqueline waved to the bartender, holding up two fingers to signal drink refills, then turned back to Adrian. "What will I do?"

"What can you do?"

She leaned her head into the palms of her hands, actually shedding real tears now but trying not to ruin her eye makeup. She needed Adrian more than ever. It wouldn't help matters to look like a hot mess. The bartender set down fresh drinks and she looked up, using the cocktail napkin to blot beneath her eyes. "I've ruined everything," she whispered. "Not just for me, but for Genevieve—I mean Ginny—too."

He seemed to come to attention now. "What do you mean?"

"Well, in this job swap, I'm supposed to hold her job for her. But if Diana fires me, what will happen to Ginny? Will she lose her job too?"

"I don't see why."

"Ginny and I contracted for sixty days. If Diana lets me go, she'll have to hire a new manager. Then what will Ginny do?"

He looked slightly perplexed, then simply shrugged. "I don't think Ginny really wanted to come back anyway. She and my mom didn't get along so well either."

This was both consoling and concerning. "Oh, Adrian, can

you talk to your mom for me? Or maybe go with me to see her? I know she'd listen to you."

"Don't be so sure about that."

"She loves you, Adrian. If you begged her to let me stay, I bet she'd keep me on." She reached for his hand again, peering deeply into his eyes. "I'd be so grateful, Adrian. I know you don't really like me as much as I like you . . ." She made a sad expression. "But you do have a good heart. Please help me."

He appeared to soften. "I do like you, Jacqueline. It's not that. But you can be, well, a little overwhelming. Ya know?"

"I know. Believe me, I know." She nodded somberly. "My therapist told me I come on too strong with guys . . ." She sighed. "He said it's because my dad left me when I was a little girl. I keep trying to make up for his abandonment by overcompensating with guys. He claims I'm worried that every man worth caring about will leave me. And I guess it's true." She opened her eyes wider. "I know you'll leave me too, Adrian. I guess *leave* isn't the right word. But I don't really expect you to stick by me on this."

"I didn't say that."

"I wouldn't even blame you." She twisted the napkin in her hand. "I mean, I realize I can be a royal pain. But if you could help me, even just a little, to straighten things out with your mom. Well, it would mean a lot."

He considered this as he slowly sipped his beer. It was hard to read his expression, but she felt a tinge of hopefulness as he set the mug down. Then suddenly his phone was ringing. He pulled it out of his T-shirt pocket and frowned. "It's Mom."

"Oh no." Her grasp on the glass stem tightened.

"Should I answer?"

"It's up to you."

He stared uncertainly at his phone before answering. "Hey, Mom." He listened for a while. "Yeah, I've seen her. In fact, she's with me right now." He held the phone away from his ear as if Diana was yelling. "Listen, Mom," he finally said. "Jacqueline is as upset as you are. She got duped by those girls. She's really upset about the whole thing."

He held the phone out far enough she could hear Diana laughing, but not in a happy way. "We could come over and talk to you about it," he eventually said. "Okay, okay, fine. I'll tell her. But if you ask me, you're being pretty harsh about it. Besides that, Jacqueline just reminded me that Ginny *can't* come back. The swap contract is for sixty days. They're just over halfway through it." With raised brows, he held the phone away from his ear again, then said, "Bye, Mom," and turned it off. "Wow. That woman can sling some words."

"She's really, really mad?" Jacqueline asked meekly.

"Enraged is more like it."

"Am I fired?"

He nodded glumly. "Sorry."

Now she really did cry, using the soggy cocktail napkin to wipe her tears. She no longer cared about her appearance, or who witnessed her breakdown. "My first real hotel job and I mess up like this," she said in a choked voice. "I'll probably never get hired again."

"Oh, come on." He reached across the table to clasp her hand. "It's no secret my mom is super hard on employees. No matter how hard they work. Ginny was the best manager ever, and my mom used to tear her to shreds from time to time."

"Yeah, but that's because you like her," Jacqueline argued. "Diana didn't want you to be involved with Ginny. The way she treated Ginny had more to do with you than Ginny's job performance."

He nodded. "That's true."

"I'm ruined," she whispered. "Just ruined."

He squeezed her hand. "You're not ruined, Jacqueline. Just having a really bad day. Things will get better. You just need to find a job at a less prestigious hotel. Work your way up."

She stared glumly down at her empty glass. "Like some sleazy roadside motel in a Podunk town. I guess I might find work there. Start at the bottom and grovel awhile." She sniffed.

"I didn't mean that."

She looked up with watery eyes. "I think it's time for me to go home."

"Back to your family's resort?" he asked.

She barely nodded. More like the *last* resort. But at least she had family there. Grandpa might've been ticked about the job swap, but he'd probably welcome her back. Okay, maybe not "welcome," exactly. But you can't turn away family. *Can you?*

GINNY GAVE ALEXI THE SHORT TOUR when they got to the lodge. Then, realizing the girl was hungry, she took her to Margie's fridge for a late lunch. "It's all very portable." She explained about the fishermen's to-go food. "We could take it down by the river if you want?"

"That'd be cool." Alexi nodded.

So they carried their lunches to the river-view bench and sat down.

"It's nice here. Kinda cool being out here in nature." Alexi popped open a soda.

"I really like it."

"And Dad's cabin is kind of cute," Alexi conceded. "But Mom would hate it."

"Because it's too rustic?"

"Yeah. Mom likes things to be perfect and new and luxurious. You know?"

"That's probably kind of like the cabin I'm staying in." She explained about Jacqueline. "She made it pretty comfortable."

"Can I see it?"

"Of course. But I have some chores to take care of first."

"For your job?" Alexi took a bite of her egg salad sandwich.

"Yeah. We're shorthanded right now. In fact, I was actually considering asking you if you'd like some part-time work."

"A paying job?"

"Absolutely."

"Does it pay more than babysitting? Mom pays me to watch my brothers, but it's pretty pathetic wages, and they can be a real pain."

"Oh, yes, I'm sure it'll be better than babysitting." Ginny wasn't positively sure, but somehow she would make it tempting. Even if she subsidized from her own pocket.

"Then, sure. I'll work for you. Might even be fun." Alexi looked out over the river. "The river is really pretty . . . but it kinda scares me too."

"Scares you?" Ginny gazed out over the rippling blue water.

"I don't think I'd like to fall in."

Ginny laughed. "Me neither. But that's not likely to happen from here."

"I know. But it looks so powerful and cold . . . like it could sweep you away."

"Well, I suppose that could happen in parts of the river. Not here though. This is a pretty calm stretch. But some of the rapids down a ways can be really strong, and there are undertows in places."

"What's an undertow?"

"A place where the current can suck something down. Your dad was explaining it to me the other day. You can't always see an undertow on the surface of the water, but underneath there could be a temperature change or a deep spot in the bottom of the river or something else that changes the current's direction and makes the water swirl around. It's really pretty interesting."

"Sounds pretty scary to me."

"Well, your dad is an expert on this river. He knows where the undertows are, and what to avoid. The river is constantly changing with snowmelt, but he knows about that too."

"That's cool." Alexi bit into her apple.

"Your dad has years of experience here, but to a newbie rafter, this river could be dangerous. Like your dad says, you have to respect it."

"Or just stay out of it." Alexi frowned as she wadded up her paper bag.

Ginny hoped she hadn't said too much. She didn't want Alexi to be afraid of the river. "Well, if you go out with your dad, you don't have to worry. He's the safest guide on the river. That's what Jack says."

"Who's Jack?"

"He owns the lodge." Ginny spied Cassie coming out of a cabin and waved. "Jack can be a little grumpy at times, but he's a good guy." She stood up. "Come on. I want you to meet my head housekeeper."

Ginny introduced Alexi to Cassie. "Alexi will be our part-time help for a while," she explained to Cassie. "But you'll have to train her."

"No problem." Cassie grinned.

Ginny turned to Alexi. "And this can be sort of a trial, you know, to see if you like working here or not."

"Maybe you won't like me." Alexi glanced at Cassie.

"How do you feel about laundry?" Cassie asked her.

Alexi shrugged. "I help out at home sometimes."

"Great." Cassie grinned at Ginny. "Thanks!"

"You can find me in my office," Ginny told Alexi.

"Cool." Alexi headed off with Cassie.

As she went to her office, Ginny felt pleased with her little plan. Not only did it help to have an extra pair of hands around here, it was a great way to occupy Alexi while Ginny did her own work and Ben was busy on the river.

Ginny had finished her afternoon tasks and was just going to see if Margie needed KP help when she heard Ben call out to her. She went out to the porch to see that several of the fishermen were already gathered, sharing drinks and fishing stories. But Ben looked worried.

"Where's Alexi?" he asked her. "She's not in the cabin. And your office was locked."

"She's helping Cassie," Ginny told him.

He frowned. "Huh?"

"I sort of offered her an impromptu part-time job," she explained.

"And she was willing to do it?"

"She seemed eager to earn some money."

"But I'd hoped to spend time with her." Ben scratched his head.

"Of course. But I thought while you and I are busy with our jobs, Alexi might as well be occupied with a bit of part-time work. And we really need the extra help."

"I guess that's a good plan." He slowly nodded. "But where do you think I might find her right now? Is she still working?"

Ginny pointed over his shoulder to where Alexi was just emerging from a cabin with a laundry basket. "There she is."

His face lit up. "Great! Thanks." He called out and waved to her.

"Hey, Dad." Alexi joined them, her laundry basket of dirty towels balanced on one hip. "What's up?"

He awkwardly hugged her, nearly knocking the basket down.

"Here, I'll get that." Ginny took the basket from her. "And I'll put you down for two and a half hours of work today, Alexi. How did you like it?"

"Better than babysitting," she said. "I like Cassie."

"Great. I'll just take this to the laundry." Ginny started to leave.

"Does that mean I'm done for the day?" Alexi acted almost disappointed.

"Well, unless you want to help in the kitchen—"

"Not today," Ben told Ginny. "She just got here, and I want her to myself for a while."

"Of course." Ginny smiled. "Thanks for your help today, Alexi."

"I want to help tomorrow too," Alexi assured her.

"And I want to show you my boat and the river." Ben took Alexi by the hand. "Come on."

Ginny watched as father and daughter walked down to the docks. It made a sweet picture. Hopefully Alexi would love the river as much as her father did. So far, the teen seemed to like the lodge well enough. And her willingness to help out was refreshing. Really, she was a sweet kid. Nothing like what Ginny had expected based on Ben's description of her. She hoped the two of them would have a delightful and memorable visit.

# twenty-five

Ginny tried not to be too concerned when Ben and Alexi weren't back in time for supper. She set aside some food and put it in the warming oven so they could have a late meal when they got back.

"Do you think they're okay?" she asked Margie as she helped clean up.

"Oh, sure. Ben's probably just showing her the river."

"I guess so. I hope Alexi's comfortable with that." Ginny picked up the table-washing bucket and dropped in a clean washrag.

"Why wouldn't she be?" Margie's brows arched.

"Well, she seemed a little frightened of the river . . . earlier."

"Then there's nobody better to introduce her to the river than Ben."

"You're probably right." She went to the dining room to wipe down the tables and sweep. She was just straightening up the coffee area when she heard raised voices. It sounded like Ben and Alexi.

"You have to give it a chance," Ben was saying.

"I gave it a chance," Alexi shot back.

"Not much of a chance!"

Ginny turned to see the father and daughter pair coming into the dining room. She greeted them, but they both looked frustrated, perhaps even angry. And Alexi hurried over to Ginny, standing close to her in a way that suggested she expected protection.

"Everything okay?" Ginny cautiously asked.

"Not really," Alexi snapped. "Dad tried to scare me to death."

"I did not." He scowled. "I told you, Alexi, it was perfectly safe. I had complete control and—"

"His boat got stuck on one of those things you told me about," Alexi said to Ginny. "A sinkhole or undertow or whatever."

"We were not stuck," Ben argued. "I just wanted to show you the power of the river. I thought you were an adventuresome girl, Alexi."

"Adventuresome enough to drown?"

"You were in no danger of drowning."

"Sounds exciting," Ginny said. "I bet you two are hungry. I saved some supper for you." She gave Alexi a little sideways hug. "Sorry your introduction to the river was rough."

"It was not rough," Ben interjected.

"Well, it felt rough to her," Ginny told him. "It's understandable. I remember being a little overwhelmed the first time I went out," she directed to Alexi. "But then I relaxed and now I love it."

Alexi frowned. "I don't want to go out again."

"Okay then, how about some food?" Ginny asked nervously. "I'll go get it."

"I'll help you." Alexi followed her to the kitchen.

"So this is Ben's daughter." Margie clasped Alexi's hand while tossing Ginny a glance that suggested she'd overheard the conversation out there. "Welcome to Frederickson's Fishing Lodge. I hear you're working with Cassie."

"Yeah, I guess." Alexi sounded sullen, nothing like the helpful girl she'd been earlier.

"Cassie told me how much she appreciated it," Margie continued. "We're really shorthanded around here."

"Yeah, I know." Alexi came over to help Ginny with the warmed plates.

"You take these out," Ginny told her. "I'll get your salads."

"I'll wait for you," Alexi said.

Ginny just nodded. Then, together, they started out with the food, but Alexi stopped in front of the swinging doors.

"Are you going to eat with us?" she asked Ginny.

"I already ate."

Alexi looked at Ginny with pleading eyes.

"But I didn't have dessert yet. And Margie made blackberry cobbler." Ginny smiled. "How about if I get some for all of us and join you."

"Yes." Alexi nodded eagerly. "That'd be good."

Soon the three of them were seated at one of the smaller tables and while Ginny picked at her cobbler and sipped coffee, she attempted to make comfortable conversation with the disgruntled father and daughter. But mostly she felt like she was talking to herself. Finally, they were all done, and Alexi insisted on clearing the table—probably just to escape them.

"I'm sorry it didn't go well with Alexi," Ginny quietly told Ben. "But I hope you won't give up on her. She told me earlier that the river scared her."

"Why should it scare her?" he demanded.

"Who knows why? Maybe just because it's new and big and unknown. And you've told me before that it's good to have a healthy fear of the river. I've heard you say that, Ben."

"A healthy respect maybe." His tone sounded sharp.

"Maybe you just need to have a healthy respect for Alexi's fear." She stopped herself at the sound of the swinging door opening. "Well, it's been a long day." She stood. "I think I'll call—"

"You were going to show me your cabin," Alexi said quickly. "*Remember?*"

Ginny glanced at Ben, trying to read him, but feeling even more confused by his creased brow. "Oh, we can do that tomorrow, Alexi. You've had a long day too."

"But I want to see it." Alexi came over and looped her arm into Ginny's. "*Please?*"

Ginny turned to Ben. "Do you mind?"

"Not at all." He carried his coffee cup toward the kitchen.

"Okay." Ginny smiled stiffly at Alexi. "Let's go."

Neither of them spoke as they went outside to where it was just getting dusky. Normally, Ginny didn't turn in this early unless the weather was bad, but she'd wanted to get away from the quarreling pair. "Here we are." Ginny unlocked her door and turned on the light.

"Wow." Alexi walked in and looked around. "Cool."

Ginny gave her the two-bit tour, explaining how Jack's granddaughter had outfitted the place. "It seemed a little over the top at first, but I have to admit I've been enjoying it."

"Can I stay here with you?"

"Stay here?" Ginny felt uneasy.

"Just for the night?" Alexi pleaded. "I'm not ready to stay in my dad's cabin. Not after today. I'm so mad at him! I can't stand to be with—"

"Okay, okay." Ginny put a hand on her shoulder. "I understand. And, if your dad doesn't mind, you're more than welcome to spend the night here." She pointed to the sofa. "You'll have to sleep there."

Alexi hugged her. "Thank you!" She flopped down on the sofa, pulling a faux-fur pillow into her lap. "Oh, this is so soft, I know I'll be totally comfortable."

Ginny sat down beside her. "Do you want to tell me about it? About what happened today?"

Alexi's lip stuck out. "I was just really, really scared. I mean seriously white-knuckled, I'm-gonna-drown-and-die scared."

"I'm sorry."

"And Dad didn't help one single bit. He was like—like I was being a *big baby*."

"Did he say that?"

"Not exactly. But I know that's what he thought. I could see it on his face. Like extreme disappointment."

"That doesn't sound like him to me . . . He's usually more empathetic and understanding."

"Not with me." Alexi folded her arms in front of her. "He always expects way too much from me. Like I should be just like him. Big and brave and strong, and all outdoorsy. Like I should've been a boy! Ben Junior!"

"I'm sure parents want their kids to take after them." Ginny tried to imagine how she would feel if she had a child of her own.

"Yeah. They want little puppets that they can control." Alexi's tone was bitter.

"Is that how you feel?"

"Sometimes." She ran her hand over the fuzzy throw pillow, then slugged it with her fist.

Ginny pursed her lips, trying to think of the right thing to say. "I know your father loves you, Alexi."

"Funny way of showing it." She pounded the pillow again.

"Well, he hasn't had much practice parenting lately."

"Thanks to Mom." She tossed the pillow aside. "Sometimes I think I'd be better off without any parents."

Struggling for words, Ginny stared at the flower arrangement on the coffee table, a sweet selection of wildflowers she'd found by the river. Did Alexi even know what she was saying?

"Seriously," Alexi proclaimed with resolve. "I should look into emancipating myself."

"What?" Ginny sat up straighter. "Emancipating yourself from your parents?"

"Yeah, who needs them? My friend Morgan got herself emancipated during spring break. She lives in a group home now."

"And she likes that?"

"It's better than what she had with her parents' nonstop custody battles. It was making her totally crazy. Seriously, she has to go to a psychiatrist for it. Now at least she's free from her parents' mess."

"Wow . . . talk about the grass being greener . . ." Ginny sighed. "Some people grow up wishing they had parents, and others can't wait to be free from them. Go figure."

"Which were you?"

Ginny wondered how much to say, then realized this girl might need to hear about the other side of the coin. "Well, my dad pretty much disappeared after my baby sister was born. I was just a kid. And when I was about your age, my mom got sick . . . and then she died." Ginny shook her head. "I kind of got emancipated, but I didn't want it."

Alexi's big blue eyes grew wide. "I guess my situation isn't as bad as I thought. You're right, my parents love me. Even if they drive me up a wall sometimes. I'm really sorry about you losing your parents, Ginny. That's so sad."

"I'm okay now. That was a long time ago." Ginny forced a smile as she stood, feeling that perhaps she'd made some headway with Alexi. "You still want to spend the night here now?"

"Yeah. If you don't mind."

Ginny shrugged. "If you don't mind the sofa."

"Because Dad probably needs some chill time." Alexi's voice cracked with emotion. "So do I."

"Then we should let him know."

"Will you do that? I'm so not ready to talk to him. Not yet anyway. Maybe tomorrow when we've both cooled off."

Ginny considered this. It wouldn't be easy to tell Ben his daughter was ditching him on her first night here. "What about your things? They're in your dad's cabin."

"Could you get them for me?" Alexi's eyes glistened with tears. "Please?"

Ginny didn't relish the idea of informing Ben about his daughter's rejection. But seeing Alexi tucked into the corner of the sofa, on the verge of tears, strengthened her. "Okay." She went for the door. "Make yourself at home."

"Thanks so much, Ginny. I really, really appreciate it."

As Ginny walked through the darkness toward Ben's cabin, she hoped she wasn't being manipulated. She knew how teen girls could be. Gillian used to be a pro at making Ginny feel guilty for one thing or another. It wasn't really a deep character flaw, Ginny realized as Gillian grew older, but just a very real part of adolescence. She braced herself and knocked on Ben's door.

"Alexi?" he said pleasantly as he opened the door, but seeing her illuminated in the light, he blinked. "Ginny? What're you doing here? Is Alexi okay?"

"Not really."

"Come in," he urged her. "What's wrong? Did I really blow it? I'm sure that I did." He ran his fingers through his hair as he stepped back to let her in. "I'm so lousy at this. Straight out of the gates and I mess up." He closed the door.

"Well, Alexi is fifteen," she said, as if that explained everything.

"I know that."

"And she's a girl."

"I know that too." He frowned. "What's your point?"

"She's trying to figure things out. It's an awkward age. You want to be a grown-up and do as you please, but you want to be protected like a child at the same time."

"How do you know all this?"

She briefly explained about raising her sister after her mom died.

"Wow, really?" He sat down. "I didn't know that."

"Anyway, the good news is that Alexi knows you love her. But she just thinks you both need a break. Just for the night." She pointed to the alarm clock on his mantel. "And you have an early trip in the morning. Maybe it's for the best."

"Well, I can't deny I'd appreciate a good night's sleep in my own bed." He glanced over to where she'd laid out bedding for him to spend the night on his sofa. "I'm guessing that thing could be a back killer."

"Can I get Alexi's bags? They're in the bedroom."

"I'll get them." As he walked, she could sense the sadness in his step. This wasn't how this evening was supposed to go. Maybe he shouldn't have gotten his hopes up. Not that she planned to point that out to him. Poor Ben.

He came out with the roller bag and backpack. "I guess this is all she brought."

"Yes." She reached for the bags, but he shook his head.

"I'll carry them over to your cabin." He glanced around the room. "I like the way you spruced this place up, Ginny." He pointed to the desk she'd set by the window. "That's nice."

"Makes your kitchen a little more functional."

He looked intently at her. "Do you think Alexi will ever want to stay here?"

She smiled. "I'm sure she will. She just needs some chill time. That's what she told me."

He opened the door. "Well, I'm glad she's warming to you." He turned to her. "But I'll admit I felt a little jealous too."

She patted his shoulder. "I'm not surprised. But I really do think things will get better. Just give her time, Ben. And don't push her too hard about the river. For whatever reason, she's a little traumatized about it." As they walked through the dark, she wondered if she might be responsible for much of it. Why had she gone on about the undertows this afternoon? Maybe she had planted those seeds of fear. If so, she needed to figure out how to undo the damage.

# twenty-six

On Monday morning, Ginny got up at the usual time and was just traipsing through the living room when she remembered her teenage houseguest. Alexi appeared to be sleeping soundly on the sofa, her clothing and bags spread across the room. Ginny had heard the TV going late into the night and suspected Alexi had stayed up well past midnight. She probably needed her sleep now.

Ginny jotted down a quick note for Alexi, putting it on the coffee table, before she tugged on her shoes and quietly let herself out the door. As usual, she saw fishermen assembling themselves down by the docks. To her relief, Ben's boat was already gone, suggesting he'd had a good night's sleep. She spotted Jack hobbling toward his favorite fishing spot and hurried down to join him.

"How are you doing?" she asked as she slowly walked beside him.

"I've been better," he grumbled. He nearly stumbled into a gopher hole but missed it.

She resisted the urge to help him. "What's wrong?"

"This ding-dang cast is getting so itchy. Kept me awake half the night."

"When do you get that walking cast?"

"This week. Margie offered to take me in." He stopped by his chair, dropping his crutches on either side, then sitting with a harrumph.

"Well, that should make life better."

"We'll see." He reached for his tackle box. "How's Ben's girl doing? Does she like it here?"

She told him about Alexi's part-time job and then a bit about the unfortunate river excursion. Jack frowned. "Ben should go easy with her. No sense in forcing anyone against their fears. I've told him that before."

"I think it's because she's his daughter. He thinks she should enjoy it as much as he does."

"Don't work that way." He grimly shook his head, and she suddenly recalled the story of how his son drowned. "Maybe I should talk to him."

"That might be helpful, Jack." She patted his shoulder. "Good luck fishing."

"Don't need luck," he said gruffly. "I'm a good fisherman."

She laughed. "Well then, *happy fishing.*"

"Yeah, that's better."

She headed on to her office to check messages, then over to the kitchen to lend a hand. Seeing Margie in the midst of her second round of cooking, Ginny went out to the dining room and was just tidying up the coffee station when her phone chimed. She checked her caller ID and did a double take. Diana Jackson was on the other end. Ginny glanced around the dining room to get her bearings. She was having a flashback to Hotel Jackson and wanted to be sure she wasn't still in Seattle. "Hello, Diana?"

"Genevieve." Diana's tone sounded exactly like it used to when she was about to make an unreasonable demand. "I need you to come back."

"Come back?" Ginny headed for the side door, slipping outside to manage this call with a little privacy. "What do you mean?"

"I mean that nincompoop you traded jobs with is trying to destroy my hotel."

"Oh, Diana, you can't be serious."

"I am dead serious. Jacqueline is worse than useless, and I insist you quit this ridiculous job swap and come home right now. *Today!*"

"I can't come . . . back." Ginny couldn't say the word *home*. "Jacqueline and I signed a sixty-day contract. It's only been a month."

"I don't care about your stinking contract, Genevieve. You must return at once."

"As I recall, you were about to fire me, Diana."

"I never said that!"

"Or maybe *I* was about to quit."

"I don't care about any of that now. You're my manager, and I've indulged your whim for this senseless swap long enough. I insist you come home. At once!"

Ginny heard Margie calling for her. "I'm sorry, Diana, I'm needed here right now. I have to get back to work. I'm sorry for your troubles, but I have to go. Bye." She hung up and, knowing Diana would not easily give up, muted her phone as she headed into the kitchen.

"Sorry about that," she told Margie as she picked up a platter of bacon and sausage with one hand and a bowl of scrambled eggs with the other. "That was my boss from Seattle calling."

"Everything okay?" Margie flipped a pancake.

"I, uh, I don't know." Ginny used her shoulder to push the swinging door open. "I'll fill you in later." She smiled at the fishermen now taking seats at the main table. These fellows were more relaxed than the early-bird diehards who thought they had to be on the river at the break of dawn.

"Good morning," she said cheerfully as she set down the food. They returned her greeting, but quickly got serious about breakfast. Margie's no-nonsense comfort-food cooking was always welcome with them. "I'll be right back with the trout and pancakes," she called over her shoulder as she returned to the kitchen. She traveled back and forth a few times until everyone had everything they needed.

"How's Ben's daughter getting along?" Margie asked as Ginny wiped down a countertop.

Ginny filled her in on last night's drama. "But she appears better today—she was sleeping soundly when I left."

"No surprise that she'd prefer your cabin to Ben's." Margie wiped down a cast-iron frying pan. "Think she'll want to stay there permanently?"

"I hope not. For Ben's sake. She told me it was just one night."

"Well, Jacqueline's cabin's pretty swanky." Margie pulled a dish scrubber from under the sink. "So what's up with Seattle? Why'd your old boss call?"

"She wants me back." Ginny set a stack of dirty dishes by the sink.

"What about the job swap? You've only been here a month." She shook the dish scrubber at her.

"Diana doesn't care about the contract. She's insisting I return ASAP."

"And what about Jacqueline?"

"Diana is finished with her."

"What a surprise." Margie snickered.

Ginny turned to look at Margie. "I don't want to go back."

"Then don't." Margie turned on the faucet.

"Really?"

"You're contracted for sixty days, right?"

"Yes." Ginny handed her a plate to rinse.

"And Jack expects you to stay for sixty days, right?"

Ginny handed over another plate. "He signed the contract."

"And your boss did too?"

"Yes. But she's changed her mind."

"Look, Ginny, that woman—Diana—does not own you, does she?"

"Of course not."

"Then honor your contract with Jack and stay put."

Ginny slowly nodded. "Okay . . . that's what I'll do."

"Good!" Margie grinned. "Now if you're not too busy and would like to finish clearing the dining room, I won't object."

"You got it." Ginny felt resolved as she returned to the dining room. She would fulfill her contract. Jack deserved that much from her. After that, well, time would tell. But she did not plan to return to Hotel Jackson. In fact, she didn't even have a desire to return to Seattle unless it was to collect her things.

With the dining room cleaned, she went into her office to check her messages again and go over her daily chores. And finally, she decided to check her phone. Naturally, Diana had called back. Nine times—with as many voice mails. The first seven messages were nothing more than whining, complaining, and spewing. But the eighth message got Ginny's attention.

"Look, Genevieve, I realize I'm not the easiest woman to work for. But I have taken you into my hotel almost as a member of my family. I deserve more loyalty than you've shown me. Please, call me back so we can talk."

Ginny actually listened to that message twice. Then she listened to the ninth one.

"Okay, Genevieve, you have me over the proverbial barrel. What will it take to get you to come home? A contract? A raise? Benefits? How can I negotiate with you if you refuse to talk to me? Please, call me back."

Ginny pocketed her phone again. It was hard to hear Diana's attempts at being nice. Practically begging Ginny to come back. It was so out of character. Ginny's heart actually went out to her. But what about the contract with Jack? What was the right thing to do?

Ginny left her office, hoping to clear her head. She walked down to the bench that overlooked the river, her favorite place to ruminate . . . or pray. She sat down, determined to gather her thoughts before she returned Diana's call. She knew she had to call back, but not until she knew what she would say. Everything in her wanted to follow Margie's advice and say, "No way, Diana." But part of her still felt guilty. Diana was no dream boss, but she had given Ginny a chance to prove herself as a manager. What was the answer?

Closing her eyes, Ginny prayed a silent prayer—asking God to guide her—then she just waited, listening to the calming sound of the river flowing, feeling the morning sunshine and a cool breeze over her face. She relaxed and savored these things . . . and waited for an answer, some direction. And then she recalled a sky-blue ceramic plaque her mother had hung in their kitchen. In fact, Ginny had saved the plaque and stored it somewhere. But what were the words on it? Suddenly, she saw the plaque in her mind's eye.

*Delight yourself in the* LORD, *and he will give you the desires of your heart.*

Looking out over the river, she ran the Bible verse through her head a few times, wondering how it applied to her prayer for direction. She thought about the word *delight*. What did it really mean? She looked up the definition on her phone to discover delight was "to take extreme pleasure or satisfaction in something." Probably similar to the way she felt about the sparkling river or the tall green trees or the star-studded night sky. She definitely took delight in nature's beauty.

And she did take delight in God, the Creator of all this beauty. That was easy enough. But what were the desires of her heart? She sighed deeply . . . *to love and be loved.* That was the strongest desire of her heart. She knew that she loved God and that God loved her. But she longed for it in human form too.

But what did this have to do with Diana? For years, Ginny had tried to love that cantankerous woman. And with God's help, she had loved her to the best of her ability. But had any love ever come back from it? Ginny sighed. Maybe that wasn't the point.

Ginny noticed Jack, dressed in his faded green fishing vest, limping along with his crutches. He spotted her, pausing to wave, then continued slowly on his way. She was happy to see him fishing again. It meant he was in better spirits. She thought about his recent words of praise. They might not have sounded like praise to anyone else, but to Ginny they were delightful. *Delightful*, she thought. Yes, delightful. She liked that word!

Ginny called Diana back, and to her relief went straight to voice mail. Taking a deep breath, she began. "Hi, Diana. Sorry to miss your calls. I appreciate how much you want me to come back, but we all signed a contract for a sixty-day job swap, and I intend to fulfill it. I'm sorry things aren't going well with Jacqueline, but I hope you can give her another chance. Remember how many times you had to give me another chance? Maybe this is your chance to teach Jacqueline in the same way you taught me. Maybe she will end up being an even better manager than me. I wish you the best, but I am going to stay here and honor my contract. Good luck." She hung up and, leaving her phone on mute, went back to her chores.

Ginny was still mulling over these thoughts as she swept the porch. Somehow everything was going to turn out just fine. As she shook out the welcome mat, she saw Alexi strolling toward her. Dressed in fashionably ragged jeans and a vintage T-shirt, she had plaited her dark hair into two long braids.

"Good morning," Ginny called out.

Alexi greeted her back, patting her mouth to cover a yawn.

"Did you sleep okay?"

"Pretty much. But I stayed up until one watching a lame movie. Sorry about getting up so late."

"It's okay."

"Am I too late to work for Cassie today?"

"Of course not. Being part-time, you have flex hours. But you should probably figure all that out with Cassie. Why don't you grab some breakfast first? Margie keeps leftovers in the warming oven until around ten. If she's not in there, just help yourself." She flopped the mat back down with a thud. "And clean up after yourself too. We run a tidy ship."

Alexi mock saluted her. "Aye, aye, Captain."

Ginny chuckled as Alexi went inside. Hopefully today would go more smoothly between Alexi and Ben. It wasn't that Ginny didn't want a roommate—although she wasn't sure how she felt about her cluttered living room. She just really wanted Alexi to spend some quality time with her father. They both needed that.

# twenty-seven

Jacqueline had felt a smidgen of hope to get Diana's text message ordering her to appear in her office at eleven o'clock on Monday morning. But now as she stood outside the door to Diana's suite, she felt slightly sick to her stomach. Jacqueline had dressed very carefully, determined to put her best foot forward as she groveled before Diana, begging not to be fired. She smoothed her hair, which was swept back into a classic French twist that really showed off her highlights. Diana had complimented her on this style once. She smoothed the front of her pale-blue jacket, adjusting the sophisticated silk scarf looped loosely around her neck—a trick she'd picked up from Diana—and then, holding her breath, she rang the bell.

It took several minutes before the door swung open and, to her surprise, Adrian was on the other side. "Mother will be out soon. She asked us to wait in her office." He led Jacqueline through the picture-perfect room, waving her to one of the luxurious chairs across from Diana's beautiful heirloom desk.

"Is she still mad?" Jacqueline whispered.

"What do you think?"

"Yeah . . . of course."

"I talked to my grandmother last night," he lowered his voice, "and she filled me in a bit."

"Huh?"

"Grandma says Mom met Mr. Wonderful on the ferry to BC."

"Well, that's nice." Jacqueline was confused.

"It could've been. I guess he promised to meet her for cocktails in Victoria." Adrian grimaced. "And then he stood her up."

"Oh dear."

"Grandma said Mom was in a royal snit over it."

"That probably won't help me." She felt like running now.

"Probably not. I guess he never even called or anything."

Jacqueline wanted to feel bad for Diana, but she was too worried about her own situation. "Do you think she might be over it by now?"

"I think she's going to—" Adrian stopped himself at the sound of a door opening. "Hey, Mom." He stood and smiled. "What's up?"

"Good morning," Diana said in an icy tone, going around to her desk chair. As always, she was dressed perfectly. Jacqueline used to dream of getting a sneak peek into Diana's closet, but now she wouldn't complain if Diana commanded her to scrub down her toilet.

"Good morning," Jacqueline muttered.

"Thank you for meeting me here." Diana sat down, then, without speaking, just looked at the two of them, her eyes moving back and forth in a way that reminded Jacqueline of a wildcat about to pounce on its prey. "As you know, Jacqueline, I am extremely disappointed in the situation with the deluxe suites. But I didn't bring you up here to go on about that."

"I am so terribly sorry, Mrs. Jackson. When I booked that group, I had no idea they—"

"Enough!" Diana snapped. "That's not why we're here."

Jacqueline felt her spine softening, sinking slightly into her chair.

"Why *are* we here, Mom?" Adrian asked in a relaxed tone. His mother obviously did not intimidate him in the least.

"We are here to discuss my plan."

"Your plan?" Adrian folded his arms in front of him. "To do what?"

"To get Genevieve back."

Adrian leaned forward. "Yeah?"

"I need both of you to help me."

Jacqueline sank even lower. So Diana really was firing her.

Diana pointed at her son. "I want you to take Jacqueline back to her family's ranch or retreat or whatever it's called."

Adrian nodded. "Okay. Then what?"

"Then bring Genevieve back, of course." She narrowed her eyes at Jacqueline. "And leave her there."

"What about the contract?" Adrian asked.

"Contracts are made to be broken." Diana drummed her perfect nails on the top of her desk. "And I expect you, Adrian, to encourage Genevieve to break it."

"What if she refuses?" he asked.

Diana opened a drawer of her desk and removed a small velvet-covered box. "Then you will offer her this."

Adrian stood up and reached for the box, opening it to reveal a rather large solitary diamond mounted in platinum. "Seriously?"

"It's what you've always wanted, isn't it, Adrian?"

"Yes, but you've been so opposed, are you—"

"I only want you to use that as a last resort, Adrian. First you will give her *this*." She picked up a legal-size white envelope. "It's a contract that includes a raise and benefits."

"Wow." Adrian picked up the envelope. "The tables are really turning around here."

Diana cleared her throat, then looked at Jacqueline. "I suppose you want to know your part in all this?"

Jacqueline reluctantly nodded.

"Well, since you are greatly responsible for this whole mess, I expect you to help clean it up."

"How?"

"You must convince your family, or whoever owns that place, to break the contract and let Genevieve leave." She locked eyes with Jacqueline. "Are you able to do that?"

"I guess so."

"Because you are finished here. Do you understand?"

Jacqueline felt a lump in her throat. "Yes . . . I am sorry. I really didn't—"

"I don't want to hear it, Jacqueline." Diana abruptly stood. "And I want this all taken care of as soon as possible. I want Genevieve back here before the weekend. *Understood?*"

"Wait, Mom." Adrian stood too. "You're not being very fair to Jacqueline."

"Fair?" Diana's eyes were fiery.

"You expect her to *help* you get Ginny back here? Why should she? What's in it for her?"

Diana's lips pursed as if considering his words.

"Seriously, Mom, why should Jacqueline help you when you treat her like this?"

Diana slowly nodded. "You make a good point, Adrian." She turned to Jacqueline with a chilly smile. "You do this for me, and I will write you a recommendation for your next job."

"A *good* recommendation?" Jacqueline asked in a shaky voice.

"You do a good job getting Genevieve back and, yes, I will write you a good recommendation." She stepped away from her desk, turning her back to them. "That's all, children. Don't let me down."

Adrian walked Jacqueline out of the suite and into the hallway where a whole troop of housekeepers was busily clearing out the deluxe suites. "I'm sorry Mom was so rough on you," he said quietly.

Jacqueline tried to smile as she blinked back tears. "It's okay, Adrian. I probably deserved it."

"No one deserves to be treated like that." He pushed the elevator button.

"I guess." She sniffed. "Thanks for standing up for me anyway."

He patted her back as the doors opened. "You're welcome."

"I didn't expect her to let me stay."

"Me neither." He followed her into the elevator. "Do you think we can talk Ginny into this? I mean, I assume your family will agree to break the contract. After all, you're family. But I'm not sure Ginny will want to come back."

"Even with that big chunk of ice your mom gave you?" Jacqueline felt the resentment in her voice.

"That was pretty surprising."

"And that contract in your pocket?" Jacqueline added. "I can't imagine she'd refuse to come back now. I know I wouldn't."

"You could be right."

As he walked her to her office to collect her personal items, Adrian talked about the plan to go to Idaho. "Since Mom wants Ginny back ASAP, I think we should just drive. I doubt we'd get a flight within the week."

"Drive? Won't that take a long time?"

He pulled out his phone. "It's near Idaho Falls, right?"

"Yeah."

"Looks like it's about twelve hours. Can you be ready to leave tomorrow?"

"Tomorrow?" She blinked, trying to hold back tears of disappointment. She was not ready for this . . . not ready to be sent home.

"If we leave early and drive straight through, we'll be there tomorrow night."

"Seriously? You want to drive that far? And all in one day?"

His smile looked slightly delusional. "If I can bring Ginny back with me, yeah, I'd happily drive that far. Can you be ready early tomorrow?"

Jacqueline swallowed against the lump in her throat. "Yeah, I'll be ready."

"Great. I need to take care of some things this afternoon. I'll pick you up at your apartment." As Adrian took off, she couldn't help but notice the new spring in his step. All because he thought he was bringing Ginny back here? The brave hero off to rescue his beloved princess . . . but the wrong princess! How had she allowed this to happen? Was there any way to stop it?

GINNY FELT SOMEWHAT REASSURED that Ben and Alexi were repairing their broken bridges when they took an hour-long hike together after Ben returned his fishing group to the dock. That was progress. But when they came into the dining room, Alexi insisted that Ginny join them for dinner. "I can't think of anything to say to him," she whispered to Ginny. "I need your help."

So Ginny sat with father and daughter, doing her best to initiate small talk but noticing the awkward silences between her cheerful injections. This was work!

"How are things going with Cassie?" she asked Alexi. "How many hours did you get in today? I need to put it into my book."

"Five hours today. And Cassie said I did good." Alexi shrugged. "But she might've just been trying to be nice. Especially after I accidentally knocked a basket of clean, folded towels in the dust." She wrinkled her nose. "I had to go do them over."

"Everyone makes mistakes," Ginny reassured her.

"And I didn't invite you here just to work," Ben told his daughter. "This should be a fun exper—"

"I *want* to work, Dad." Alexi's brow creased. "You should be glad that I'm earning money."

"I can give you money," he argued.

"I know that. But this is my *own* money. Don't you get it?"

"Don't you have everything you could possibly want? What do you need your own money for?"

Ginny laughed. "Are you kidding, Ben? What does any normal teenage girl need spending money for?"

"Clothes?" he tried.

Alexi just rolled her eyes, tossing Ginny a look.

"I guess I just don't understand women," he said.

"Accepting your shortcomings is the first step to recovery," Alexi told him.

"Thanks a lot." Ben waved Jack over to their table, and soon the two men were chatting away about the river and today's fishing. Ginny started to clear the table, and Alexi followed her lead, going into the kitchen with her.

"Can I spend tonight at your place again?" Alexi asked as they stacked dishes by the sink.

"I don't mind, but I'm worried it'll hurt your dad's feelings," Ginny told her.

"Dad doesn't care. I asked him on our hike, and he said it was okay."

"Then I guess it's okay." Ginny noticed Margie tossing her an I-told-you-so look. "I'm enjoying your company." She smiled at Alexi. "But it'd make me feel better if you spent more time with your dad this evening."

Alexi tipped her head to one side. "I will if you will."

"Well, I need to help Margie first."

"I can help too. And I won't even charge you for it." Alexi winked at Margie.

As the three worked together, Margie started making suggestions for things Alexi might enjoy doing during her visit, but Alexi wasn't showing much interest. Margie pulled out the basket with chocolate bars, marshmallows, and graham crackers. "How about making s'mores by the campfire?"

"S'mores?" Alexi grinned. "Sure, that'd be fun."

"Are you going to join us?" Ginny asked Margie.

"Depends . . . My bedtime comes early these days."

"I'll ask Ben to start the fire earlier," Ginny told her.

"Why don't you talk Jack into playing his ukulele," Margie suggested. "He's pretty good."

So it was that Jack, Margie, Ben, Alexi, Ginny, and several guests gathered around the campfire even before the sun had gone down, singing funny old songs and eating s'mores. As Ginny looked around at this unexpected, diverse group, she felt a strange sense of belonging. Like she was really at home.

Finally, after the sun was down, Margie and Jack excused themselves. The guests claimed they needed to be up early, and Alexi offered to carry the s'mores things back to the kitchen. It was just Ben and Ginny.

"I really appreciate the time you're spending with Alexi," he said quietly. "And I want to apologize for being such a stick-in-the-mud."

"Stick-in-the-mud?"

"I'm so clueless when it comes to parenting a teenage girl. You're a natural."

"Like I told you, I had experience with my baby sister."

"Well, I do appreciate it. I know Alexi wants to spend the night in your cabin again. I hope you don't mind."

"Not at all. She's really a delightful girl."

"Delightful?" He looked doubtful.

"Okay, she can be mouthy and difficult too. But that's her age. Beyond that, she's truly *delightful*." Ginny grinned to realize how comfortable she was getting with that word. "And I think I've figured something out about you two."

"Really?"

"Yeah. You're both very similar. I think that's why you don't get along so well. At least right now. I'm guessing it'll get better . . . in time."

"How are we alike?"

"You're both very hard workers. You're both very strong and confident in yourselves. But you're also very tenderhearted."

"Tenderhearted?" His frown was accentuated by the flickering campfire flames.

"Yes. But you try to hide it. Anyway, Alexi does. And I think you do too, at least when you're around her. You seem to have your guard up."

"Hmm." He rubbed his chin. "That could be true. I never thought of it quite like that." He studied her. "You're very ten-derhearted too, Ginny. Except you don't try to hide it. That's why everyone is so drawn to you."

"Really?" She considered this. "Everyone?"

He nodded. "Including me."

She felt her cheeks flushing, and not from the fire. He leaned toward her, and for a moment, she thought he was about to kiss her. She wouldn't object. But then Alexi was coming back, and Ben simply reached over and flicked a cinder off her sweatshirt sleeve. "Don't want you to catch on fire," he said lightly.

She thanked him, and then, saying she was tired, excused herself to bed. She wasn't really tired but simply hoped Alexi would linger awhile with her dad. But Ginny had been in the cabin for just a few minutes when Alexi came in. At least the girl was in good spirits and didn't have anything negative to say about her dad. That was something.

# twenty-eight

Jacqueline had planned to start packing that evening but just couldn't manage to dig her bags out from beneath her bed. She still hoped something might happen to slam the brakes on this whole stupid mess. Maybe Diana would have a change of heart by tomorrow morning. Or Adrian might come to his senses and realize he was madly in love with her and beg her to remain in Seattle.

Not surprisingly, Rhonda wasn't overly concerned when Jacqueline broke the news she was leaving. While stewing in her bedroom, Jacqueline overheard Rhonda on the phone, clearly making plans for a new roommate. When the conversation stopped, Jacqueline went out to give Rhonda a little advice.

"You know that Ginny still has a lease on this apartment," she reminded her.

"Yeah. But she's not coming back."

"You might be surprised about that." As Jacqueline gathered a few stray items of her clothing from the living room, she considered pushing the matter, then decided it was Ginny's problem. After all, Rhonda had been her roommate first. Let them sort it out.

Still, she wasn't ready to start packing. Instead, she gave herself a facial, touched up her mani-pedi, whitened her teeth, and addressed a few other neglected beauty maintenance chores. If she had to go back to the lodge, at least she could go back in style. Finally, it was past midnight and too late to get serious about packing.

It was the sound of someone knocking on the apartment door that woke her up in the morning. Thinking Rhonda would answer, she ignored it. Then, her phone rang. Adrian called to remind her they were supposed to be on the road by now. "I'm sorry," she told him. "I had a rough night. I need more time."

And she kept taking more time, delaying the inevitable as much as possible. By the time she was ready, or nearly ready, it was past eleven, and Adrian was pacing back and forth in the living room, livid. "You promised to be ready early," he grumbled as she set her bags by the door. "I've literally been waiting for hours!"

"I'm really sorry. Everything just takes longer than I think. It's like I'm in a dream, trying to run, but I'm wading through thick strawberry Jell-O."

"Strawberry Jell-O?" He picked up a bag and opened the door. "Ready now?"

"Almost." She attempted a smile as she pointed to her cosmetics case. "Just need to get a few things from the bathroom."

"Well, then do it!" Adrian picked up another bag with a loud growl that reminded her of Grandpa. She couldn't help it if her feet were stuck in Jell-O. What did he expect? She gathered her expensive toiletries from the tiny bathroom, carefully packing them, one by one, into the individual slots of her designer cosmetic case. Just because Adrian wanted to drive all day and half the night to reach Idaho Falls didn't mean she did!

Finally, with her bags loaded into the back of his car, they were on their way amid a Seattle downpour. "Almost noon." Adrian growled as he waited for a light to change. "At this rate we won't be in Idaho Falls until after midnight."

"And it's another half hour to the fishing lodge from there."

"Fishing lodge?" Adrian turned to look at her. "That's your family's resort? A *fishing lodge?*"

She folded her arms across her front with a shrug.

"I thought it was a fancy tourist resort."

"Did I tell you that?"

"I don't know. Maybe Ginny did. I can't remember now."

"The light is green, Adrian." She exhaled loudly. "What difference is it to you if my family owns a run-down fishing lodge or a fancy-schmancy resort? Why should you care?"

"You're right." He nodded firmly. "Actually, it's good news."

"Huh?" She turned to look at him—he was smiling!

"I'm glad it's just a fishing lodge. It'll make it easier to get Ginny out of there."

"Right . . ." She turned to gaze out the side window, watching the rain drizzling down in streaks. The weather suited her mood. Dark and damp and dreary. For a long time, neither of them spoke. Jacqueline briefly considered calling Grandpa to let him know they were coming. But what if he scolded her for her failure? She just couldn't take any more negativity or criticism right now. By the time they got onto the freeway, thanks to the weather, traffic was moving like *it* was stuck in strawberry Jell-O.

"So how's the fishing there?" Adrian's tone was surprisingly bright.

"I don't know. Okay, I guess."

"I'm thinking it's probably not a good idea to arrive at the fishing lodge in the middle of the night."

"Yeah. Everything will be shut down. Fishermen all go to bed with the chickens and get up with them too." She felt tired just remembering.

"We'll stop somewhere for the night." He edged his car into the "fast" lane, which was crawling along. "No need to hurry now."

"Not like you can, anyway."

"I checked my maps app while I was waiting for you this

morning. Looks like we'll make Boise by evening. Tomorrow we'll leave around eight—eight for real this time—which should put us at the fishing lodge around noon on Wednesday."

"Great." She rolled her eyes. "Can't wait."

"You did let them know we're coming, right?"

"Not yet." She still wasn't eager to announce her failure to Grandpa.

"And I checked the weather forecast for Idaho Falls," he continued in his cheery voice. "Sunny and warm for the next ten days."

"Oh, goody."

"Well, I sure won't mind leaving this chilly rain behind."

"Uh-huh."

"Thanks to your slo-mo morning, I did some more weather research, and it sounds like that part of the country, unlike here, is known for sunshine and blue skies." Adrian continued to drone on in his irritatingly cheerful tone. Did he think this was a pleasure trip? An unexpected, fun-filled vacation? She wouldn't be surprised if he took up fishing too. Good grief!

ALEXI'S THIRD DAY at the lodge went surprisingly well. Since Ben didn't have a group to take out, he took his daughter fishing— from the riverbank—and according to Ben she'd been over the moon to catch a fish.

As they ate supper, including the trout caught by Alexi, Ginny felt like father and daughter had finally moved solidly forward. So much so that, as Alexi went to get her dad a second dessert serving, Ginny quietly asked Ben if he wanted to invite Alexi to relocate to his cabin for the rest of her visit.

"You tired of having her with you?" His brow creased.

"No, not at all." Ginny shook her head. "We even worked out a system for her to keep her clothes in the hall closet instead of splayed all over the living room."

He laughed. "Well, I'm fine either way. Want to let Alexi choose?"

"Sure. I'm just so relieved to see you two getting along."

"Me too. And I have an idea, Ginny. It probably won't work, but I'd like to give it a try."

"What's that?"

"I thought if I invited both you and Alexi to go fishing on the river, well, maybe she'd feel more comfortable. What do you think?"

"It might work." Ginny looked to where Alexi was coming through the swinging kitchen doors. "Here she comes."

"How about if you ask her?" Ben suggested. "She might be more agreeable."

Ginny wasn't so sure about that but decided to give it a shot. "Hey, Alexi, your dad doesn't have to take a fishing group out tomorrow, and I'd sort of like to get out on the river again. I've really been loving it. Are you interested in coming too?"

Alexi set the piece of chocolate cake in front of her dad with a perplexed look.

"No pressure, Lex," Ben told her.

"That's right," Ginny agreed. "I can only go out for a couple of hours. It'd be a short trip."

"And you're not scared?" Alexi asked her.

Ginny's smile grew wide. "Not in the least. Your dad is such a pro. I feel perfectly safe in his boat."

"What about getting stuck again?" Alexi asked him. "Will you promise not to do your little dramatic demonstration about the power of water?"

"You have my word." His expression grew even more sincere. "I'm sorry I did that. I think I was trying to compete with Disneyland." His smile looked sheepish.

"Yeah . . . right."

"I honestly thought it'd be fun for you."

"It wasn't."

"I know. I'm really sorry. I hope you can forgive me."

She tipped her chin in a nod. "Okay then, I'll go out."

They exchanged high fives and made plans for where to meet and what to bring and then, like the previous night, they all gathered around the campfire again. Ginny felt happier than ever as she watched Alexi and Ben joking back and forth. And they all applauded when Alexi sang along with Jack, every verse, to "The Fox Went Out on a Chilly Night."

"I can't believe you know all the words," Jack said.

Ben patted Alexi on the back. "That was amazing!"

They sang a few more songs until they were interrupted by Alexi's phone chiming. She answered without enthusiasm, then stepped away from the group. Ginny and Ben exchanged glances and when Alexi finally returned, she looked angry.

"That was my mom. I have to go home tomorrow," she announced. Of course, this was followed by everyone's questions. Alexi said it was school related, something she'd signed up for months ago. "Mom won't let me ditch it." She poked the fire with a stick, then looked up. "But she did say I can come back here." She looked hopefully at Ben. "I mean, if it's okay with you."

"Of course, it's okay. It's more than okay," he assured her.

"When ya coming back?" Jack asked her.

"Mom mentioned the Fourth of July week," she told him.

"Perfect!" Jack clapped his hands. "We'll have a barbecue and music, and we'll shoot fireworks over the widest part of the river."

"Really?" Margie sounded surprised. "We haven't done that in a while."

"Then it's about doggone time we did," he growled back at her.

"Sounds great." Ben slapped Jack on the back. "Let me know what I can do to help, Jack."

"Yes, same for me," Ginny told Jack.

"We'll have a planning meeting tomorrow after supper," Jack told them. "I'm hitting the hay now. Good night."

"Me too." Margie walked off with him, and soon the rest of

them were dispersing as well. Including Ginny. But she was glad to see Alexi remain behind with her dad. She acted like he needed her help to put out the campfire, but Ginny thought she just wanted to be with him. And that was oh so sweet!

About an hour passed before Alexi came into the cabin. Ginny was already in her pajamas and just brushing her teeth. "Hey, there," she said with a foamy mouth.

"Sorry to intrude." Alexi sat down on the closed toilet seat. "But I wanted to talk to you before you went to bed."

Ginny spit and rinsed. "Sure. No problem."

"So, Dad told me about this three-day rafting trip he wants to do right after the Fourth of July. *White water rafting.*"

"White water?" Ginny reached for her dental floss.

"And he wants me to go on it."

She paused from flossing. "How do you feel about that?"

"I think I'd be okay. He said he'd take you and me out on his boat before the raft trip. A couple of times if I need it. Just to help me get comfortable on the river."

"Uh-huh?" Ginny studied Alexi.

"What do you think?"

Ginny threw her floss into the trash. "I think if you're okay with it, you should definitely go. I've heard those trips are amazing. They camp out at night and eat lots of great food. They'll probably even sing around the campfire. By the way, that was really impressive how you knew that song. Jack just ate it up. You have a really good voice, Alexi."

"Thanks. But here's the deal." Alexi stood. "I told Dad I would only go on the raft trip if you went too."

"Oh?"

"He's totally down with that, Ginny. And it'd be so much better if you were there with me. Honestly, I don't think I can go if you don't come."

"I appreciate that, but I have my job responsibilities here and—"

"Dad said he'd talk to Jack about it. He seemed pretty sure that Jack will let you go."

"Well, if Jack agrees, I'd love to go with you. It sounds like fun."

Alexi hugged her. "Thank you so much. It's going to be awesome. I just know it."

Ginny nodded. "So about tomorrow . . . when do you have to leave? Do you need a ride to the airport or anything?"

Alexi frowned. "My mom's driving here. She'll pick me up around ten."

"I'll miss you." Ginny tugged one of Alexi's braids. "But I'm glad you're coming back so soon. July Fourth is right around the corner."

"And Mom said I can stay here longer next time. Maybe the rest of the summer."

"That's fantastic! I bet your dad is thrilled." Ginny rubbed lotion into her elbows and hands.

"He acted pretty happy." Alexi reached for her toothbrush. "I probably shouldn't keep yapping about it. You look tired."

Ginny let out a yawn. "I guess I am." She told Alexi good night and headed for bed. As she closed her eyes, she remembered to thank God for the way Ben and Alexi seemed to have repaired their broken bridges. It felt good to have played a small part in the restored relationship. Hopefully they'd have lots more good times together. Maybe all three of them.

# twenty-nine

After a very busy morning of catching up on some management chores and witnessing Alexi being picked up by her mother—an impeccably groomed blond driving a silver Mercedes—Ginny eagerly got ready for today's fishing trip. Despite Alexi not joining them, Ben had insisted on taking Ginny out.

By now, thanks to an online sporting goods site, Ginny had proper—and not unattractive—fishing clothing. Outfitted in her olive-green cargo shorts with lots of pockets, a crisp white sun-blocker shirt, a bandanna tied perkily around her neck, and a khaki canvas hat, she felt ready to fish.

"You look sporty," Ben said as he met her at the dock. "And pretty too."

"Thanks. I was hoping I didn't look like an ad for women's fishing apparel."

"You look ready for the river." He took her thermal pack of food, then gave her a hand as she stepped into the boat.

"I just wish Alexi could've come." She reached out for the food pack and tucked it under her seat.

"Me too." He untethered the rope and climbed in, giving the boat a little shove away from the dock as he started the motor.

Ginny pulled her sunglasses from a shirt pocket and slipped them on. "The good news is she's really looking forward to it now." She paused as he looked up and down the river.

"I know." He revved the engine slightly. "I'm hoping missing out today will make her even more eager to go out when she gets back."

Ginny leaned her head back, drinking in the warm sunshine along with a cooling river breeze. "What a perfect day."

"What's that?" Ben asked.

Suddenly Ginny heard someone yelling from the shore. Opening her eyes, she saw a woman running down the grassy slope toward the dock. Dressed in a pale-blue pantsuit, she waved her hands wildly. "Stop, stop!"

"Who is that?" Ginny tipped her glasses up to see more clearly.

"Ben! Ben!" the woman screamed loudly. "Wait!"

"*What?*" Ben turned the boat.

"Oh my goodness, it's Jacqueline!" Ginny exclaimed.

"You gotta be kidding." Ben waved unenthusiastically as he piloted the boat back toward the dock.

"I need to talk to you," Jacqueline yelled from the bank.

"We're just going out," Ben called back. "Is this an emergency?"

"Yes!" she screamed. "It is!"

"What happened?" he called back.

"Do you think it's Jack?" Ginny asked in alarm.

"Nah. I just saw him. He looked fine. Heading to his office for his afternoon nap."

"But she seems really upset," Ginny said. "We should go in."

He let out a loud sigh but continued toward the dock, staying close enough to hear but not close enough to tie up. "What is it, Jacqueline?" he asked.

"We need to talk," she told him.

"We're just going out," he told her again. "Can it wait?"

"Is it about Jack?" Ginny called out with concern.

"Uh, not exactly. Sort of." Jacqueline waved for them to come closer.

Now Ginny noticed Adrian coming down the hill, approaching the dock. "There's Adrian," she said with astonishment. What was he doing here?

"Who's Adrian?" Ben asked her.

"He's Diana's son. Diana's my old boss—from Seattle."

"Wonder what he's doing here?"

"I have no idea." She frowned. "Maybe we should go in."

"I don't know." He lowered his voice. "Jacqueline can be a real drama queen sometimes. I bet it can wait. Unless you really want to go in."

"Not particularly."

"Hey, Ginny." Adrian waved to her.

"Hey," she called back. "What's up? Is there some kind of emergency?"

"Nah." He shook his head with a forced blasé expression. "I just brought Jacqueline back. We, uh, can catch you later."

"We need to talk! Now!" Jacqueline elbowed Adrian as if to hush him. "Come back in!"

"We'll see you later," Ginny said lightly. She didn't like being ordered around like that. She turned to Ben. "Ready when you are."

"Good. Fish are waiting." He grinned as he gunned the motor, steering it straight up the river with Jacqueline still yelling at them from the shore. They rode along quietly, hearing Jacqueline's voice steadily fade into the sound of the motor and the water until it finally vanished altogether. Ginny leaned back and breathed deeply. She had her suspicions about what Jacqueline was so eager to discuss, but was in no hurry to find out for sure.

"I wonder what that was all about." Ben slowed the boat as he guided it through the water.

"I think I know." Ginny blew out a sigh.

"Let me guess." He turned the boat up his favorite fork. "She got canned, right?"

"Yep."

"And she wants her job back?"

"Probably." She felt an unexpected wave of sadness.

"Wonder what Jack will say about that?"

"What can he say?" Ginny pursed her lips, determined to not let this ruin their afternoon. "How about this?" Ginny turned around to look at him. "How about we just pretend that didn't happen. Jacqueline isn't back there right now. Let's just enjoy this time like we don't have a care in the world. Okay?"

He nodded. "Spoken like a true fisherwoman. Leave your troubles behind and go fishing. You got it."

And that is exactly what they did for the next two hours. They didn't even catch a single fish, but it didn't matter. They had a picnic on an island and visited about all things—except Jacqueline—and it was one of the loveliest afternoons Ginny could remember.

JACQUELINE WAS MAD. Bad enough to come back here like a kicked pup, tail between her legs, but seeing Ginny like that! All tanned and happy in her fancy fishing clothes, looking so pleased with herself, like she owned the world. At least the fishing lodge world. And going out on the boat with Ben! The cherry on top! Well, it was more than Jacqueline could handle, and she honestly hoped Ben's boat would hit a rock and sink to the bottom of the river! Not so that the despicable pair would drown, necessarily, but at least get a decent dunking—just what they deserved!

"This is quite a place," Adrian observed as they walked up to the lodge. "Beautiful river, pretty landscape, attractive lodge—"

"Oh, shut up," she snapped.

"Glad you're so happy to be home sweet home."

"Just thrilled, *Pollyanna!*"

"Yeah, and *thanks for the ride, Adrian.*" He playfully elbowed her. "Come on, Jacqueline, lighten up."

"*Excuse* me." She narrowed her eyes. "I need to find Grandpa."

"Is there a restaurant in there?" He pointed to the lodge. "Some place to get a bite?"

"There's an old fridge in the dining room full of nasty, old fisherman sandwiches. And probably a few cartons of worms. Help yourself."

"Thanks a lot." His brow furrowed. "You really have a *hospitality* degree?"

"Argh!" She stormed off toward Grandpa's office. She knew she'd be interrupting his afternoon nap, although he would claim he was working, but she didn't care. She pounded on the door, then, without waiting for him to answer, burst in to see him fumbling with some metal crutches before he clumsily flopped into his recliner with a loud groan.

"Jacqueline?" He blinked in surprise. "What the devil are you doing here?"

"I'm home," she declared. "Ready to take my job back."

He rubbed his grizzly chin. "But our trade contract was for sixty days and I—"

"Contracts are made to be broken," she parroted Diana.

"That all depends." His expression grew sober as he pointed to a chair. "Why don't you sit down and tell me what's going on?"

She wanted to weave a heartbreaking tale about how she'd been treated unfairly, but something about his expression stopped her. He looked almost sad. Still, as she explained about her departure from Hotel Jackson, she was careful not to take all the blame for her unfortunate dismissal. After all, Diana was not the easiest boss in the world. "Even Ginny didn't get along with her," she finally said.

"That's too bad." He shook his head. "I thought Ginny could get along with anyone."

"No one gets along with Diana Jackson. The woman is a real witch!"

"Sorry to hear that." He pursed his lips.

"So I want my job back," she declared. "I can start today."

"Easier said than done."

"What do you mean?"

"I mean there's Ginny to consider. She signed the contract too."

"Ginny won't care. She'll probably be glad to get out of this place." Even as she said this, she wasn't so sure. Ginny had looked pretty satisfied—like the cat who'd swallowed the canary—out on the boat with Ben.

"You might be surprised, Jackie. Ginny seems perfectly happy here. Happier than you ever were." His eyes narrowed slightly.

She tried to hide her irritation at being called Jackie. "I'll be happy now." She leaned forward to peer into his face. "I've learned that city living isn't all it's cracked up to be, Grandpa."

"Really?" He still looked doubtful.

"Yeah." She described some of her disappointments with Seattle, probably painting it blacker than it was, but enjoying his concern. "I want my job back. I really do."

He exhaled loudly. "I need to think about this, Jackie."

"Right." She stood, smiling hopefully. "I know you won't let me down, Grandpa." She leaned over and kissed him on the cheek. Out of character perhaps, but whatever it took to win him over. She needed that good recommendation from Diana.

"Yeah . . ." He groaned as he reclined his chair. She wasn't sure if it was from physical pain or if he was that displeased to see her. Maybe both. As she closed his office door, she realized she'd forgotten to inquire about his injured foot. Well, that could come later. Right now, she had other fish to fry. She planned to take her bags to her cabin and make herself at home. And while Ginny was out on the river with Ben, Jacqueline would move the interloper out! She chuckled to imagine Ginny's face when she discovered her belongings splayed out across the front porch.

But when she got to Adrian's car to retrieve her luggage, she discovered the vehicle locked. Thinking he was probably eating some stale tuna sandwich, she went inside the lodge, surprised to find him casually chatting with Margie in the dining room.

"This place is totally charming," he told Margie. "Really unique."

"Here, have another." Margie held out a plate of cookies. "While they're still warm."

"Thanks, ma'am."

Jacqueline cleared her throat as she approached them.

Margie's smile was crooked. "Well now, look what the cat drug in."

"Thanks a lot." Jacqueline scowled.

"I'm sorry, honey. *Welcome home.*" Margie hugged her with one arm. "You know me and my big mouth."

"Yeah. I remember."

"So I met your friend, but I still don't know what you're doing here," Margie asked. "Vacationing?"

"No, I'm home to stay." Jacqueline helped herself to a cookie.

"Really?" Margie's brows shot up. "Does Jack know?"

"Of course." She paused to glance around. "Everything looks different around here. What happened?"

"Ginny's doing. That girl's just full of clever ideas."

"Yeah, I'll bet." Jacqueline chewed with a vengeance. "Well, I'm moving back into my cabin now. Adrian, your car's locked and I want my bags."

"Hold on there, Jackie." Margie stepped in front of her. "Not so fast."

"Whaddya mean?" Jacqueline glared back at her.

"Ginny is using that cabin now."

"It's *my* cabin!" she shot back.

"It's the *manager's* cabin." Margie's expression looked grim. "Ginny is the manager right now. She keeps the cabin until Jack says anything different."

"But she is done here," Jacqueline argued. "I'm back. I'm the manager. Don't you get it?" She stormed past Margie and into the living room. "What're these stupid blankets doing out here?" She jerked one from the back of the sofa, holding it out at arm's length with a turned-up nose.

"Ginny put those out." Margie grabbed the blanket in a territorial way. "They belonged to your grandmother. We've all enjoyed seeing them out again. You leave them be."

"They look cheesy." Jacqueline folded her arms.

"I think they're pretty cool." Adrian bit into his cookie, nodding with approval. "Very lodgey."

"*Lodgey?* Is that even a word?"

"I don't know, Jacqueline. Seriously, does it matter? Why are you so down on anything Ginny did to better this place?" His eyes bored into her. "Do you really hate her that much?"

"No, no, of course not." Jacqueline knew she needed to rein it in.

"Ginny's done a lot around here." Margie tossed the blanket back on the sofa, taking time to smooth it out. "That girl's a breath of fresh air. Have you looked around, Jackie? In only a month, Ginny's done amazing things. Without hardly spending a dime. She's a magician."

"A magician?" Jacqueline silently counted to ten, trying not to explode.

"Ginny's always been good at making improvements on a budget," Adrian told Margie. "She helped make Hotel Jackson what it is today."

"Whose side are you on anyway?" She jabbed him in the chest.

"Ouch." He glared at her. "Take it easy, *Jackie.*"

"Do not call me Jackie!" She glared at him. "Don't you remember what your mom told you—why we came here?"

"Huh?" He looked confused, then slowly nodded with realization.

Jacqueline turned to Margie. "I'm getting the spare key to my cabin from the office. Please do not try to stop me." She stormed past her.

"Don't bother. The office is locked."

Jacqueline spun around with clenched fists. "Then where am I supposed to stay, Margie? I need some place to call my own. At least until Ginny moves on, which will probably be before the end of the day if I have anything to say about it."

"Take one of the rooms up there." Margie pointed to the staircase. "They're all vacant at the moment."

"Up there?" Jacqueline made a face. "You gotta be kidding. Those rooms are a nasty mess. No one stays up there."

"Then take one of the back cabins."

"The *back cabins*?" Jacqueline felt like screaming. "With the pack rats?"

"Ginny started fixing some of them up and—"

"Fine!" Jacqueline yelled. "I'll take an upstairs room." She turned to Adrian with an angry smirk. "Would you mind bringing up my bags?" Without waiting for an answer, she headed for the stairs.

"Want a key?" Margie followed her.

"*Whatever*." Jacqueline stomped back and stuck out her hand.

"The one on the east side is in the best shape." She pulled a key from her apron pocket. "Ginny started fixing it up already."

"Of course she did." Jacqueline suppressed the urge to grab Grandpa's prized bronze elk sculpture from the mantel and dash it against the wall, and then she paused. "Where did *that* come from?" She pointed to the river landscape hanging above the fireplace. "I never saw it before."

"Ginny got it from Jack's cabin. It was one that your grandmother particularly liked. She used to keep it there too."

Jacqueline studied the painting for a long moment. "It's nice."

Margie put a gentle hand on Jacqueline's shoulder. "Yes, it is. Now how about you go up and just try to relax a little? You seem all worked up, Jackie." She held out the platter. "Cookie?"

Jacqueline snatched two, then, blinking back angry tears, she ran up the stairs. Clearly, she was a totally displaced person now. Unwanted, unloved, and practically homeless. Her only hope was to get Ginny out of here. She needed that usurper to leave ASAP. Then Jacqueline could get Diana to write her that recommendation letter, and she'd be out of this place for good!

# thirty

Ginny felt a little guilty for staying out on the river so long, but since it was the middle of the week, the lodge wasn't terribly busy yet. And her work in the office was caught up. Still, it was getting late, and she knew Margie might want help preparing supper.

"I hate to say it, but I need to get back," she finally said.

"I know." He revved the engine slightly, turning the boat around.

She still didn't want to talk about why Jacqueline had been acting like something was so terribly urgent earlier. Really, she didn't want to know. Not yet anyway. Neither of them spoke as the boat steadily moved back down the river. She let her hand dip into the water, leaving a trail as they went.

"I'm really looking forward to seeing Alexi out here," she finally said. "I think she's going to learn to love it."

"I sure hope so."

"She sounded pretty enthused about the raft trip last night."

"Only if you go," he reminded her.

"And that's only if you talk Jack into it."

"I mentioned it to him at breakfast, and he seemed okay with it. He said you're going to hire more staff. Think you'll have them by then?"

"I already scheduled several interviews for tomorrow morning."

"Hopefully you'll find someone good. I told Jack that as a manager, you really do need to experience a rafting trip. I said you could get photos to add to the website, and he agreed that was a good idea."

The dock was coming into view now. Other fishing boats had already come in, but no one was lingering by the dock. Including Jacqueline. But just in case she was lurking nearby, Ginny hurried to gather her things and get out.

"Thanks so much for today," she told Ben as he took her hand, helping her onto the dock. "That was so relaxing."

"Sorry about not catching anything." He continued to hold her hand, looking into her eyes. "Maybe next time."

She smiled. "Yes, definitely." She looped the handle of the thermal lunch sack over her shoulder. "I better go see if Margie needs help." Eager to avoid Jacqueline, just in case she was around, Ginny hurried up the hill and slipped through the back door into the kitchen.

"There you are." Margie took the thermal pack. "Good fishing?"

"We didn't catch anything. But it was delightful. Sorry if I stayed out too long."

"Dinner's pretty simple tonight. And Cassie offered to help."

"Then maybe I'll get cleaned up."

Margie put a hand on Ginny's arm. "You know Jackie's back, don't you?"

She nodded somberly.

"She's been making quite a fuss. She wants her cabin back, but I made her take an upstairs room for now."

"Thank you. But she can have her cabin if she—"

"You need to leave that up to Jack." Margie's brow creased. "Jackie doesn't run this show, and she needs to know that."

"Well . . . I don't know." Ginny bit her lip. "I mean, she is family."

"Maybe . . . but don't worry, Jack will sort it out."

Ginny forced a smile. "Yeah, sure. Thanks, Margie." She went out the back door and, hoping not to bump into Jacqueline, took the shortcut through the trees to her cabin. At least it had felt like "her" cabin for the past month. What would happen now? She'd just stepped onto her porch when she heard her name called. Adrian. Smiling and waving, he jogged over. "Hey, I've been looking all over for you."

"Sorry. I just got back."

"You do know Jacqueline's on the warpath?"

"The warpath? I had a feeling she was unhappy. But what's going on?"

"She wants her job back. She already talked to Jack about it."

"Oh?" She nodded. "How'd that go?"

"She makes it sound like it's a done deal."

Ginny wasn't that surprised but felt a tightness in her throat. Naturally, Jack had to give Jacqueline her job back. She was his granddaughter. It was understandable. "So I guess the contract doesn't matter," she said more to herself than Adrian.

"Apparently not. Diana and Jacqueline have dissolved their part of the contract. Apparently Jack agrees. Not much you can do, Ginny."

"Right." She unlocked the door. "I need to clean up for supper, Adrian."

"Wait, I'd like to talk to you." He placed a hand on her shoulder. "I know this is hard on you. I've heard what a fabulous job you've done here. No surprise there."

"Really?"

"You should've heard Margie singing your praises. She's a real sweet gal."

"She is." She nodded.

"Anyway, I really do need to talk to you." He handed her a legal-size envelope with her name on it. "This is from Mom. She wants you to read it and then talk to me."

"Okay." She nodded with uncertainty as she opened the door. "I think I'll read it inside."

He pointed to a porch chair. "Mind if I wait here?"

"That's fine."

"Take your time. We'll talk when you're ready."

She went inside and sat down on the sofa. Curious as to what Diana wrote, she opened the envelope and slowly read the neatly typed one-page letter, which was actually a contract proposal. Then she read it again. Diana appeared to be offering Ginny everything she'd longed for these last several years. She was offering a substantial raise, more benefits, and even profit sharing. Was this for real? She studied the curly signature at the bottom. It was definitely Diana's. In a way, this was all very touching. But at the same time, it felt too late. There was a handwritten note too. Ginny slowly read it—twice.

*Dear Genevieve,*

*I know I owe you an apology. I have taken you too much for granted. I realize that now. You were a loyal employee and an efficient manager, but I was too busy to properly notice. I hope you will forgive me. If you agree to come back, I will honor the contract enclosed. And I assure you that I will treat you differently. I also promise not to raise any objections if you and Adrian want to be romantically involved. I realize now that I never should have interfered. Please accept my apology and come back home at once.*

*Sincerely,*
*Diana E. Jackson*
*Hotel Jackson Seattle*

Ginny's mind was spinning as she cleaned up. She knew Diana well enough to take the apology letter with a grain of salt, but a contract was a contract. And perhaps she had no choice in the matter. If Jacqueline wanted to manage the lodge, Ginny would have to move on. She tried not to dwell on all this as she changed into a pretty sundress, another online purchase, topping it with a lightweight cotton cardigan. She rubbed some lavender lotion onto her legs and slid into her favorite leather sandals. Not fancy, but practical. Then she went outside to talk to Adrian.

"That was quite the letter your mom wrote." She sat in the chair next to him. "Did you read it?"

"Are you kidding?" He shook his head. "I'm surprised Mom didn't seal it with wax to make sure I didn't peek."

"Well, she's offering quite a generous contract."

He brightened. "Really? I know she's had a real change of heart toward you. Thanks to Jacqueline."

"What did Jacqueline *do*?" she asked.

"Oh, a lot of things. Some that were really stupid. Some that were just plain unlucky. But Mom is very done with her."

"Poor Jacqueline."

"Poor Jacqueline?" His brows arched. "Seriously? You feel sorry for her?"

"I sort of do."

"That figures." He smiled, reaching for her hand. "Do you know how good it is to see you?"

"You too. You were always such a good friend to me in Seattle." She studied him. "But I heard you and Jacqueline were pretty good friends too."

He shrugged. "She's a funny girl. Sometimes I want to protect her and sometimes I want to throttle her."

Ginny smiled and then noticed Ben emerging from his cabin across the way. He'd already cleaned up and appeared to be heading to the lodge for dinner. He waved at them with a curious expression. Feeling slightly confused and a bit lost, she waved back.

"Jacqueline got herself into a big mess." He explained about the damaged deluxe suites. "Mom was furious. But that's what helped her realize what she'd lost in letting you go. She desperately wants you back, Ginny." He continued to hold her hand. "She begged me to bring you back with me."

Ginny sighed. "I suppose that's what I should do. I mean, I wish I could stay on here, but this place isn't big enough for two managers."

"I'm pretty sure Jacqueline wouldn't stand for it anyway."

Ginny felt a lump in her throat, but hearing cheerful voices over by the lodge, she now noticed that Jacqueline was greeting Ben with a big bear hug. For a couple minutes the two of them seemed to be chatting congenially in front of the porch. And then Jack joined them, and the happy reunion continued. Finally the three of them went inside.

"It's suppertime," Ginny said in a flat tone. "But I'm not too hungry."

"Me neither," Adrian told her. "I had a couple sandwiches from the fishermen's fridge and too many of Margie's oatmeal cookies."

"Margie's a great cook," she said glumly.

"You sure you're not hungry?" he asked.

"I'm sure." She felt like a large rock was sitting in the pit of her stomach.

"I have an idea." He pulled her to her feet with a wide grin. "Let's take a ride."

"A ride?"

"Yeah. I saw something in town you might like."

"What?"

"Come on." He led her over to where his car was parked. "It'll be a surprise."

She didn't argue, but as he drove them to town, she felt like she was leaving the fishing lodge for good. Oh, she knew she wasn't really gone yet, but as they drove past the COME AGAIN! sign, something inside her felt severed from Frederickson's Fishing Lodge. Like this pleasant little bit of her life had just ended. Of course, they wouldn't need her help anymore. She wasn't family.

"I always knew that if anyone could change my mother into a nicer person, it would be you, Ginny. I'm just sorry it took so long."

"Me too." She looked out the window toward the mountains.

"And no one would blame you for refusing to go back to Hotel Jackson," he continued. "But I hope you will. At least for long enough to see how it goes. I mean, you know my mom, she could wind up going back to her old tricks."

"Yes, I've thought about that already."

"If I were you, I'd make a condition in the contract. Just in case, you know? Leave yourself with an exit plan."

"Right."

For a long spell, neither of them said anything. But Ginny's head felt like the host to dozens of ping-pong-ball thoughts bouncing all over the place. Finally, town was coming into sight, and she knew she needed to pull herself together. "So where are we going, Adrian? What's this big mystery?"

"Still like sushi?" he asked.

"Yes."

"When did you last have any?"

"Not since Ono's with you in Seattle."

"Well, I saw this place earlier today. I googled it, and it's got good ratings. Wanna give it a try?"

"Why not?" She felt bad for her unenthusiastic response. Adrian was trying to cheer her up. Why make him feel bad? So she pasted a stiff smile on her face and pretended to be hungry for sushi. And while they ate and talked, she did slowly begin to feel better. But not good. Would she ever feel good again?

AS THE THREE OF THEM went into the lodge, Jacqueline insisted that Ben join her and Grandpa for supper. After talking to Grandpa earlier, she'd decided the smartest way to handle this slightly dicey situation was to become Miss Congeniality. So far it was working.

"I'll save a chair for Ginny," Ben told her as they sat at a round table.

"And one for Adrian too." She sat next to Ben, using her purse to save a spot for Adrian.

"Where are they anyway?" She glanced around.

"They were talking on Ginny's porch," Ben said.

"You mean *my* porch." She grinned as she playfully punched his shoulder. "I'm glad she's been enjoying it, but I plan to move back in tomorrow."

"Tomorrow?" Jack frowned. "Where will Ginny stay?"

"She'll be headed back to Seattle by then." Jacqueline poured herself a glass of iced tea, then handed the pitcher to Ben.

"What makes you so sure of that?" he asked as he filled his glass.

"I just know." She smiled smugly as she reached for the salad bowl. "Call it inside information."

"Inside information?" Jack frowned.

Jacqueline paused as Cassie set a shepherd's pie on their table. Then she glanced around the dining room and lowered her voice. "It's top secret."

"What're you talking about?" Jack grumbled as he served himself salad.

"I can only tell you if I swear you both to silence," she said mysteriously.

"What is it?" Ben looked exasperated.

"Yeah, spill the beans." Jack reached for the shepherd's pie.

"Well, you see, Adrian and Ginny were sort of involved in Seattle. Kind of undercover. Because Adrian's mom, Diana, who was also Ginny's boss, *disapproved.*"

"Why should she disapprove?" Jack asked as he chewed. "Ginny's a real sweet girl."

"Oh, I know that. But Diana can be a real tyrant. Believe me, I know. And she didn't want her hotel manager marrying her son."

"So what are you saying?" Ben demanded.

"I'm saying Diana has had a complete change of heart. In fact, Ginny should be grateful to me for it."

"Why's that?" Ben asked.

Jacqueline laughed. "Well, I made such a mess of things in Seattle that Diana suddenly realized she wanted Ginny back. So really, Ginny should thank me that Diana suddenly approves of Ginny and Adrian getting married." Jacqueline beamed at them, pleased that they were both speechless. "And do not repeat this, because I don't want to ruin Ginny's surprise, but right this minute, Adrian has a gorgeous engagement ring in his pocket."

"He's going to propose to Ginny?" Ben asked.

Jack looked alarmed. "You think she'll accept?"

Jacqueline nodded firmly. "Most definitely. Adrian is an awesome catch. He's a nice guy and his family is loaded. They've been secretly dating for years. You know, to keep Diana in the dark. But I wouldn't be surprised if they got married as soon as they get back to Seattle. Adrian is over the moon for her."

"That doesn't mean Ginny feels the same." Ben reached for the shepherd's pie, a fixed nonchalant expression on his face, as if he was hiding something.

Jacqueline's curiosity was piquing, but she knew better than to question Ben about Ginny. That would shut him down completely. "That's true," she said lightly. "I guess we'll just have to wait and see." She looked out the window toward the back parking area. "But Adrian's car is gone."

"So?" Jack reached for a roll.

"Do you think they already left for Seattle? I know Adrian's eager to get back."

"No way." Ben shook his head. "Ginny wouldn't leave without saying goodbye."

"That's right," Jack chimed in. "She's more thoughtful than that."

"Maybe . . ." She shrugged. "But I'll bet you guys anything, those two went off somewhere together."

"Where would they go?" Jack asked her.

"Someplace romantic." Jacqueline sighed. "Adrian told me he planned to do this right. He wanted to make it memorable."

For a while the three of them just ate quietly, which worried Jacqueline. Had she said too much? Overplayed her hand? Perhaps it was time to lighten up. She began to make casual conversation, keeping her tone cheery and hopeful. As dessert was served, she went over to get a deck of cards. "When did you guys last play gin rummy?"

"Probably with you," Jack said in a grumpy tone. "It's been a while."

She handed the deck to Ben. "You deal first."

He looked reluctant, but with a little urging, began to shuffle.

"Remember how much fun we used to have," she said as she put their names on the score sheet. "I've really missed that." She beamed at both of them. "I'm so happy to be back here. It's like old home week."

"Really? You're happy?" Jack questioned. "You sure weren't happy before you left here for Seattle. You said you never wanted to come back."

"I know. And I'm sorry about that. I guess it took being gone to make me appreciate this place . . . and my good friends here. It's so good to be home." She picked up her cards, arranging them in her hand.

Jack made a half smile. "You remind me of when you first came here, Jackie. You were full of life and fun back then." His smile faded. "But is this for real? Or are you just playing me?"

"Oh, Grandpa." She leaned over and wrapped an arm around him. "You know I love you. I'm not playing you." She pointed to her cards. "Well, unless you're talking about cards. I could be playing you then." She laughed. "I'm gonna cream you guys!"

As they played cards, she continued to talk about how much she loved this place, loved the river, loved playing cards . . . and how sorry she was that she'd ever left. Of course she wasn't being totally honest, but she wanted to make Grandpa happy . . . If being a little disingenuous cheered him up, what was the harm?

# thirty-one

The sky was just getting dusky as Adrian drove them back to the fishing lodge. It had been a quiet ride, but Ginny appreciated him not trying to get her to talk. He seemed to understand this was hard on her. After he parked his car, they walked past the lodge, and she couldn't help but look in one of the big front windows. It looked so sweet in there—the golden glow of the interior lights; the rich, warm brown of wooden surfaces; the colorful blankets here and there. So welcoming. She paused to see a small group playing cards, surprised to see it was Ben and Jacqueline and Jack. They were laughing and talking and appeared to be having a pretty good time.

"Want to go in there?" Adrian asked.

"No . . . no, I don't think so." She watched as Ben and Jack laughed hard about something Jacqueline must've said or done.

"Looks like fun," he said.

"Yeah." She nodded glumly, feeling like the kid pressing her nose to the candy shop window.

"Jacqueline's in hog heaven." Adrian chuckled.

"Hog heaven?" Ginny made a face at him. "Seriously?"

"Oh, yeah. She was so thrilled about seeing Ben again. You know she's in love with the guy?"

"I didn't know." Ginny noticed Ben looking their direction and, not wanting to be seen spying, backed away from the window.

"She went on and on about Ben on the drive here," he continued. "Couldn't wait to see Mr. Perfect again. She bragged about how handsome he is, and what an outdoorsman, and an attorney to boot. Did you know he's writing a novel? A thriller, according to Jacqueline."

"So I've heard."

"Quite a guy." Adrian sounded more than a little jealous.

"Well, it's nice to see they're all having fun." Ginny turned away. "I haven't seen Jack laugh like that before. Must be glad to have his granddaughter back."

"I guess so."

"I think I'll turn in." She left the porch, walking toward her cabin, hoping to be alone . . . but Adrian continued along with her.

"I know it's hard for you to leave," he said quietly. "I'm sorry about that. You've done lots of great things here, Ginny, and I know they really appreciated all you did. You're such a hard worker."

"Don't you mean *workaholic?*"

"I didn't say that. It was refreshing to see you out on that fishing boat. Looked like you really were having fun. I was pretty impressed."

They were on her porch now, and Ginny was ready to say good night, but Adrian lingered. "We need to talk, Ginny," he said gently. "Before I leave tomorrow."

She shivered in the night air. "Okay. Come inside." She opened the door, turned on the lights, and waved him in. Not inviting him to sit, she waited. "What do we need to talk about, Adrian?"

"I want to hear what your plans are, Ginny."

"Plans?" She frowned.

"You know. Mom's letter to you . . . the contract . . . what do you plan to do about it? Even if you want to decline, I'd like to let her know. She kind of assigned this task to me." He attempted a meek smile.

"Right . . . Well, it was a generous offer." She picked up the letter she'd left on the coffee table, skimming over it again. "I guess I'd be crazy to pass it up."

"Even if you only take her up on it temporarily," he urged. "Just until you figure out what you really want to do."

She nodded. "You're right."

"And Hotel Jackson isn't such a terrible place, is it?"

"Not at all. I actually miss it a little."

"And if Mom lives up to her promises, well, it might not be bad at all."

"What time are you leaving tomorrow?" she asked.

"Early. Like seven. I'd like to make Seattle before dark."

"Can I think about this some?"

"Of course." He stepped closer to her. "No pressure. I just don't want to leave you here, Ginny. You know . . . if you decide to come back to Seattle."

"Of course." She refolded the letter from Diana. "And no matter what, I'll need to go back sometime. I've got my apartment lease . . . a lot of things stored there."

"I'd really enjoy your company on the drive." He reached for her hand, squeezing it. "You've always been such a good friend to me."

"You've been a good friend too." She tried to smile but felt close to tears. Was it because of Adrian's kindness? Or because she was leaving Ben?

"It's going to be okay, Ginny." He hugged her. "Whatever you decide to do. You're such a good person and such a hard worker— you'll land on your feet no matter where you go."

"Thanks." She stepped away, looking at him with teary eyes. "I'm pretty sure I'll be leaving with you in the morning. But I want to sleep on it. Okay?"

"Absolutely. Like I said, no pressure." He went for the door. "Good night."

After Adrian left, she reread Diana's letter and the contract proposal. It really was more than she'd ever hoped for before. Still, it was hard to think about leaving. This place, the river, the lodge, the people . . . Ben . . . had all gotten into her heart. How was she supposed to just walk away now? But it was meant to be a job swap, a temporary arrangement. She knew that from the start. She jumped at the sound of knocking on her door. Hoping it was Ben, she hurried to open it. But there was Jacqueline, with a wide smile.

"I hope it's not too late. But I saw you standing there, with the lights on. I just thought I'd pop in to say hello . . . or goodbye. Since I suspect you'll be leaving with Adrian in the morning."

"What makes you think that?" She suddenly felt like digging in, holding her ground. After all, they had a contract.

"Well, I'm back, Ginny. I'll be managing the lodge. You've done a good job, but the swap is over now."

"We agreed to sixty days," Ginny reminded her.

"I know. But since Diana and Jack and I . . . well, we've all stepped out of the contract. So it's pretty moot. I'm sorry, but it's time to go." She looked around the cabin. "It's so good to be home again. I can't wait to move back in here tomorrow. The room in the lodge is better than I thought, but nothing like this." Jacqueline flopped down on the comfy sofa. "Lots better than your apartment. Which reminds me. Rhonda already got a new roommate. She said you'd be okay with it."

Ginny bristled. She didn't even have a place to live in Seattle now?

"But don't worry," Jacqueline assured her. "Adrian told Diana all about it, and she said she's going to offer you a suite at the hotel." She shook her head. "Wish she would've offered me one. Maybe I'd still be there."

Ginny wanted to remind her that she'd been fired but didn't see the point. She suddenly got another idea. "You're shorthanded here, Jacqueline," she began carefully. "I've fixed up more cabins and booked more guests. But it's too much for just Cassie. What if I stayed on for a while? I could help out."

Jacqueline frowned. "Oh, that's not going to work. Sorry."

"Why not? You wouldn't even need to train me."

"It's a bad idea. You're a manager, Ginny. You'd want to manage and—"

"I wouldn't. Really, I'm used to cleaning and doing laundry and KP. That's all I'd do. It wouldn't even have to be full-time. And I'd work for just room and board." She felt herself pleading now. That was an offer no smart manager would refuse.

"No." Jacqueline firmly shook her head. "It won't work."

"But Jack likes me and—"

"I am the manager. And I say no." Jacqueline stood up with a stiff-looking smile. "Anyway, I just wanted to come say hey to you. To connect with you before you leave. You've done a good job here, Ginny. I hope you understand why you can't stay."

Ginny simply nodded. She did understand. Jacqueline didn't want the competition. In a way, she was like Diana. Really, it was time to go.

Jacqueline paused by the door. "But I want to thank you too, Ginny."

"Thank me?" Ginny studied her. "For what?"

"If you hadn't swapped jobs with me, I wouldn't have realized this is where I belong."

"Really?" Ginny's skepticism rose. What had made this change in the girl who hated the grungy old lodge?

"Yes. It's like that old saying. You don't know what you got until it's gone."

"Right." Perhaps Jacqueline could see the beauty of the lodge and river now. That was something. Ginny felt a tinge of happiness for her.

"That's how it is with Ben and me."

"With Ben and you?" Ginny blinked.

"Yes. I'm sure you heard about our big fight, the one we had before I left."

"No, I didn't hear." Ginny studied her closely. Was this for real?

"That was probably the biggest reason I wanted out of here. I thought it was all over between Ben and me. But it looks like my absence has made his heart grow fonder. Mine too." She sighed with a dreamy look. "We're back to where we were before . . . only way better now." She beamed at Ginny. "And I have *you* to thank for it." She threw her arms around Ginny. "Thanks so much! You're the best!"

"Well . . . I guess you're welcome, then." Ginny felt seriously confused as she stepped away from the embrace. Ben and Jacqueline were involved? Really? It just didn't make sense.

"And it's all so perfect, Ginny. My grandpa's been like a dad to Ben for years. It makes Ben just like family. And this is a family business. It all works out so beautifully. We can all see it now. I honestly don't know if we would've gotten back together if you hadn't done the job swap with me. So truly I'm grateful . . . and happy."

Ginny felt speechless now.

"And I know you'll be happy to get back to Hotel Jackson. It's such a beautiful, comfortable place. Diana will be thrilled to have you back."

Ginny simply nodded.

"I'm sure you need to get to bed. And you'll need to pack. I know Adrian wants to leave early tomorrow. I must admit I'm going to miss that guy. He's a real sweetheart. And he's quite fond of you." Jacqueline winked as she opened the door. "I wouldn't be surprised if there were wedding bells in your future, Ginny. Please keep me in the loop."

GINNY DID PACK. After setting her bags by the door, she wrote Jack a heartfelt note, thanking him for everything and wishing him well. She felt slightly cowardly about it but knew she'd probably start blubbering if she had to tell him to his face. She got up extra early the next morning. First she texted

Adrian saying she was almost certainly going back to Seattle with him. Then she dropped Jack's letter in the mailbox by his office and went down to the docks in hopes of seeing Ben . . . for one last time.

Shivering in the morning cold, she waited until she finally saw him coming toward the dock with a couple of fishermen in tow. She made a feeble wave, calling out to him. He came over with a furrowed brow. "I thought you'd be gone by now," he told her.

"Not yet. I'm packed. But I just wanted to, uh, talk to you first." She glanced at the fishermen, waiting on the dock. "If you have a minute."

"Sure. Go ahead."

"Well, I wanted to thank you for everything. For your friendship, for introducing me to your river, for teaching me to fish . . . everything."

He nodded, his lips like a firm line. "Okay. You're welcome."

"And I wish you the best with . . ." She wanted to say "Jacqueline," but couldn't.

"Thanks. I wish you the best too." He rubbed his chin. "Have a good trip back to Seattle. Adrian seems like a good guy. I hope you'll be very happy."

"Hey, Ben," a fisherman called out. "Fish are waiting!"

"I'm coming." Ben turned back to Ginny. "I gotta go. Sorry. Really, have a good life." And then he hurried down to his boat. She watched as he quickly loaded, everyone got seated, and they were putt-putting down the river.

Goodbye.

GINNY DIDN'T REALLY KNOW what a time warp felt like, but when Adrian pulled up to the Hotel Jackson that night, she thought she must be experiencing one. She didn't recall loading his car, driving the long distance, or anything along the way. Had she been sleeping the whole time?

"Here we are," Adrian said cheerfully as the bellhop hurried out to greet them. "Mom texted me that she's got a suite set up for you. Not a deluxe suite. It's the one on the second floor. Near your office."

"Thanks," she said woodenly.

"Welcome back, Miss Masters," the bellhop said as she got out.

"Hi, Ronnie," she said. "Thank you."

Grateful it was nighttime, Ginny went directly to her room and, without even changing into her pajamas, fell into bed. Maybe tomorrow would be better.

The next day was a tiny bit better, but she still felt like she was stuck in a bad dream. Not a nightmare. Just a frustrating dream that had no end. Fortunately, the steps in her day were familiar. Oh, she had some snags to sort out. Things that Jacqueline had snared up. But it was a relief to have something to focus on, something to absorb her attention. Maybe she really was a workaholic. Maybe this was exactly what she needed to do—feed her addiction to busyness.

Diana was tolerable. She hadn't turned over a completely new leaf, but the woman was trying. And after Ginny had been back for a few days, Adrian stopped by to tell her some "good news." Ginny wished the good news would be that Diana had decided to give Jacqueline a second chance and honor their sixty-day agreement. Although it would probably be pointless now, since Ginny no longer had any hope of reigniting what she thought had been going on between her and Ben. And being back at the river, well, it just wouldn't be the same.

"Okay." Ginny waited as Adrian leaned against her office console with a slightly smug expression. "What is it?"

"Mom is in a pretty good mood."

"Oh?" She felt only mildly interested.

"You see, she met this guy she really liked on a trip up to BC.

She'd thought they were going to meet up, but he appeared to have blown her off. As it turned out, he'd gotten mixed up and gone to the wrong place."

"Uh-huh." Ginny still wondered why he thought this should interest her.

"Anyway, he tracked her down here and they've gone out a couple of times."

"That's nice." Ginny glanced at her notepad. "Speaking of your mom, she wants me to come up for coffee this morning. I should probably get going."

"Yeah, me too. I have a phone call at ten."

After they parted ways, Ginny grew more curious about Diana. She was glad her boss was in good spirits, but what did that have to do with her? As she went into Diana's suite, she didn't know what to expect, so she decided to expect nothing. But as she sat down in Diana's office, she felt something was different about Diana.

"Are you settling in okay?" Diana asked as they sipped their coffee.

Ginny nodded. "I'm fine."

"Fine." Diana frowned. "My therapist has an acronym for that. It's not very proper, but sometimes appropriate."

"Oh?" Ginny studied Diana. "You have a therapist?"

Diana waved a hand. "You didn't guess that?"

Ginny just shook her head.

"Well, I know you're not happy," Diana declared. "Weirdly enough, you used to be happy. Or at least content. But you are unhappy now. Care to tell me why?"

Ginny considered this. "The truth?"

"Why not?"

"I think I have a broken heart."

Diana leaned forward. "Seriously? I suspect my son is not to blame."

"Adrian has been very sweet, but no."

"Then who is it? Someone at that fish camp place?"

"Frederickson's Fishing Lodge."

"Yes, that. So who broke your heart?" Diana's brows arched.

Ginny's instincts warned her to stay quiet, but what difference did it make? "His name is Ben. He's a fishing guide."

"A fishing guide broke your heart?" Diana frowned. "Really?"

Ginny found herself suddenly explaining everything, down to the smallest details. Perhaps even more amazing, Diana was actually listening. Maybe this "Mr. Wonderful" Adrian had told her about really had made an impact.

"Wow, you fell hard, didn't you?"

Ginny barely nodded.

"And you really think he's in love with Jacqueline?" Diana scowled. "I mean, she's pretty enough, but talk about an airhead. If I'd let her stay a day longer, the hotel would probably have gone up in smoke."

Ginny felt a smidgen of amusement. "I don't think her management skills were as great as we originally thought."

"That's an understatement."

"Anyway, it doesn't matter now." Ginny sighed.

"You miss my point, Genevieve. I'm saying how could this intelligent, sensitive, sweet guy—the man you just described—how could he prefer someone like Jacqueline over you?"

Ginny felt close to tears again. "Jacqueline is very pretty. And she's—she's fun. Adrian tells me all the time that I'm a workaholic."

Diana pursed her lips. "Well, I hate to admit that I can relate to that myself."

"I know it's true—I mean, about me."

"Maybe so, but it's not too late for a person to change." She stood up, turning her back to Ginny as she looked out the window. "I wish someone had told me this when I was younger."

"What do you mean?"

"I mean there was a man . . . before I married Adrian's dad. A kind, sensitive, intelligent man. I was in love with him."

"What happened?"

"He was a fisherman too."

"Really?" Ginny's attention perked up.

"Not like your river fisherman who's also an attorney and author. No, Tom was just a fisherman from a fishing family. They ran a big outfit right down there." She pointed to the Sound. "They still do."

"What happened?"

"Tom asked me to marry him." She turned around to look at Ginny. "But I was too good to be a fisherman's wife. Or so I thought. I didn't grow up with money. And I wanted to marry a rich man."

"Oh?"

"And so I married Gary Jackson."

"Did you love him?"

"I made myself believe that I did. But I loved his family, his name, his money . . . more than I loved him. He eventually figured that out and found someone who really did love him."

Ginny knew Diana's marriage had failed when Adrian was a boy.

Diana waved her hands. "And this hotel was part of my divorce settlement."

"You've done pretty well with it."

"You helped with that," she admitted. "And I've been rotten to you."

"That's water under the bridge now." Ginny felt strangely warm toward her boss. "I think I get why you've been so protective of Adrian. You probably didn't want me, or anyone, to marry him because of his money or family . . . right?"

Diana nodded. "But I want to be done with that now. Adrian is free to marry anyone he likes."

Ginny wasn't so sure about that but didn't think it mattered anyway. "Well, Adrian is a smart guy, Diana. I'm pretty sure he'd never marry a gold digger."

"I know." She sat back down with a slight smile. "It's about time we all started to live our own lives, Genevieve—to follow our own dreams. Don't you think so too?"

Ginny didn't know how to answer that. She was still stunned that Diana was opening up like this. And it was great, but what was she supposed to do with it now?

"Look, I'm glad you came back, Ginny. I really needed you." Diana sighed. "But I don't want you to feel trapped here. Don't make the same mistakes I did and wait to figure it all out until you're my age." She chuckled quietly as she turned back around in her chair, looking out over the Sound again. "That's all."

Ginny wanted to thank her but knew Diana would prefer she just quietly leave her office. And that's what she did . . . feeling more sad and confused than when she'd gone in there. What good was it for Diana to become so understanding now that it was too late?

# thirty-two

Jacqueline had received her letter of recommendation from Diana, via email, the day after Ginny got back to Seattle. Before fully reading it, she'd eagerly printed several copies. Then, seeing that Diana had included the time frame, stating that "Jacqueline has been in my employ for less than a month," she realized the letter was worthless.

Even so, she filed the copies in her personal file. She knew she'd never snag a management position in an upscale hotel now. She also knew that Ben had zero romantic interest in her. She'd probably known this all along but had made herself believe the overblown fairy tale she'd used to get Ginny out and attain her letter of recommendation. Now what?

"I don't know why you came back, Jackie." Her grandpa was scolding her after catching her grumbling at Margie in the kitchen—again. "You obviously don't want to be here."

"It's sure not much fun!" She tossed down the damp dish towel.

"Fun?" He growled. "Life isn't supposed to be *fun, fun, fun.*"

"Don't you have fun when you go fishing?" she challenged.

He rubbed his grizzly chin. "I guess so. But it's *hard-earned* fun."

"Well, even if I work hard, I don't have any fun. Not *here* anyway."

"Then leave," he told her. "No one's forcing you to stay. Go find yourself a hotel where you can work as well as have fun. I don't care."

"I did that already!" she shouted at him. "It was Hotel Jackson in Seattle."

"Then why did you come back?" Margie asked in a gentler tone.

"I got fired!" Jacqueline confessed. Until now she'd concocted a story about a mutual agreement to move on. "I failed, okay? My boss wanted Ginny back. Diana hated me. Are you satisfied now?" She felt like crying. "No one likes me!"

"That's not true," Margie told her.

"It is true. My real dad left because he didn't like me. My stepdad sent me away because he doesn't like me. And you!" She pointed at her grandpa. "You don't like me either."

"That's not true," Jack argued. "I love you, Jackie. I just don't understand you. You seemed happy when you first came to work here."

"Yeah," Margie chimed in. "You were fun and lively back then. But over the years . . . well, you sure haven't been happy."

"I *know* that!" she shouted. "That's why I wanted to leave."

"Then why did you come back?" Jack demanded.

"And why did you make Ginny leave?" Margie asked. "She was happy here."

"I don't know." Jacqueline choked out a sob. "I guess I'm just an awful, terrible, horrible person."

Her grandpa wrapped his arms around her now. "You're not an awful, terrible, horrible person, Jackie. You've just gotten yourself stuck in a place that doesn't fit you."

"I know." She sobbed. "How do I get out? Where do I go? What do I do?"

"I'm not sure," her grandpa said as he released her from his bear hug. "But I'll do what I can to help you figure out something."

Jacqueline picked up the discarded dish towel, wiping tears from her face.

"Why *did* you get fired?" Margie gently but firmly asked.

"Because I messed up." She paused to think about that final week at Hotel Jackson. "I was probably too distracted with all the fun things Seattle had to offer. I guess I didn't take my job seriously enough."

"Maybe you weren't prepared to take on such a fancy hotel," Jack suggested.

"Ya think?" Jacqueline loudly blew her nose on the towel.

"Maybe you needed someone to take you under their wing, to sort of show you the ropes," Margie said.

"Not Diana. She was mean and cold and awful." Jacqueline cringed to remember.

"You needed someone like Ginny." Margie hung a pan up.

"Yup." Jack blew out a sigh. "That's what you needed, alright."

"Well, too late for that." Jacqueline couldn't imagine that Ginny would ever speak to her again. "That ship's sailed." *And sunk.*

"Maybe so . . . but you never know . . ." Jack exchanged glances with Margie, then, excusing himself from the kitchen, grabbed his cane and hobbled off on his walking cast.

GINNY HAD JUST GONE into her suite when her phone rang. Tempted to let it go since this was her lunch break, she took a quick peek at caller ID and couldn't have been more surprised to see Jack Frederickson's name. Worried something might be wrong, she answered. "Jack, is that you?"

"Yep," his gruff voice confirmed. "I need to talk to you. Got time for an old coot like me?"

"Of course." She went over to look out her window. The view of the Sound wasn't nearly as spectacular as Diana's, but it wasn't half bad either. "How are you? How's your foot?"

"I'm alright. The walking cast is okay. But I called to ask you a favor, Ginny. A real big favor."

"Okay." She sat down on the sofa, slipping off her heels and pulling her legs up under her. "What is it?"

"I know this is a lot to ask," he said solemnly, "but Jackie's in a real bad way. She really needs your help."

"What kind of help?"

He explained how unhappy she was at the lodge. "She needs to work in a bigger hotel. Kind of like where you're at, Ginny. But she doesn't have the right kind of references or experience. So I got to thinking . . . what if you took her on? Not as a manager, of course. But as a trainee, working for minimum wage. Or even working for free. I could subsidize her for a while, just while she's learning the ropes."

"I don't know, Jack. She and Diana kind of locked horns when she was here."

"But you're the manager. Aren't you in charge of hiring your personnel?"

"Yes. That's true."

"Couldn't you give Jackie one more chance? I think she's learned some lessons. And you're so good at what you do, Ginny. I know it's asking a lot, but it would be a real gift to me if you could help us out here."

Ginny considered what Diana would say if she hired Jacqueline, then decided it might be a good test. Who was really in charge here? Diana or Ginny? "Okay, I'll give her a second chance. But tell her I expect her to work. I mean, really work. If she doesn't want to work hard, tell her not to even come."

"I'll do that. Thank you, Ginny. If anyone can help Jacqueline, it's you. I just know it."

"I hope you're right." But as she hung up, her doubts increased. How would Jacqueline respond to Ginny as her boss? And what would Diana say? It sounded like a lose-lose situation for Ginny.

And yet, it was a favor for Jack. And she really liked Jack. So she would give it her best shot . . . for his sake.

She wondered if she should tell someone. Not that she normally informed anyone when she filled a new position at the hotel, other than letting the manager involved know. She never mentioned a low-level hiring to Diana. It was a waste of time. She vaguely considered telling Adrian about it. After all, he probably knew Jacqueline better than anyone else here, but he'd been pretty frosty to Ginny lately. Ever since she'd discouraged his attentions, finally telling him, flat-out, she was not up for any kind of romantic entanglements right now. If ever!

Since returning to Seattle, Ginny had decided that romance was highly overrated. Just a fairy tale for starry-eyed little girls. Not middle-aged hotel managers. Okay, she knew that she wasn't really middle-aged, but she wasn't much younger than her mom had been when she passed away. Anyway, Ginny was determined to stick to her no-nonsense, hardworking way of life from now on. She should've known from experience that letting herself slide down the slippery slope with handsome Ben Tanninger and his "romantic" river was just plain foolishness.

As Ginny got a yogurt from her fridge, she wondered about Jacqueline's relationship with Ben. Would she even want to leave him? Or was that all over with? Really, it had nothing to do with Ginny. Why even think about it now?

JACQUELINE FELT SLIGHTLY SICK to her stomach as she walked into Hotel Jackson the next evening. Hopefully she wasn't about to lose her cookies right there in the beautiful lobby, but her nerves were a wreck. How on earth had she let Grandpa talk her into this? It was ridiculous! All that could possibly come out of returning to this place would be complete and total public humiliation.

"What are *you* doing here?" Jeremy asked with arched brows.

"I'm here to see Genevieve." She bit her lip. "For a job."

"What kind of job?" He leaned forward on the registration desk, all ears now.

"Whatever she decides to give me." She forced a shaky smile. "For all I know, I might be working in the laundry."

He chuckled. "Is she expecting you?"

"I just texted her."

"How about I give her a jingle and let her know you're here." He reached for the desk phone. Did he think she was lying? That Ginny wasn't expecting her? Instead of waiting for him to announce her presence, she grabbed her rolling bag and hurried for the elevators. Hopefully she wouldn't bump into Diana. She pounded the Up button several times, holding her head down just in case.

Talk about eating humble pie! Being back here with all the employees she had so recently been over. She used to boss them . . . and she'd be one of them. What had she been thinking to return to this? But what other options did she have? As the elevator went up, she thought about Grandpa's offer to financially support her until she found a real job. Was that generosity or just eagerness to be rid of her? She imagined him limping about in his walking cast, trying to manage the lodge on his own. How long would that last?

As she got out of the elevator on Ginny's floor, she noticed the head maid, Rosaria, coming toward her with an armload of towels—and looking so shocked, Jacqueline thought she'd probably drop her linens.

"What are *you* doing here?" Rosaria asked. "I thought you got fired?"

Jacqueline quickly explained. "So who knows, I might be working under you."

Rosaria chuckled. "That might be fun."

"For you." Jacqueline smirked. "Wouldn't you enjoy bossing me around?"

"I would." She nodded. "I really would."

Jacqueline knocked on the door to Ginny's suite. Hopefully she was in there. These random encounters with staff were awkward and painful.

Ginny opened the door wide with a furrowed brow. "Please, come in, Jackie."

Jacqueline wanted to tell Ginny not to call her Jackie but didn't want to sound uppity to her new boss. Instead, she rolled in her bag and stood by the door. "Thank you for letting me come, uh, Ms. Masters."

Ginny waved a hand. "I use my first name."

"Okay. Well, I appreciate you giving me a second chance. I know Grandpa kind of pressured you into this. Margie filled me in on the details."

"He didn't pressure me exactly." Ginny led her into the living area. It wasn't as fancy as the deluxe suites, but it looked very comfortable. "It's just that he loves you and thought this might help." She pointed to a chair. "Please, sit."

Jacqueline sat on the edge of the chair, nervously folding her hands in her lap.

"Before we get too far along in this, I want to be absolutely sure you understand the terms, Jackie."

Jacqueline cringed at the use of the nickname again. Was Ginny trying to put her in her place? Biting her tongue, she waited.

"You are my employee, which means you will show me the respect you would show any manager over you. And there will be several. Are you okay with that?"

Jacqueline somberly nodded.

"You will work a variety of jobs here. Just like I did when I was learning about management . . . from the bottom up. It's the best way to really understand how the hotel operates. The faster you learn to do these lower-level jobs, the faster you will move up."

"So I will be able to move up?" Jacqueline asked.

"That is the plan. I guess it's up to you."

"Do I start in the laundry?"

"That's right."

Jaqueline nodded. "Tomorrow?"

"Yes. At six in the morning."

"Fine. Where will I be staying?"

"Back with Rhonda." Ginny seemed to be studying her for a reaction.

"I thought Rhonda had a new roommate."

"She does. But since my name's still on the lease, I encouraged her to let you come back temporarily. You'll be sleeping on the couch."

Jacqueline felt her nostrils flare. Ginny was putting her on the couch in that horrid little apartment? Why not just make her sleep in the parking garage? Maybe she could pitch a tent. She kept these thoughts to herself.

"Unless you have another option." Ginny's eyes remained fixed on her. "You could rent a room here, but it would exceed your wages. You'd go in the hole fast."

"Fine. I'll go back to the apartment."

"Are you sure?" Ginny pursed her lips.

"I don't really have a choice, do I?"

Ginny shrugged. "I don't know. But if it works out, if you can handle the work, with a good attitude . . . well, your accommodations *might* improve. But I'm not making any promises."

Jacqueline stood. "Well, if I have to be here at six tomorrow, I should probably go. Does Rhonda know I'm coming?"

"She does." Ginny stood with a sad smile. "I hope this works out, Jackie. I know it probably sounds like I'm being tough on you, but it's the same way I was treated when I first came here."

"Right." She headed for the door, then turned. "I do have one question."

"Yes?"

"Diana knows I'm here, right? And she's okay with it?"

"I'm the manager." Ginny's smile turned all business. "Report

252

to Lindsey in the laundry. She'll train you. I'll check on you later in the day tomorrow."

"Thanks." Jacqueline opened the door.

"And, please, don't forget to use the service entrance in back from now on. And the service elevator too. You're not a guest here."

"You've made that crystal clear." As Jacqueline left, she wondered if it was worth it. Her job at the river lodge might not be fun, but it was far better than this. And what if it didn't pan out like Grandpa had told her? He acted like she was enrolling in a special management program with all kinds of potential. But what if Ginny simply wanted revenge? What if she'd brought her here for punishment?

As she walked toward the apartment, rolling her bag behind her, she wondered if perhaps she deserved some punishment. After all, she'd pulled a fast one on Ginny by pretending Ben was in love with her. Just to get rid of her. Ruining Ginny's management job at the lodge—when Jacqueline hadn't even wanted it. Just to get that useless letter of recommendation from Diana.

Maybe these were her just deserts. Like on her thirteenth birthday when she'd "pranked" her stepdad by keying his car. Her mom had gotten a coconut cream pie for Jacqueline's birthday, knowing full well that she hated coconut cream ... hence her just "desserts." But Robert had sure enjoyed it.

GINNY DIDN'T CHECK on Jacqueline until the next afternoon. She halfway expected to hear that Jacqueline had flown the coop. But to her surprise, there she was, dressed in jeans and a baggy sweatshirt, looking a bit damp and rumpled as she worked the pressing machine to iron a sheet. Relieved that Jacqueline didn't see her spying, Ginny glanced at Lindsey. The older woman jutted out her lower lip with a shoulder shrug. Ginny took that to mean "so-so," which was better than a frown and a thumbs-down.

As she returned to her office, she felt a smidgen of guilt. Was she being too hard on Jacqueline? She'd just sat down at her desk when Adrian popped his head through the still-open door. "Busy?" he asked.

"Not too." She smiled stiffly. "What's up?"

"Not much. Just haven't seen much of you lately." He came in and, closing the door, leaned back onto the console, arms folded across his chest, with a furrowed brow.

"I've been busy." She waved to a stack of still-unopened mail and a flashing phone.

"Right . . ."

"Is there something I can do for you?" she asked crisply.

"Not exactly. Mom asked me to check on you."

"Check on me?" She frowned. "Does she think I'm not doing my job?"

"No, of course not. She just thinks you've been different . . . somehow." He peered curiously at her.

"I've just been busy. That's all."

"The way you're acting, Ginny. It reminds me of my mom."

"How so?" She flicked a letter opener up and down with impatience.

"All business." He tilted his head to one side. "You haven't even noticed that my mom's been acting differently too."

"You mean besides being nicer to me?"

"You haven't even wondered why she is nicer."

"I haven't really given it much thought."

"You know she's got a beau?"

"Yes. Are you saying it's serious?" Ginny felt mildly curious.

"Yes. I finally got to meet him. He's a pretty cool dude too."

"Well, I'm happy for Diana." Ginny opened a letter, as in *hint,*

*hint.* "Thanks for enlightening me about her." She looked up at him. "Anything else?"

"Yeah . . . I heard a rumor . . ."

"What kind of rumor?"

"Ginny, I heard you've got Jacqueline slaving away in the laundry. Is it true?"

She extracted the letter, then solemnly nodded. "That's true."

"*Seriously?*" He stepped away from the console, placing his palms down on her desk with an exasperated look.

"You think I'm wicked?"

"No, of course not. I'm just confused. Bamboozled, in fact."

She explained Jack's plan for his granddaughter. "I'm supposed to be teaching Jackie the ropes. Helping her to learn how to be a good manager."

"No kidding?" He sounded skeptical.

"It might seem crazy. I realize she's the one with the hotel management diploma. But it's how I learned."

"But the laundry?" He grimly shook his head. "Sounds more like punishment than training."

"It's to help change her attitude. That's a big part of her problem. She has this entitled superiority complex going on. You haven't noticed?"

"Of course. But that's just Jacqueline. To be honest, it's that sassiness that makes her kind of fun."

Now Ginny felt slightly confused. Was he serious? "Well, you might like her sassiness, as you put it, but it's not a very good management quality."

"Maybe so." He stood up straight. "It's nice you're helping her, Ginny, but maybe you should let her help you."

"Huh?" How could Jacqueline possibly help her?

"She could give you lessons." His smile was crooked.

"Lessons in what?" She frowned.

"In how to have fun." He opened the door. "At the rate you're going, you'll be old before your time. Even Mom's concerned. You're a real workaholic. Get help."

She didn't know what to say as he left. Adrian had never talked to her like that before. Was he just wounded from her rejection? Or was he genuinely concerned? And, really, what did it matter anyway?

# thirty-three

After five long days of slogging away in the hot laundry, Jacqueline was promoted to housekeeping—and the ugliest uniform imaginable. Ironing linens had been bad enough, but at least she'd been allowed to wear her own clothes down there.

"Do I really have to wear this?" she asked Rosaria as she studied the drab gray tunic and baggy trousers.

"Of course." Rosaria gave her a little shove. "Now get dressed. And do something with that hair."

"What?" Jacqueline smoothed her hair. It was almost back to normal after the steam treatment it'd been receiving in the laundry.

"Hurry up," Rosaria insisted. "We've got a lot of rooms to do."

As Jacqueline changed clothes, she remembered her last conversation with Ginny. "You're doing great," Ginny had said. "Maintain a good attitude and your time in purgatory will be over before you know it."

As Jacqueline zipped up the tunic and looked into the mirror in the changing room, she knew she'd need to try harder. But what was she supposed to do with her hair? She thought about the other housekeepers and how they always kept their hair pulled back. Was that what Rosaria meant? She opened a jar filled with bobby pins and hair ties, quickly made a ponytail, and pinned it into a bun. Hopefully that would do.

"Ready?" Rosaria asked as Jacqueline emerged.

"Reporting for duty." She made a mock salute and smiled.

Rosaria looked slightly surprised. "Okay, let's get going."

As they headed for the service elevator, Rosaria complimented Jacqueline's hairdo. "I'm glad to see you're trying," she said as they went up.

If Jacqueline thought the laundry was difficult, she soon realized that housekeeping was even harder. Instead of doing the same repetitive tasks all day, there were all sorts of cleaning chores to perform and much more to remember. By the end of her shift, and after a multitude of mistakes, Jacqueline was exhausted.

"Aren't you tired?" she asked Rosaria as they rode down the elevator together.

"No more than usual." Rosaria turned to look at Jacqueline. "Although you look pretty worn out."

"I am." She nodded. "I don't know how you do all that, day after day."

"It gets easier . . . as you get better." The elevator doors opened. "But it's hard work."

"I can see that." Jacqueline followed her out. "Thank you for helping me."

"Tomorrow you'll be on your own."

"On my own?" Jacqueline felt alarmed as they went into the changing room.

"Not exactly on your own. You'll be working with the Johnson twins. But as you might remember, those girls are quite a team." Rosaria's dark eyes twinkled. "And they like to work fast."

"Okay." Jacqueline had to control herself from complaining as she unzipped the tunic. Everything inside of her was screaming, *Get me outta this!* Unfortunately, her feet were screaming even louder. "I'll see you tomorrow morning," she muttered as she tugged on her hoodie. "Thanks for your help today."

Rosaria's smile looked genuine. "You did good, Jackie. For your first day."

Jacqueline smiled back. "Thanks again."

GINNY FELT A DARK-GRAY CLOUD had taken up permanent occupancy overhead. And it wasn't just the Seattle weather. Despite her raise in salary, improved accommodations, and Diana's concessions, Ginny wasn't happy. In fact, over the many years she'd worked at Hotel Jackson, she'd never felt worse. And it wasn't the hotel. Since returning to her position and fixing some of Jacqueline's snafus, the hotel was running more smoothly than ever. Or maybe it was just that Diana complained so much less. But still, Ginny was miserable.

By now Diana was aware of Jacqueline's "training program." Although she'd questioned it at first, now, probably because of Adrian, she appeared to accept it. And Ginny had to admit that Jacqueline, according to her supervisors' reports, was pulling her weight . . . and maintaining a good attitude. Ginny had just learned that Jacqueline had worked every day since arriving in Seattle.

Ginny had scheduled a meeting with her for this afternoon. But when Jacqueline appeared in her office wearing the housekeeping uniform, neatly pulled-back hair, and a nervous smile, Ginny did a double take. "Come in." She waved her to a chair opposite her desk. "How's it going?"

"Okay, I think." Jacqueline sat down.

"That's what I've heard." Ginny felt a twinge of guilt, remembering how Adrian had accused her of punishing Jacqueline. Hopefully, that hadn't been her motivation. "Do you feel like this has been an educational experience?"

"I guess so. I mean, to be honest, it's been exhausting. I didn't realize the staff worked so hard. I guess I appreciate them more now."

"And do you understand the workings of the hotel better?"

Jacqueline solemnly nodded. "I really do."

"I just heard you've put in over a week without a day off. Is that right?"

She nodded again.

"I didn't mean for that to happen. I want you to take the rest of today off and tomorrow too."

"Okay. Thanks."

"And when you come back, I'd like you to start working as my assistant manager."

"Really?" Jacqueline's eyes lit up.

"Yes." Ginny felt another wave of guilt. "How is it going at the apartment?"

Jacqueline's frown was enough of an answer.

"Okay, since you'll be my assistant, you're welcome to share my suite. The sofa in the living room pulls out into a bed. I don't know how comfortable it is, but it's yours if you want it."

"Oh, Ginny, thank you so much!" Jacqueline looked almost tearful. "When can I move in?"

"As soon as you like. I'll tell the front desk to give you a key." Ginny stood.

"I know I haven't done everything perfectly, but I've been trying my best." Jacqueline stood too. "And I really do want to learn more."

"Good." Ginny smiled stiffly. "You'll probably make a really good manager . . . someday. And I'll let Rosaria know that you've been promoted."

Jacqueline thanked her again and then left. But as Ginny returned to work, she hoped she wouldn't be sorry about offering to share the suite. What if Jacqueline got all uppity again and tried to take over? Or what if she left her things all over the place and the suite became chaotic and unlivable? Well, perhaps this would be a good test. Time would tell.

When Ginny's workday was over, she felt unsure about going to her suite. She was tired of her ho-hum routine—work in the hotel and live in the hotel—but at the same time, she didn't know what else to do. Besides that, she was worried that she'd get an unhappy surprise when she went up to find her suite occupied by Jacqueline. She imagined the worst-case scenario as she rode the elevator up—TV blaring, clothes and fast-food containers strewn about, and Jacqueline's "fun" personality taking over.

But when she went into her suite, all was quiet and almost exactly as she'd left it that morning. The only trace that she had a roommate was Jacqueline's fancy roller bag next to the door. "Hello?" Ginny called out as she closed the door behind her.

"Coming," Jacqueline called back from the bathroom. When she came out, dressed in comfy-looking sweats and slippers and with her hair down, she looked more like the woman Ginny remembered. "I hope it's okay that I put my toiletries in the bathroom," she said. "I put them in the cabinet, so they're not even in sight."

"That's fine, of course. And I realize you'll have to use my master bath for showering."

"Yes. I actually already did that. But you won't even know I was in there." Jacqueline grinned. "Because I know how the housekeepers like it cleaned."

"Thank you." Ginny tried to hide her surprise.

"I put my clothes in the coat closet. I hope that's okay. And I'll take my bag down to be stored so it's not in the way."

"Well, you seem to have thought of everything." Ginny kicked off her shoes.

"I'm so grateful you're letting me stay up here." Jacqueline held up what looked like a menu. "As a thank you, I ordered sushi for us. Adrian told me Ono is your favorite restaurant and which kind you like. Does that sound good?"

Ginny nodded. "Sure. I haven't had their sushi since I've been back."

"Oh, good. It should be here in about half an hour. I wanted to give you time to relax."

Ginny went over to the island in the kitchen. "Flowers?" She looked at the pretty bouquet. "Where did these come from?"

"I hope you don't mind. They were left over from a guest who checked out—not hotel flowers. But they still looked pretty, so I brought them up here."

"Nice recycling." Ginny pulled a stool out and sat.

"Can I offer you a glass of wine?" Jacqueline opened the fridge. "I'm chilling some pinot gris, sort of to celebrate, you know? Want some?"

"That sounds nice. Thanks." Ginny stared at Jacqueline with amazement as she uncorked the bottle and removed stemmed glasses, then carefully poured. "You seem like a different person, Jackie." She stopped herself. "I mean, Jacqueline."

Jacqueline beamed at her as she set the glasses on the table. "Thank you."

"So . . . you mentioned Adrian. I assume that means you've seen him."

She nodded eagerly. "He's been the highlight of my day lately. We meet for coffee during my break."

"How's he doing?" Ginny took a sip of her wine.

"I think he's getting over his broken heart."

"Broken heart?"

"You know . . . over you. I hear you refused his proposal."

"It wasn't exactly a proposal, but yes, I did tell him I don't love him."

"Apparently, it wasn't the first time either. He admitted that to me just yesterday."

"He's a good guy, and he's been a good friend." A friend that Ginny had been missing lately.

"Ben was a good friend too, wasn't he?" Jacqueline appeared to be studying Ginny now.

"Yes. At least I thought so. He was a little chilly right before I left."

Jacqueline looked down at her glass. "That's because of me."

Ginny sighed. "Yeah, I thought so. I didn't realize you two were still involved."

"That's because we weren't." Jacqueline looked up. "I'm sorry, Ginny. I tried to make it seem like we were. And that's not all."

"What do you mean?"

"I mean I might've given Ben the impression that you were involved with Adrian."

Ginny nodded. "Oh . . ."

"I did it so you would leave." Jacqueline reached over, putting a hand on Ginny's forearm. "I'm so sorry I did that, Ginny. Here, you've been so good to me. And I feel guilty because of what I did back at the lodge. I made it sound like you and Adrian were going to get married. I told Ben about the engagement ring Diana had sent with him and everything."

Ginny didn't know what to say, but she pulled her arm away.

"I'm so sorry. I know Ben has feelings for you."

Ginny considered this. "I tried to talk to him." She felt a lump in her throat. "But he didn't want to listen."

"Because he was hurt."

"Maybe . . . but he hasn't tried to contact me."

"He probably thinks you and Adrian are . . . well, you know." Jacqueline slapped her hand on the island top. "I hate to interfere, Ginny. But you need to let Ben know that you and Adrian aren't married . . . or even engaged, for that matter."

"Oh, I don't think so." Ginny set down her wineglass. "And if you don't mind, I'd rather not talk about this again. Okay?"

Jacqueline pursed her lips, then nodded.

"I have an idea," Ginny told her. "Why don't we start going over some management things? Put our time together to good use."

"Sure. Whatever you think is best."

So Ginny got a tablet and pen and told Jacqueline to take

notes. Then, while waiting for the sushi to arrive, and even while they dined, Ginny went over the many things Jacqueline had overlooked or messed up while working at Hotel Jackson. Jacqueline seemed to be taking it seriously and even asked some intelligent questions. By the time they called it a night, Ginny thought there might be hope for Jacqueline as an efficient manager. But as she tried to quiet her mind and get sleepy, most of her thoughts were about Ben . . . and the lodge and Jack. Finally, she just gave it all to God, repeating, "Your will be done . . . your will be done . . ." Eventually she drifted off to sleep . . . and into a dream about drifting on the river.

THE NEXT FEW DAYS of having Jacqueline as her new roomie and assistant manager went relatively smoothly. Oh, they had a few little mishaps and power struggles, but for the most part Jacqueline was getting it. Ginny was impressed. And when she bumped into Diana by the elevators, she paused to describe Jacqueline's recent progress.

"I'm glad to hear it." Diana paused as the elevator doors opened. "Come on up with me," she said. "We need to talk."

Ginny didn't like those four words. Had Diana's romance soured? Was she about to return to her mean ways? Bracing herself for an old rerun of a Diana tirade, or lecture, or accusation, Ginny accompanied her.

"What's up?" Ginny casually asked as they went into the fancy top-floor suite. Would she even care if Diana suddenly returned to her old self and fired her?

"I'm worried about you." Diana sat down, pointing to a chair for Ginny.

"Seriously?" Ginny said. "Why?"

"You're not the same Genevieve."

"Oh?"

"Adrian thinks so too." Diana played with a pen, spinning it back and forth between her palms.

"Have I been neglectful in my duties here?"

"No, of course not. You work harder than ever."

"So?"

"You used to be happier. At least, you seemed happier. Now you're, well, different. Adrian thinks you're depressed."

"Depressed?" She considered this. "I guess I've been a little gloomy."

"Is it because of that fisherman back at the lodge?" She locked eyes with Ginny, and Ginny looked away.

"No, no, of course not. That's all over with now." Ginny knew it was a lie but didn't want to go into that again. If Ben was interested in her, he would've contacted her by now. End of story.

"Really?" Diana sounded unconvinced. "Well, then, is it from having Jacqueline here?"

"No, not at all." Ginny firmly shook her head. "In fact, I've almost enjoyed her company lately. It's not like we're best friends or anything. But she does lighten things up."

"Oh, good. Adrian has mentioned that to me. Jacqueline may have her faults, but she does know how to have a good time."

Ginny leaned forward, eager to keep this conversation on anything besides Ben. "So do you think Adrian is interested in her? I mean, romantically?"

Diana frowned. "Oh, I don't think so . . ."

"What if he was?" Ginny pressed, remembering Diana's claim that Adrian could go his own way. Was she changing her tune now?

"To be perfectly honest, I'm not totally sure." Diana stood, turning to face the window.

"Well, you might want to think about it. I'm pretty sure that Jacqueline has."

Diana turned back around, taking in a deep breath. "I guess I want Adrian to be happy. If Jacqueline makes him happy . . .

well, he could do worse." She almost smiled. "I would've preferred you, Genevieve."

Ginny didn't know what to say. Feeling partially flattered and partially irked, she stood. "I'll try to be more cheerful," she said woodenly. "Now, I should probably get back to—"

"Wait." Diana held up a hand. "I still need to know something."

"What?"

"Adrian told me even more about that romance you were having with the river guide. He made it sound like it was something pretty serious. Is that true?"

"Calling it a romance might be a stretch." Ginny paused. "Or if so, it was a one-sided one."

"You mean he liked you more than you liked him?"

Ginny sort of laughed. "No, just the opposite."

"Then maybe that's for the best." Diana got a canny look in her eyes. "Because I cannot imagine you being happy with an ordinary river guide, Genevieve. You're too sophisticated for a life like that. And a rustic, old river lodge? I just can't see that for you." Diana's tone sounded taunting, like a challenge. "Yes, you made the right choice."

"First of all, Ben's much more than just a river guide," Ginny defended. "I told you—he's also an attorney and an author."

Diana's brows arched with dramatic interest. "Oh, you mean *that* fisherman?"

"And more importantly, he's a very decent human being." Ginny stood up straighter. "And as to being too sophisticated, I'm not the least bit sophisticated, Diana, and I don't even want to be. I've never been happier than I was at that *rustic, old river lodge.*"

Diana looked thoroughly amused now. "I'm surprised I was able to coax you to come back here. I honestly thought it was Adrian who enticed you initially, but I understand that wasn't the case." She pointed to Ginny. "So I have a question. Why *did* you come back here, Genevieve?"

Ginny thought hard. "It was several things. Partly because I felt guilty for leaving you high and dry without a manager. Partly because I thought Jacqueline wanted her managerial job back at the lodge. After all, she's family. And to be perfectly honest, mostly because I thought Ben didn't care for me."

Diana nodded with a sad expression. "I'm sorry to hear that. Ben must not be quite the man you've imagined him ... if he can't see what a great girl he's passed up."

Ginny smiled with misty eyes. "It's kind of you to say that, Diana. Thank you."

"Okay then ... I'm sure you have work to do." Diana waved a hand. "That's all."

As Ginny returned to her office, she noticed Adrian and Jacqueline in the hotel coffee shop. With their heads bent together, laughing with amusement at something, they didn't even notice her walking by. Or maybe she'd simply become invisible. She certainly felt that way.

# thirty-four

As Ginny went over the schedule for Hotel Jackson's upcoming Fourth of July celebration, she couldn't help but notice that Jacqueline, in higher spirits than ever, was working exceptionally hard to make all the pieces fall into place. Ginny listened as Jacqueline went over the details of their usual rooftop terrace celebration.

"I ordered extra rental chairs and tables," she explained, "after I saw how many guests would be here."

"How many extra chairs and tables?" Ginny questioned. "And are you sure they'll all fit up there?"

"Absolutely. Adrian helped me measure it all out. And he agreed we should have enough to accommodate anyone and everyone who wants to be up there. As you know, the hotel is fully booked."

"But not all the guests will want to go up there," Ginny protested.

"They might. And we sure don't want anyone feeling left out, do we? Or to end up with standing room only? Watching the fireworks over the Sound from up there sounds so romantic. And we're going to put out hurricane lanterns with candles, and complimentary beverages and appetizers. Diana suggested that."

Ginny sighed. "Well, then I suppose the rental items are a good idea. It'll probably be quite a crowd."

"I know. I can't wait!" Jacqueline explained a few more ideas she and Adrian had decided to implement. "With Diana's blessing, of course."

"Of course." Ginny appreciated that Jacqueline's confidence had returned. And she was pleased to see the old uppity, self-centered cockiness seemed to be a thing of the past. But at the same time, this bright-spirited helpfulness was a bit disconcerting. "I'll have to watch out for you," Ginny teased. "You're becoming so efficient, you'll soon have my job."

"Maybe that wouldn't be such a bad idea." Jacqueline winked.

"Maybe not." Ginny leaned back in her desk chair. For some reason she felt more tired than usual. Especially this early in the week. Perhaps it really was a good thing Jacqueline was here to help out. Or maybe Adrian had pegged it right when he'd told Ginny she would grow old before her time. Was that what was happening?

She watched as Jacqueline went over more details for the celebration. She acted so energetic and young and happy. It probably didn't hurt that she and Adrian were now considered an "item" by much of the staff. Or that Diana, with her own newfound romance, wasn't objecting. Ginny was glad for them. All four of them. But their happiness cast an even greater shadow over her gloominess.

"You seem to have things under control here," Ginny said in a weary tone. "I think I'll call it a day. I'm tired."

"Are you feeling okay?" Jacqueline peered closely at her. "I heard there's a summer flu going around."

"I'm fine. Just a little tired."

"Well, you can enjoy a quiet evening." Jacqueline grinned as she tugged a baseball cap from her bag. "Adrian is taking me to the Mariners game."

"Have fun," Ginny said as she gathered her things. "Later." As

Ginny walked toward the elevator, her feet felt leaden. Maybe she *was* getting sick. Or maybe she was just tired of this. All the glitz and glitter of a big July Fourth celebration on the hotel rooftop sounded dull and tiresome to her. Let Jacqueline have at it. Ginny planned to be in bed early that night!

She'd just entered her suite when her phone chimed. Hopefully it wasn't Jacqueline needing her help with something. But the caller ID said Alexi. Ginny answered as she kicked off her shoes. "Alexi?"

"Oh, Ginny. I got here this afternoon. You know, at the river lodge. Dad's still out on a fishing trip, but Jack just told me you're gone! He said you went back to your old job in Seattle. Is that really true?"

Ginny sank into the sofa. "Yeah, it's true. How are you doing, Alexi?"

"Not so good *now*. Don't you remember you promised to go on the white water trip with me? You agreed to go with me. *Remember?*"

"I'm sorry. I guess I sort of forgot about that." Okay, that wasn't completely true. She'd been *trying* to forget.

"You have to come back, Ginny. I won't go on the trip without you."

"Oh, Alexi, you *need* to go. You'll have so much fun."

"Not if you don't go."

"I wish I could come back—"

"Then just do it!" Alexi insisted.

"But I have my job here. I can't just—"

"Jack told me his granddaughter's there with you, and that she can manage the hotel, and that you can come back here."

"Jack said *that*?" Ginny just shook her head. Leave it to Jack to oversimplify her situation.

"Yeah. He said you've been training his granddaughter to take over your job."

"To take over my job?" Ginny considered this. "Really?"

"Jack's here with me now, Ginny. Wanna talk to him?"

"Sure . . . why not." Ginny waited for the sound of Jack's gruff hello. "Hey, Jack. Sounds like you're giving Alexi ideas."

"It's time for you to come back here, Ginny. Jackie's had plenty of time to get used to managing the hotel. And my lodge is going to rack and ruin in the meantime."

"I thought you were managing things, Jack."

He laughed. "More like mismanaging." He described some of his troubles, particularly with the computer bookings.

"I'm sorry to hear that. But it won't be hard to fix."

"You're right. It won't be hard. Not for you. Listen, Ginny, I've got an old buddy. He's in Seattle right now. Buck's flying his private plane to Idaho Falls *tonight*. Coming fishing here. I already mentioned this idea to him, but I'm gonna call him right now and have him bring you with him."

"I can't just leave—"

"Yes, you can. Jackie already told me you're not happy there."

"She told you that?" Ginny sat up straight.

"Yep. Just a couple days ago. And Ben and I were talking late last night. I told him what Jackie said, and you know what Ben told me?"

"Of course not. How would I?"

"Ben told me to get you back here. And that's just what I'm doing, Ginny. You are coming back here. *Tonight!* You are still under contract to me, young lady. You have more than a week left to fulfill your agreement. And Ben is a lawyer. If I have to, we'll take you to court. Do you understand?"

"You're serious?"

"Serious as a heart attack, and don't you make me have one!"

"Maybe you should calm down, Jack."

"I'll calm down once you get here. And your first order of business, well, after you straighten out my computer snafu, is to go on that white water rafting trip. I want my manager to understand what that's all about."

Ginny didn't know what to say.

"Now I'm going to call Buck and tell him to get you at your hotel. He's an old coot like me and a darn good pilot. He'll probably be there within the hour. You understand? And if you don't show up here with him tonight, you can expect to hear from my lawyer."

"Ben?"

"That's right. Don't make me play hardball with you, Ginny." He chuckled.

Ginny promised to see what she could do, reminding him that she had a boss here in Seattle, but he simply reminded her he could "lawyer up." She hung up and then called Diana. To her amazement, Diana didn't act the least bit surprised.

"You've put in enough time here, Genevieve. Go to the fishing lodge. See if your fishing guide has come to his senses."

"What about your hotel?" Ginny asked in disbelief.

"Well, Adrian and I can help Jacqueline with management. And I'll probably hire someone else too. We'll get along. It's time for you to have a life."

Ginny felt tears in her eyes as she thanked Diana . . . for everything. And then she packed her bag, wrote a note for Jacqueline, and went down to the lobby to wait for Buck, the old coot, to pick her up.

BUCK TURNED OUT to be much nicer than an "old coot." He told her all kinds of flying stories—some that were terrifying—as he flew them to Idaho Falls. When they got there, Margie was waiting for them. After a good, long welcome-back hug, Margie drove them both to the lodge. She and Buck visited like old friends, which they apparently were. Meanwhile, Ginny sat in back fretting over what her reunion with Ben would be like. It was interesting to know that Jack had talked to Ben about her, and that Ben had been in favor of her return. But was it for Jack and the lodge's sake, or for Ben's? Maybe it didn't matter. As they drove onto the lodge property, everything looked dark and quiet. Like everyone had gone to bed. Even so, she experienced a surge of real happiness as she got out of the van—a feeling that she'd come home.

Alexi was waiting in the parking lot and ran over to greet her. "Thanks so much for coming back," she said as they embraced. "I really don't think I could've gone on the raft trip if you hadn't."

"Well, I must admit it feels good to be back."

Alexi reached for her bag. "I'll take this to your cabin for you. Jack's in his office. He told me to send you there to talk to him."

Ginny thanked her, then headed off to find Jack—but not until she paused in the darkness to look up at the night sky . . . admiring how bright the stars looked. When she knocked on Jack's office door, she noticed it was dark inside.

"He's not there." Ben walked onto the porch.

"Oh." She nodded nervously. "Alexi said he wanted to meet me here."

"Sorry about that. I made my daughter tell a lie." He stepped closer. "But it was for a good reason."

"What's that?"

"I wanted to talk to you alone."

"Okay . . ."

He pointed to one of the rockers on Jack's small porch. "Have a seat."

She sat in one and he sat in the other, and for a long moment, neither of them spoke. She was tempted to break the silence but reminded herself that he was the one who wanted to talk. Let him.

"First of all, I want to say I'm sorry," he finally began. "On the day you left here, I was a little confused. I believed something that someone told me about you. Something I only recently discovered was untrue."

"Something Jacqueline told you?"

He nodded. "She's apologized for it. And she even encouraged me to talk to you." He sighed. "But I wasn't sure what to say . . . or how to say it."

"Uh-huh?"

"I wanted to apologize for brushing you off on that day. I thought it was the right thing to do at the time, but it felt lousy afterward."

"There was a lot of misunderstanding going on right then."

"I'll say." He ran his fingers through his hair. "So, after I heard what was really going on—that you hadn't eloped with Adrian—I wasn't sure what to do. I wanted to ask you to come back here. But I knew if I asked you to come back, it would have to be for a very good reason."

She still didn't know what to say.

"Because I realized you had your life in Seattle . . . your career to consider. How could I call you up and ask you to come back here? Especially when you originally came here for a sixty-day job swap. What right did I have to ask you to give up everything and come back? I don't even live here for more than just the summer myself."

"That's true." She could see his reasoning.

"But then I didn't know how I was going to continue to get to know you better. With you there . . . and me here."

"That's a good point."

"And I wanted to get to know you better." Standing, he reached for her hand and pulled her to her feet. "And I was hoping you might feel the same."

"I do want to get to know you better, Ben." She felt a warmth rush through her as he stepped closer. "I've missed you a lot."

"I've missed you too." He cupped her chin in his hand and kissed her.

Ginny had just been marveling at the stars in the heavens, but now she felt like the stars shimmering inside her shone even brighter. As he kissed her again, she felt herself melting in his arms. Finally, he stopped and looked into her eyes.

"And the reason I wanted to get to know you better, Ginny, is because I'm pretty sure I'm in love with you."

This time she kissed him. "I'm pretty sure I'm in love with you too, Ben."

"Then all we need to find out is whether my daughter approves. Want to go tell her what we're thinking?"

Just then, they both turned to a loud rustling sound nearby. "Is it a bear?" Ginny grabbed more tightly to Ben, suddenly remembering that first night when he'd warned her about the wild animals. He acted unafraid as he led the way to the overgrown bushes alongside Jack's office.

"I don't think so." As Ben spread the brushy branches apart, Ginny heard a gruff laughing sound followed by shrill giggles, and suddenly Jack and Alexi stepped out of the brush with sheepish-looking grins.

"You guys don't have to tell me, Dad," Alexi announced. "I already knew."

"So did I." Jack came over to shake both their hands. "Sorry to interrupt your private moment, but I got curious when I saw Alexi prowling around in the dark."

Hugs were exchanged all around, and then Jack, tugging Alexi by the hand, went back into the lodge. Once again, Ben gathered Ginny into his arms. "So I take it you're staying, then?"

"I love it here at the lodge," she confessed. "And I love that gorgeous river. Almost as much as I love you."

TURN THE PAGE
FOR A SNEAK PEEK AT A
## SECOND CHANCE ...

*Everyone moves on.*

Everyone except for Mallory Farrell. At least that's how she felt as she drove home after her daughter's wedding. Mallory sighed. Dear Louisa had made such a beautiful bride and, thanks to all of Mallory's careful planning, it had been a gorgeous wedding. Picture-perfect down to the tiniest detail. Well, almost.

Mallory had suppressed the urge to growl when her ex-husband, dressed in a sleek black tux, escorted their youngest child down the aisle. Vince, who'd been mostly absent from their lives for nearly twenty years and now had a new wife with two young kids, had the gall to take center stage with the daughter Mallory had raised by herself. And when asked, "Who gives away the bride?" he proudly proclaimed, "I do." Oh, sure, he'd added "on behalf of the family" in a quieter tone, but Mallory had felt the sting.

Despite her pasted-on smile throughout the day's wedding festivities, Mallory was left with a bad taste in her mouth. She'd only learned Vince planned on coming during the wedding rehearsal. After she'd been so pleased to see her older son, Seth, practice-walk Louisa down the aisle, she'd imagined a repeat performance for today. But as they left the church, her younger son, Micah, had spilled the beans.

"Dad just texted me that his flight was delayed," he'd whispered, "but he'll be here in time tomorrow." She could tell by Micah's half smile that he'd felt conflicted too.

When her kids had questioned why her boyfriend wouldn't be there to share in the nuptial celebrations, Mallory had feigned nonchalance, saying she and Marcus were taking a break. After all, she didn't need her personal life to detract from Louisa's limelight. She sure didn't want them all to feel sorry for her when the truth was that Marcus, after almost four years, had suddenly decided he, too, wanted to move on. Just three days before the wedding where he was supposed to be her plus-one.

Despite Marcus's usual bad timing, Mallory had told herself it was for the best. Sure, the relationship had been handy when it came to social functions. Marcus was charming and attractive and well-connected, but he'd always been more about Marcus than Mallory. Was it possible he'd viewed her as nothing more than the consummate escort? And maybe she deserved that. After all, everyone moved on eventually.

Mallory felt a weight fall upon her as she pulled up to the house she and Vince had purchased when Louisa was still in diapers. She'd loved this house then and loved it even more now. She'd been the one to urge Vince that it was a fantastic deal "for a fixer-upper." But the once-neglected property had quickly evolved into a serious money pit. Still, they'd been young and strong and motivated . . . at first. But this house put their unrealistic DIY dreams, as well as their marriage, to a severe test. A test that first drained them—and their bank account—then thrust them into two different directions and two completely new career paths. Well, that was water under the bridge now. Mallory was beyond this. Wasn't she?

Still, she felt an indescribable lostness as she unlocked the massive front door and walked into her big, lovely, *lonely* house. By now she'd fixed and renovated every square inch of the stately old Victorian. Her friends called it a showplace, which came in handy for her interior design business. In her effort to be a stay-at-home mom, Mallory had converted the basement into a workspace years ago. But she'd always welcomed clients at her front door in order to show off the fruits of her efforts in her own home. Vain perhaps, but useful too.

She set her handbag on the cherry buffet in the foyer and picked up the small stack of mail she'd tossed there this morning. But before thumbing through it, she paused to admire the sunflowers, cosmos, and ferns she'd arranged in a bottle green vase. Sweet but simple perfection. Although this house had been built in the overly frilly Victorian era of gingerbread and fussy frills, Mallory had given it a more "grown-up" style—something all its own. People were usually surprised to discover her historical home wasn't filled with floral wallpaper and ornately carved antiques. Oh, there were a few well-selected old pieces, but the overall feel was more clean and sophisticated than fluffy and stuffy.

She'd offered to host the wedding reception in her home, especially since it had an early end time, but Marshall's parents had packed the guest list so full that everyone agreed a hotel reception was more practical. Still, Mallory had handled all the decorations, at both the church and the hotel, and she suspected some of the guests were still talking about it.

She kicked off her shoes and sighed. Life was good . . . *right*? She strolled through the living room where the last of the evening sunlight filtered through the massive maple tree outside. The yard looked so pretty in late May. But there was no one but her to enjoy it today. Mallory's sons and significant others had opted to stay over in the hotel. They hadn't said as much, but she imagined it was so they could whoop it up late into the night without bothering her. And that was fine. After all, everyone moves on.

"Oh, get over yourself," she said aloud as she opened a legal-size envelope. Talking to herself was a habit she'd acquired after Louisa had left home for college six years ago. "Be grateful your children have their own lives now and that they're not living under your roof, raiding your fridge, cluttering up your house—not like some of your friends' kids." But even as the thought crossed her mind, she wondered which was worse.

She turned her attention to the letterhead she'd pulled from the envelope. It was from an attorney named Lloyd Henley, from a law firm in Portside, Oregon—the town Grandma Bess had resided in for most of her life, before passing away several months ago. Mallory had attended the funeral, which had been arranged by her mother's sister, Aunt Cindy. According to Aunt Cindy, all Grandma Bess left behind was a "'worthless' little tourist shop and a mountain of debt." Not that Mallory had cared about any of that. Mostly she'd regretted not having spent more time with Grandma Bess in recent years. Especially since there was no good excuse.

Portside had felt like a second home during her childhood. How many summers had Mallory spent with Grandma Bess after her mother had died? She'd even taken her own children to visit when they were young—before adolescent lives grew too busy. Prior to her grandma's funeral, Mallory hadn't been to Portside for nearly ten years. She tried to maintain contact with cards and notes and phone calls on Grandma's birthday, but she regretted not making it over there more often.

Mallory reread the letter more carefully. According to Mr. Henley, Grandma Bess left Mallory her small tourist shop, including the small apartment above it. Mallory, pacing, reread the letter a third time. Aunt Cindy must've been wrong about Grandma's assets. Mr. Henley's letter claimed he had the title and keys and some paperwork and would present them to Mallory when she came to pick them up in the near future.

How strangely intriguing. Mallory was now the owner of a beachy tourist trap. Oh, she'd loved that dusty cluttered shop as a child. She'd laughed over the silly gag items, played with the cheap plastic toys, and been completely charmed by the seashells and glass balls that Grandma had wisely displayed on a higher shelf. Mallory had even worked in the shop as she'd grown older. Dusting, stocking, and sweeping until she was old enough to run the old cash register. What fun she'd had waiting on customers. She'd sometimes dreamed of having a shop just like Grandma's when she grew up. But then she grew up and things changed.

Still, the idea of taking a trip to the coast was surprisingly appealing. And if she hadn't invited her sons for Sunday brunch tomorrow, she'd take off right now. But all things in good time. She would spend the day with her boys and their girlfriends tomorrow. Then on Monday morning, she'd reschedule this week's appointments, make a hotel reservation, and leisurely venture on over for what she hoped would be an interesting trip down memory lane. It might even turn into a much-needed vacation. Perhaps she could pretend that, like everyone else, she was moving on too. At least for a week anyway.

Because she had no doubts that after her restful week in Portside, she'd come back here and get her nose to the grindstone again. That was what she did. And she had a long list of impatient clients with high expectations. Mrs. Denton wanted her entire house finished by early August for her family reunion. Sunshine Estate Realty wanted a bid to redo their lobby, and Alice Moore was still waiting for her high-end kitchen appliances to arrive. Perhaps Mallory would track those down from the coast.

Mallory was aware she'd inherited more than just her father's dark brown eyes, height, and prematurely gray hair. She ran her fingers through her thick, shoulder-length hair. It took her years to give up the dark brown dye she'd hidden behind since her late twenties, but ironically now that it was shiny and silver, people often assumed she had it done at the salon!

Besides Dad's physical looks, Mallory had been "blessed" with his workaholic ways. Early on she'd blamed her obsessive work ethic on being the only breadwinner, after Vince's disappearing act, but she suspected these habits went deeper than that, and although she'd always promised herself she'd slow down after the kids were launched, she was still going strong. And her clientele list was as demanding as ever. And growing. She'd get one client satisfied and, like Whac-A-Mole, two more would pop up. More people than ever wanted their homes redone these days.

Sometimes, usually around three in the morning, Mallory grew worried. What if she continued this hectic path—would she work herself to death and follow her father into an early grave? Sometimes, again only at three in the morning, she'd even feel her heart fluttering frantically, imagining it was giving out on her. But her last doctor's visit had confirmed she was in generally good health for her age.

Although death was one surefire way to move on, it wasn't something she felt ready for. Despite knowing fifty wasn't too far in her distant future, she still felt fairly young and fit. And if Louisa and Marshall had children as soon as Louisa hoped, Mallory could become a grandmother. Perhaps it was time to slow down some and reevaluate her life plan. And perhaps Grandma Bess was offering her the opportunity. God willing and the creek don't rise, she planned to check it out!

**Melody Carlson** is the award-winning author of more than 250 books with sales of more than 7.5 million, including many best-selling Christmas novellas, young adult titles, and contemporary romances. She received a *Romantic Times* Career Achievement Award, her novel *All Summer Long* has been made into a Hallmark movie, and the movie based on her novel *The Happy Camper* premiered on UPtv in 2023. She and her husband live in central Oregon. Learn more at MelodyCarlson.com.

"A glorious setting in California wine country, a family business in danger of going under, and emotionally real characters dealing with life combine to yield a memorable novel."

**—LAURAINE SNELLING**

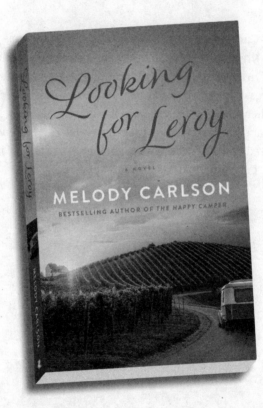

Brynna Philips is ready to give up on love. But when a fellow teacher invites her on a trip through Sonoma wine country, she's reminded of her first crush, whose family owned a vineyard there. Is there any chance she can find him . . . and one last chance for love?

Ⓡ Revell
*a division of Baker Publishing Group*
RevellBooks.com